He'd known the plan would be dangerous, but he'd thought the danger would only be to him...

"Are you all right, Emilie?"

"I think so, not sure what put me out, a shot of some kind. We're in a bomb shelter. Out by the old test site. I heard that much on the way. They had to use a GPS, and I gathered there were a whole lot of shelters out here."

He craned his neck painfully and the walls doubled up on him. Two Emilies merged, moved apart. "They were used to test soldiers for radioactivity back in the fifties." It hurt even to talk. "Who's behind this, you know?"

"I thought I heard Binaggio, but they could've been saying Bellagio, the casino. One of them sapped you hard. He was worried it might have been too hard, so they must want us alive. Are you all right?"

"Yeah." The only thing they had going was the release of materials upon their death, and torture could probably make him tell how the stuff could be accessed. Except for the fact that Cobb had removed the tubes and had them reburied. If they hurt him too badly, he'd just go with death, but he couldn't stand the thought of Emilie in pain and danger.

This was his fault, all his fault, and now they were in for it. She didn't know the details of the whereabouts and subsequent release of materials, but that could be worse than knowing if these people were not sophisticated inter-rogators. If they were, they were not about to let her go, anyway. His mind raced, getting nowhere. Concrete walls, floors, steel door, and crappy ventilation system. He deserved what he'd get. He knew that.

But she didn't.

Travis Meachem, a disillusioned middle-aged man, flies to Daytona to visit his dying father, Reno Pete. On his deathbed, Reno confesses his darkest secrets then commits suicide, leaving his son absolute proof of his part in the JFK assassination, along with instructions on how Travis can profit from it. Following his father's cryptic advice, Travis heads to his uncle's house in the Marais Des Cygne Wildlife Refuge, where they hatch a plot to ruin the days of those who destroyed their family. It's an endeavor that will shake up the power corridors from New Orleans to Washington DC, and beyond. Along the way, Travis attracts some unlikely allies, among them a stunning creole girl, a streetwise rasta character, and a Dallas, Texas, police detective. But some allies are not what they appear to be, and Travis's enemies aren't the only ones in danger of having their days ruined for good. Is revenge hollow? It depends on who's seeking it.

And why.

KUDOS for *Ruined Days*

In *Ruined Days* by Guinotte Wise, Travis Meachem, is called home to see his dying father. As the two aren't close, home is the last place Travis wants to be but, like the dutiful son he isn't, he flies home to see his father one last time and say goodbye. But instead of a touching reunion and tearful goodbye, Travis's father, a former undercover operative for the CIA, confesses to Travis that he's the one who killed JFK. He gives Travis an envelope he says will help him get both money and revenge on the people who ruined his family's lives, then promptly eats his gun, leaving Travis with nothing but unanswered questions. As Travis follows the clues left by his father and uncovers some deep dark secrets, he ends up with ammunition that makes some powerful people very nervous. When his friends and family start dying, Travis realizes that these people play for keeps. If he's is going to survive, he needs to learn—fast. The story is complicated, clever, and very fast paced. It will grab you by the throat and not let go. If you want to figure out who the good guys and who the bad guys are in this mystery/thriller, you'll need to pay close attention, or you'll miss important clues. And, even then, you probably won't figure it out until the very end. ~ *Taylor Jones, Reviewer*

Ruined Days by Guinotte Wise is the story of lies, betrayal, and deep dark secrets—dangerous ones. Our protagonist, Travis, is a middle-aged self-employed flooring contractor, living his mundane life—mundane, that is, until his dying father sends for him. Against his better judgment, Travis flies home to say goodbye to his father and, hopefully, repair their damaged relationship. But when he gets there, his father, Reno Pete, starts confessing all the things he did while working as an assassin for the CIA. Travis is caught completely by surprise, never having known his father even worked for the clandestine agency. To top it off, Reno tells his son that his inheritance is buried in the yard of the house where they used to live, but it's not money, gold, or jewelry. Oh, no. It's information. Information that certain powerful people will do anything to keep from becoming public knowledge. But Travis isn't the only one who's heard of Reno Pete's death, and the assassins are coming after him. If he going to not only survive, but thrive, he's going to have to be smarter, faster, and more determined than his enemies—just like his father was. *Ruined Days* is a fun, exciting, and sometimes scary read. I loved Travis's subtle humor, clever mind, and devil-may-care attitude—a down-to-earth guy, you can't help rooting for. The story will catch and hold your interest from the very first page, so plan on missing some sleep until you finish.

~ Regan Murphy, Reviewer

ACKNOWLEDGEMENTS

Thanks to Tim Trabon for reading a piece of flash fiction and saying, "This should be a novel..." And to him, Kathleen Jones, Eric Baumgartner, Ann Reckling, Jim Carns, and Jim Long for reading the original manuscript and making vastly helpful suggestions.

To Cameron Ashley, editor of *Crime Factory Review* for publishing the flash fiction that became *Ruined Days*, and for saying, "Jesus, don't stop writing!" which I have pasted on my computer.

To Walt Brown, the JFK researcher/author who steered me through some conspiracy scenarios, and who has proved the lone nuttiness of the lone nut/magic bullet theory.

To Ben Carmean for his marvelous cover designs of past, present, and future books.

To Francine Edelman who worked so hard to get *Ruined Days* published.

To Tony Bony for gun stuff, and Jenny for that day she spent hours landing a fourteen-pound catfish on five-pound test, inspiring the Reno letter to Travis (p. 109).

And to friends and family for constant enthusiasm and support. It ain't easy, this journey from thought to ink. Bob Shacochis calls it a birth canal. "Push!"

RUINED DAYS

DAYS

GUINOTTE WISE

A Black Opal Books Publication

Black Opal Books

BECAUSE SOME STORIES JUST HAVE TO BE TOLD

GENRE: MYSTERY/THRILLER/SUSPENSE

This is a work of fiction. Names, places, characters and incidents are either the product of the author's imagination or are used fictitiously, and any resemblance to any actual persons, living or dead, businesses, organizations, events or locales is entirely coincidental. All trademarks, service marks, registered trademarks, and registered service marks are the property of their respective owners and are used herein for identification purposes only. The publisher does not have any control over or assume any responsibility for author or third-party websites or their contents.

For Freddie

"Made 'em pay dear for their frolic."
~ Miguel de Cervantes

CHAPTER 1

Travis sighed, tilting back the last of his tepid Coors to wash down three aspirin. His old man's shitbox home in Daytona was the last place he'd wanted to go in this world, other than maybe Kabul.

"But he's dying," she'd said on the phone.

His first thought had been, finally.

And the guilt started again. He snapped the cap back on the aspirin bottle. Laying floor tile was torture on his back. Now this. But he could use some time off from the relentlessly unrewarding business he'd gotten himself into. A forced retiree and his son were looking at buying it, god knew why. Maybe while he was in Daytona, they'd come to their senses, or maybe even say yes.

A shooter of pain seemed to bounce from temple to temple then subsided. His feet on the coffee table, he caught his reflection in the blank black flat screen directly across from him, the big TV he rarely turned on. Thinning hair, broken beak from the ring, still-square shoulders, not too bad a gut.

All in all, the outside Travis was holding up okay for fifty-three, going on ninety, or feeling like it.

"Pete wants to see you. He has something important to give you," Flame had said.

Travis rather liked Flame. She'd been with his dad the longest yet. She was the last in a line of way-younger-than-his-old-man's lady friends. "Mail it," he'd said.

"Please, Travis?"

He thought back to when he was a kid, a lifetime ago, when they'd lived in Vegas and his mom was still alive. The old man had come home in a sweat one afternoon and said to his mom, "Pack up everything you can get in the car, now. We're leaving." And they did. Travis shook his. They'd moved to fucking Kansas, leaving Travis's almost new bike in the garage, his carefully plastic-wrapped Captain America comic collection up for grabs.

The old man was crossways with ATF in some bull-shit scheme to ship a load of AK-47s to a guy in one of his banana hot spots.

Kansas had turned out okay, actually, and Travis would return there often to stay with his dad's brother, his uncle Cobb and Vinita, his aunt. Kansas was what he remembered as home now. Cobb lived in the Marais de Cygne Wildlife Refuge, which was unlike any other part of Kansas. Lush, green, Amazonian, the Marais de Cygne River snaked through the refuge and huge birds took off almost lazily like overloaded C-5 transports from the jungle encroached banks. It was a Huck Finn world for Travis, still was.

They'd moved to Mexico for a while. Bored, Travis had opened some boxes in the shed and found land mines. He didn't know what they were—olive drab things with military printing on them. The old man caught him. He'd grabbed him by his skinny kid arms, slammed him up against the wall, and looked at him with those water-blue eyes. "Those fuckers will ruin your day a lot worse than I ever will."

Travis got it. The old man could ruin your day. Reno Pete, they called him. Always sniffing out the next bo-

nanza. He did some time for arms trafficking, tax eva-
sion, once for breaking and entering. He always got out
early. Half the prison time he did was for someone else
and he never talked. Cobb had told Travis that, in Pete's
defense.

Now, the dyed redhead said he was croaking. Travis
called her Flame, Reno's name for her, though she preferred Myrna. Maybe fifty-five, she soaked up the tropical sun over the years, smoked and drank too much, had
that fine-lined sun-leathered skin and fake tits, and could
have been a looker back in the day. She'd sounded sober
when she called.

CHAPTER 2

Flame was there, waiting as the herd milled out into the airport. Travis hoped she didn't expect hugging and all that. She was deeply tanned, wearing baggy linen cargo shorts, a linen blouse with palm fronds on it, silver jangly bracelets, and hoop earrings. She didn't look half bad for an old lush with false eyelashes and elephant skin.

"Travis," she said, "You look so…prosperous."

He didn't know what to say to that. He was wearing an old khaki sport coat and jeans. Maybe it was the watch. It would pass for a Rolex, if you didn't look too closely. It was his ex-wife's ex's, and that asshole probably stole it.

"Hi, Flame. You're looking good."

The car was an older Crown Vic. It sounded like the tailpipes were leaking. Everything rusted down here. She lit up as she drove, raised her head, and blew a plume out her mouth. The AC fought to keep up with the humidity. Her tanned legs still had shape to them. *Maybe she's quit drinking*, he thought. She seemed more alert, less sarcastic.

"So how's the flooring business?" she asked, cutting a look over at him, flicking ashes into an overfull ashtray.

"I'm selling it," he said, "Actually got a buyer."

Silence.

"Pete is really sick, Travis. The doctor says a month, maybe six. He's…I don't know…making amends or something."

He doesn't have enough time if he lives to be a hundred, Travis thought but didn't say.

⁓⁓⁓

The house looked better than it did last time—fresh coat of paint maybe, plants well-tended, even lush. A breeze made the palm leaves clack, a sound he associated with vacations, a few good times.

Pete was stretched out on a ratty lounge chair, watching TV. He turned when they came in and tried to sit up.

"Look what the cat drug in," he attempted to say, half of it lost in a coughing spasm.

Flame helped him up to a sitting position, held a glass of water from the side table to his lips, and the coughing subsided. He looked like he should in his condition—his aloha shirt hanging too large on his frame, his legs emphatically skinny in the khaki shorts.

"Pops," Travis said, "How you doing?"

"Fuck's it look like?" he said, but not in an angry way. He smiled, those blue eyes lighting a little. Residual cough.

Flame had Travis put his bag in the tiny back bedroom. Reno slept in the living room now, wouldn't go to a hospital. He kept a Glock 23 under a towel on the Barcalounger. No surprise there. Drop guns were part of him. Flame slept in the other bedroom. Travis heard her in the small kitchen, banging an ice tray on the sink, then clinks in a glass.

"Drink, Travis?"

"Bourbon and water, thanks," he said.

"Make it two," Reno said, gazing at Travis. He'd gone downhill fast since the last visit, Travis noted. As usual he had the AC at freezing.

It was a hospice situation, Flame the caregiver. On days she wanted out, they got a nurse type from down the road. Pete wouldn't stand for any contract nurses, and no more doctors since the last clinic visit. "I'm kakking. I don't need to pay some sonofabitch in a white coat to tell me that. I'll do it my way. Ashes in a cardboard box. Scatter 'em in Tulsa, anywhere by the Glenn Pool field. Finis."

❧❧❧

One shot, in the night. Travis crawled on his hands and knees in his skivvies, peered around the corner. Pete had wrapped his head in a towel, spread a plastic sheet under himself, ate the Glock.

It's not like TV, Travis thought. No tape, no finger-printing. It was perfunctory. Flame was okay, down, but okay. Pete had willed her three grand a month from some oil lease in Louisiana. He had no social security, it turned out, at least not a valid number. He was a ghost back then, Travis thought. A real one now.

CHAPTER 3

What he'd left his son was a fat manila envelope which Travis opened on the plane back to Kansas City after ordering a drink from a flight attendant about Flame's age. In it was a diagram of Dealey Plaza in Dallas, lines from various places converging on a rectangle labeled *Limo.* The writing was Reno's—spelling errors, bad punctuation, and all.

One line of two, *grassy knoll/fence,* was in red. *My shot, head, purposely breaching round—see Z-film to see how that worked,* it said. *The other fence shooter got him in the neck. Shots come from the Dal-Tex Building, Book Depository, Storm Drain, seven in all, three from the Depository. Two missed, one hit curb, curb chips hit Tague, 4 hit JFK, one gets gov. Remember Gene from Vegas? He fired from Dal-Tex bldg. I didn't know the others. Whole story buried in plastic tubes in back yard of Kansas house. Handle it how I say and you can make a bundle. Screw it up and they'll ruin your day.*

Travis was transfixed. Suddenly aware his mouth was open, he looked around him to make sure no one could see the crude map, folded it, and returned it to the envelope. His hand trembled a bit when he lifted the drink to his lips. Holy shit, the old man was nuts, he thought.

Grassy Knoll, my lame ass. This is crazy. Is he fucking with me? He had seemed quite lucid the evening he'd talked to him in Daytona. Calm and at peace, somehow.

Travis picked up the envelope again, pulled the contents from it, and spread them on the fold-out tray after checking behind him. The passenger in the aisle seat was asleep, a businessman type. The middle seat was empty. There was the map. A thick, hand-written letter, folded, maybe ten pages. Another map, apparently of the yard in Kansas. A yellowed snapshot with an Elko border around it, the kind one sees in old albums and antique shops. He held the photo. It was his dad as a young man, in a police uniform, smiling, the blue eyes colorless in the faded black and white picture. He was holding an odd weapon, a long-barreled pistol with a shoulder stock. On the back was scrawled, *Noon, 11-22-63.*

Travis thought back. When that thing had happened, he was in school in Kansas, how old? Maybe five or six. Living with his mom at Cobb and Vinita's little tenant house. He remembered the old man was gone, but he was gone a lot. He wasn't exactly a "show and tell" daddy as in "what's your father do for a living," in grade school. What the hell did he used to tell people who asked? His old man told him the term manufacturer's rep, a guy who repped various products and travelled, import/export business. He just didn't tell anyone what the products were. M-16s. Bouncing Bettys. Berdan primered Polish ammo.

That tenant house back in the woods. His mom had helped make it comfortable insisting on good beds, decent furniture, rehab, and painting. Water-tight against the storms, bright curtains, and toys for Travis. Window air conditioning. Good smells from the kitchen. It was small. Like a playhouse. Maybe that's why he liked it so much. His old man could live in a tent, he didn't care, probably rather live outside, face painted, belly-crawling with a gun. But Pete was in love with Travis's mom. That was evident. He smiled at her a lot and treated her nice. Sometimes, in fun, he'd grab her butt and she'd smack his hand away, and say "Pete! That's tacky!"

"Can't help myself, Rose." He'd laugh. "Your mom should be in the movies," he'd say to Travis and his mom would smile.

Travis started reading the letter again. *You don't have to do this,* it said. *If you do decide to go ahead, relize what your up against. Badass. These people* do not *fuck around. I will warn you again, when and if you dig up the tubes, but for now, just know this: do not do this for any reason other than you are fine with the chance of getting dusted or a big payoff ($4 mill, I'd go for). It'll take guts and I know you have that, but I don't want you in this unless your sure. Total committment. The payoff will set you up for good.*

If you decide not to go for it, burn all this stuff, and leave the tubes near Cobb's tenent house in place. No-body'll ever find them there and if they do, who cares? It'll be 100 years from now.

Another thing. Your mom never knew about this, and some other things I did back in the day. She thought I was a better person than I was, and I like that she thought that. But it kept us in groceries and shoes and she and I took some real fine trips together in some pretty places. I was very careful never to put you guys in danger, but that backfired on me. You can't live a certain kind of life and have a family too. Not that you care about. Rose was my life when I wasn't doing what I did. (and when I was, too) And when you were born, it was a happy day, bud. Just want you to know.

CHAPTER 4

Travis laid the letter down. The typos tugged at his heart a little. Reno had a high IQ but little schooling. So many inconsistencies with that man. Land mines in the shed. *And he never put us in danger, what a crock.* Travis pushed the call button for another bourbon and water. Out the window were fleecy cloud tops, sun, the glare of the wing. It looked real. What he was reading seemed way out in fantasyland. If it was true, his own father had altered world events in the most audacious, head-snapping violent crime of the century. While Travis didn't doubt for a moment that Reno was capable of ending someone's earthly tenure, this seemed out of scale, too public, too—

Another, younger stewardess, maybe forty, checked on him, and went back to get him the drink. He watched her smoothly skirted bottom and calves as she receded up the aisle toward first class. The plane must be climbing slightly. She seemed to walk uphill, using the seatbacks some to pull herself along. She looked around at him, caught him eyeing her legs. Busted, he shrugged, smiled. She smiled too. She was no spring chicken but attractive. His own mother had been a stewardess when she'd met his dad-to-be. How had he known that? he wondered.

Maybe Cobb told him. She'd been in her twenties, a looker all her life. Her short life.

Reno Pete must have been a glamorous guy back then, man of action, global dude. She'd met him on a flight to Florida where some cover company was doing business and JM Wave, the covert group, was preparing for a Cuban invasion. Travis had read all about this stuff after he'd had an inkling of what his old man was up to. There was no end to the shenanigans. Covert this, black ops that. All these guys playing spy games and sucking air through a reed in some swamp.

Cobb said that whenever action broke out in a hot spot, the guys with Harley luggage tags were in every airport that pointed there. They were the mercs and adrenaline freaks. Cobb also said Reno Pete was the real deal. Always where the action was. He wasn't playing at it. He was shadow government, deep black. Not to be discussed.

Cobb idolized his older brother Pete, even though Cobb was a legend on his own. Travis was sure he was on crank though, last time he'd been at the house. Vinita had slipped into a part-time dementia and was quietly going away. Cobb was philosophical about it but the pain was in his eyes.

Travis loved them both, had been their surrogate child over the years, as they had no children of their own. When his mother died, he'd lived with them in the main house. Cobb told him she'd been in an accident. Reno Pete disappeared for a time, and Travis thought little of it—Reno was always gone for varying lengths of time. This time, when he returned he didn't bring anyone anything. He was quiet and took the johnboat out on the Marais Des Cygne River late at night, said he was checking trotlines, and maybe he was. He was often out all night, filthy and bug-bitten when he returned.

The stewardess interrupted Travis's reverie, asked if he wanted a pillow, set his small bottle and plastic cup of ice with stirrer and bottled water on his tray.

"Pillow, really? I didn't know you guys did stuff like that anymore."

She smiled, nice laugh lines fanning from the corners of her eyes. "You looked tired, is all. Want one? Or two?" He noted her short blonde, streaky hair, hazel eyes, nice chest straining at her white blouse, the rub-off of makeup on the open collar as she leaned over him, one arm on the seatback, her other hand on his armrest.

He smiled back, and hoped he looked half as good as she did. "I would. Two. Thank you."

He finished the drink quickly, then he slept.

"...approach, tray table in upright position..." woke him up, his face mashed into one of the pillows, the other on the seat next to him. He looked around, the seats next to him were empty, then the business type on the aisle seat returned, buckled in. The guy opened a Wall Street Journal. There was moisture on the pillow. Travis had been out like a light. Mouth obviously open, probably snoring. He began gathering things around him, a book, the envelope, his ticket. Too late to go to the head, he'd wait until the "buh-byes" were said. The stewardess hurried by, turned, and smiled at him again. He winked before he could stop himself, still half asleep. She winked back.

At the door she handed him her card. *Miss* had been written in before her name, Melissa Bradley. On the back was written, *Downtown Marriott.*

He turned, partway down the corridor after he'd read it, gave her a thumbs up. She returned it.

He had nowhere to go anyway, except his bleak apartment. Plantless. Petless. No appointments for tomorrow. Weird trip. He could use some companionship, and

Melissa Bradley was great looking and friendly. She was maybe ten pounds over, just on the cusp of plump, but cute as hell. Pretty face, great rack. Worth at least a couple of drinks in the bar, see where that went. He wondered if he should have offered her a ride. Stews always had transportation, and he didn't want her to see the dusty interior of his crappy Nova with tools all over the floor, wood and tile samples on the seats.

CHAPTER 5

"Melissa. Over here." He waved to her from a booth he had settled in, with his envelope of Reno-weirdness and a Manhattan on the Rocks—a more potent drink than he usually ordered, but it was a what-the-hell afternoon. She had changed. Short clingy jersey dress and huaraches. She looked fresh and happy.

She slid into the booth next to him and patted his thigh. "You talk in your sleep. I already know that about you. Troubled dreams, I think. Maybe we can lighten your mood."

"Ahh. What did I say?"

"You talked about Reno, and a boat and cobs, all kinds of stuff that made no sense, mostly mumbling. I stopped and was going to wake you, but then you slept soundly and I left."

He reflexively slid the envelope off the table. He'd have to be more careful of it, if it was for real. "Where you from, Melissa?"

"Waxahachie. I live in Dallas, but it was a hassle to get home tonight, and they paid for this..." She waved a hand around. "I don't hustle travelers, by the way, I just...you remind me of someone."

"So this guy must have been a real dreamboat, huh," he said, lifting his drink in a toast.

They both laughed as the waitress arrived. "What'll you have?"

Melissa ordered a vodka tonic and described the man who'd brought Travis to mind. "...and his eyes turned down at the ends like yours. He was such fun." She looked into her drink, her hazel eyes glistened. "He never made it back from Iraq," she said. Then she shook it off and smiled. "What a way to start a conversation, right?"

"No, I get it. I was in Afghanistan. PSC." He put his hand over hers as he said it.

"PFC?"

He laughed. "No, PSC. Private Security Company."

She looked incredulous. "You mean like a rent-a-cop?"

"Oh God, no. We provided security for some embassy people, my...unit. You ever hear of RedZone? Armor-Group?"

"Oh. Yes. Like bodyguards, sort of?"

"Sort of." This subject needed changing before it touched on Fallujah and the fact that a shadow army of over 100,000 guys like him were there, making big money and observing no laws or conventions. Like father like son. In some ways.

"Your accent is pure Texas," he said. "Waxahachie is close to Dallas, isn't it?" And he got her telling funny stories about her cheerleading days in Waxahachie, but he drifted as she talked.

He felt oddly disengaged from Reno's violent departure. Maybe it just hadn't hit him yet. It was his old man, after all. Why didn't he feel more grief? Less like, well that's over with? He felt badly for Flame. She was alone now and had taken care of the old man, all the way to the end.

He'd have to call her and check on her now and then.

Melissa had finished her vodka tonic and was fooling with her stirrer, gazing at him, a half smile on her lips. *Back in the moment, bud*, he told himself. *Quit spacing out.*

"Hey, how about dinner?" he asked her. "I know some great spots here and there, and I have my car. Or, there's a good steak house in walking distance. Want to try it?"

"Sure, it's nice out. Let's just walk somewhere."

Hot KC dusk. Downtown had emptied of office workers, some activity going on in The Power & Light District, energetic rock music wafted to them. She watched their reflections in the upscale store windows they passed. Streetlights began to come on and neon signs shone brighter in the distance. Melissa had his arm and he felt her breast on his bicep.

The jersey pullover dress was revealing and enticing. He put his arm around her and let his hand fall to her waist, then farther. She leaned into him and raised her face to his. They shared a natural kiss.

As they approached a dark alley, she pulled him a bit off balance. "Wait up. Come here."

They made a sharp right and stopped. She kissed him hard and he returned it, holding her to him. He could feel her smile through the kiss as she felt him harden. Then, impishly, she quit and pulled him back into the light of the sidewalk.

He laughed. "Hey, wait, hang on."

"Why is it so *hard* to get you to moving, Travis?" Her Texas drawl was sexy.

He noted the looks she drew from the male half of other couples. Damn, he felt good for just having lost his father.

❧❧❧

The feeling continued until he showered before bed, and suddenly he was overtaken by a fatigue he hadn't experienced since the worst of his flooring jobs. When he crawled into the big comfortable hotel bed, he was out.

He awoke to bright sunlight and a view of Melissa he'd not seen. She was bent over in a short green nightgown, looking into the room safe. In her hand was his manila envelope which he'd asked her to put in the safe for the night.

"What are you doing?" he said, a little too urgently.

She whooped and pulled the skirt of the little nightgown down over her buttocks. Turning to him, she dropped the envelope. "God, could you just scare me a little bit?"

"Sorry, but the envelope, uh, what are you doing with that?"

"Nothing, I'm looking for my tennis bracelet, and this was on top of it, is that okay? Jeez…I mean who's paying for this fucking room, anyway?"

"Aww, Melinda, I'm sorry, I really am. I just wake up weird—"

"What did you just call me?"

"Melissa. Come here."

"I don't think so. I'm pretty much over it. You know, dinner was great, the walk back, the drinks in the bar— then blooey—you were zapped out. I tried to wake you up, and very specifically, too. You—"

"Specifically?"

She flushed. "Mouth-to-whatever resuscitation." She gestured to his mid-section. "Didn't work. In fact, it gave you nightmares, I think."

"Oh, man. I'm sorry." He sat on the side of the bed and told her some of what his last few days had contained.

She sat next to him after a bit and gave him an "Aw-www," and then a kiss.

He pulled her down to the bed gently, raised her short nightgown above her breasts. He filled his hands with them, aware of his rough calloused palms on her smooth skin. She crossed her arms, tugging the nightie over her head, tossing it, and sat astride him, smiling as she guided him into her. The smile, her sleep-tousled hair were the last images he saw clearly as they entered a realm he'd not experienced for too long.

ⱭⱭⱭ

By the time she had to leave to make her flight, they'd exchanged email and phone numbers and promises to keep in touch.

She emerged from the bathroom in black slacks, heels, and a white shirt that fit her snugly. Her makeup was simple and her short streaked blonde hair artfully ar-ranged. She zipped her efficient luggage and wheeled it past him.

"All yours," she said, waving at the bathroom. "Just get out of here before checkout."

"You sure I can't drive you to the airport?"

"Shuttle is fine, but thanks, Travis." She sat on the bed next to him and put her cool hand on his cheek. "I hope things work out for you, hon. I'll say a prayer for you. And your dad."

He kissed the palm of her hand, pulled her gently to him.

"Nope, nope, nope. The shuttle leaves with or without me. We'll see each other again. I really don't pick up passengers you know."

"Do I still remind you of your buddy?"

"You have a cuter butt." She thought for a moment.

"And you're not all ripped and chiseled like some fitness club freak. You look…natural."

They both laughed.

"You mean like a chub?"

"No, like you maybe played college ball and then said to heck with it, got a little…fleshy. Love handles." She patted his side then got up briskly. "Enough about you, what about me?"

"You're stunning. Fucking stunning. You have a good heart. Oh, and you're stunning."

"Good answer. Buh-bye, thanks for flying me."

"Thank *you*."

After she left, he dressed, grabbed his envelope, and hung the housekeeping sign out. Talking with her about his old man's death had released a flood of feelings and memories. He was a little embarrassed about telling her. Had he done it for effect? To get her back in the sack? Nah, but it was unusual for him to spill anything about Reno Pete and his own past with the man. Too soon to tell, but Melissa might just be a keeper.

In the coffee shop, he opened the envelope again, shoving his breakfast dishes aside. Where was the picture? A little panicked, he riffled through the materials. All there but the picture was gone. Had she gone through the envelope while he was asleep? He shook the envelope and the picture floated out and onto the floor. He leaned down to pick it up and saw a pair of wingtip shoes as he did.

He looked up. A young man with a military haircut, white shirt and tie, gray suit said, "Sorry to bother you, could I borrow your ketchup?" Unblinking eye contact, no smile. It was like he was filing Travis away.

Travis palmed the snapshot. "Sure." He handed the bottle to him, noticing empty tables with similar bottles on them.

The young man moved to the booth behind him where he'd apparently been sitting. No ketchup on that table. Don't be paranoid, he thought. Yet that feeling of things being a hair off center was what he credited with keeping him alive in the provinces. This table was closest. Maybe he just didn't notice the bottles on other tables.

When Travis left, he observed the guy paid no attention to him at all. He even backtracked from outside the restaurant to look again. The man was sitting, reading a newspaper, and absentmindedly stirring his coffee.

℘℘℘

The parking garage was like any other—spooky, poorly lit. His footsteps echoed. He thought he remembered the floor, P3 or was it P5. There it was. He saw the aging Nova between an immaculate Audi and a huge high-platform pickup. How the hell was he supposed to get into his car with that thing practically up against it? The dumbass.

Whoa, there was a pile of glass on the concrete beneath the rear quarter window. Why would anyone break into his blue-collar crappy car? Damn. He edged sideways between the vehicles and got the door open against the pickup, smacked the truck with it hard enough to set off the alarm. The big truck issued siren sounds and horn honks, lights flashed. Shit! He managed to get in his car and start it, backed out over the crunchy glass, and sped away from the noise. He looked in the rearview mirror but saw a blank. His trunk lid had come up. He stopped, went back to shut it and noticed the contents were strewn about. They didn't take the tools that were there, a good Makita drill, a new Milwaukee grinder, some loose wrenches, and air hose fittings. Strange.

He'd have to get the window fixed, needless damned

expense. Why would they break in? Were "they" after him already? The bad asses his old man mentioned? *Calm down, strange shit happens, it just does. Could be coincidence.*

Did someone follow him from the airport? He thought back, nothing stuck out. Why wouldn't they take the tools if they were just petty thieves? Maybe they were interrupted. Sure, that had to be it. They'd probably pried open half a dozen cars. It happened all the time, looking for small things, radar detectors, stuff they could convert to cash quickly. Assholes.

Then he relaxed his tight jaws, smiled, in spite of the circumstances, thinking back to Melissa and the early day. He'd look her up again, for sure. He liked her, and he knew it was mutual. But there was that shadow over both of them that could have drawn them together—his resemblance to a dead…what?…lover, husband, brother? He hadn't pursued it. And the death of his old man was maybe making him more susceptible to human contact. Whatever. The mixed chemistry had proven good. Funny how you could tell a relative stranger things it was tough to open up and tell family.

At his Overland Park apartment, in the suburbs of Kansas City, the AC was on a chilly seventy. He'd meant to turn it up to eighty when he'd left. There were messages on the answering machine. One from the son of the pair who were negotiating to buy him out. He listened to that one intently and took down the number to call.

The second was "a business matter" with an 800 number. He knew what that was. Late payment. Fuck it.

The next message was an automatic political message. He erased it. Then a silent one with a hang up.

He called the father/son team. They wanted to pay eight grand down, a grand a month for a year as they built up business, the remainder after the first year was done.

They would draw up papers and send them. After his lawyer checked them over, he'd return them. Sounded fine he said. He hated the business but had dutifully built it up, had a decent rep, four stars on merchant.com, some good reviews. What he'd do after that he had no idea. Pay a couple bills. Get a job. His fighting career after college ended with his fifth knockout—him, not his opponent. He could run grass and crank for Cobb.

Or go after the four mil in his old man's dream scheme. He snorted. He snapped the top off a Coors, grabbed the manila envelope, and sat down on the couch with the mail.

e⁄ɔe⁄ɔ

A smaller envelope inside the manila envelope contained, among other items, a patch insignia roughly cut from a blue uniform—a Dallas police patch. It appeared to be the same patch on the sleeve of the uniform in the black and white snapshot. There was a casing from a .221 Remington bullet. An official looking Dallas Police Department ID card with his father's picture, and the name John T. Harrison. A matchbook from Jack Ruby's Carousel Club. A free admission coupon, same club. A key with a circular tag on it that said *32*—It looked like a safe deposit box key—1963 deposit receipts from a number of banks, all for $9000 each.

As he handled each item, he expected some sort of buzz, like electrification, coming down through the years, heat, a crackle that might make him throw it to the floor. Nothing occurred, except a heightened sense of *shit this is for real*, these things were part of a century-shaping crime in Dallas. Everyone knew, or most anyone who wasn't in denial, that a shot, or shots, came from the fence behind the grassy knoll. Few, if any, knew who pulled the trigger—who aimed with a blue-eyed shallow breathing steadiness that he, Travis, had seen a hundred times before something died clean, or a bottle at sniper's range had burst, or a wasp had exploded in a blast of bark on a tree trunk fifty feet away.

He replaced the items in the smaller envelope, sucked the rest of the beer down, sighed, belched. The other mail was mainly bills, an Esquire magazine, a Dish TV circular, junk. He opened the bills, laid them in a pile, and began writing checks for some of the most urgent in that stack.

Then he stopped.

It was time to go home. Visit Cobb and Vinita. Cobb would give him the straight scoop on this JFK thing and answer some questions. It had been months since he'd been back to see them.

ఛఎఛఎ

The Marais Des Cygne River and wildlife refuge was some fifty miles south of Kansas City and wilder than some stretches of the Amazon, as far as Travis was concerned. People had disappeared there. Cobb had sixty or so acres back against the refuge, but he actually had 7,500 acres and 550 refuges—the Marais Des Cygne was his for the roaming. Marsh of the Swan in French, it was the flyover and feeding area for thousands of Canada geese and home to countless wild animals. The river wound through it, coursing as wide as a mile in deceptively quiet backwater areas and becoming a rushing narrow creek in others.

Cobb knew it all. So had Reno Pete. On hot summer nights, the three of them checking trotlines, Reno would slip over the side of the john boat naked but for shorts, and disappear soundlessly into the inky black water, reappear when they would use the humming trolling motor to head back upriver to Cobb's, a mile away. Travis's old man would meet them on the mud bank, a mud creature himself, teeth in a white grin, sometimes with a catfish, already cleaned. Cobb would just shake his head when Reno was gone, say, "Hope he don't get snake bit," and pull another line up from its plastic Clorox bottle bobber to check it.

Their French ancestors, fur trappers, had settled along the Missouri River and the Little Blue, become prosperous traders all the way to St. Louis and New Orleans on the Mississippi. Some few had preferred the Marais Des Cygne, against intruding civilization and for the replaceable revenue of steady, even flourishing, trapping and fishing. Of the Chouteaus, St. Cyrs, Brouchards, Piccards, and the others, all interrelated, some more closely than others, St. Cyrs still carried the blood of those early moody trappers who preferred knives to muskets and a star-filled night to friends.

Travis knew his last name was St. Cyr, like Cobb's but his old man had changed their name so the relatives wouldn't be involved in any blowback from his "work." Sometimes the name was Meachem, sometimes Wood, after a patriot-relative in the war of 1776. Often, Reno's last name was different from his son's and his wife's last name. It was just something Travis had lived with, confusing though it was, in grade schools he'd attended.

⌘⌘⌘

Travis hit the button on his cellphone.

"Yep?"

"Cobb. It's me, Travis."

"Meat head? I don't know any meat head. 'Cept my nephew."

"How's Vinita?"

"Oh, she's got good days, not so good days. Good right now."

"Need some help checking trotlines?"

"You and me and Jack should battle some mosquitos I think."

"Jack the dog?" All Cobb's dogs were named Jack.

"Jack the Daniels."

"I'll see you in a few hours."

Travis unpacked and packed again. Cargo shorts, jeans, socks, undershorts, a denim shirt. Showered. Set the AC at eighty and did some minor cleanup around the small apartment. He put stamps on the envelopes to be mailed and set them on top of his suitcase. Dressed in jeans, T-shirt that said *Die Trying*, and black Converse low-cuts, he thought for a moment, went to the kitchen, and pulled a tube of OFF from a cabinet, tossed it on his bag. He pulled a jean jacket from his closet. He dug out some duct tape and a plastic bag for his rear quarter window. After he'd gone out and taped the broken window up satisfactorily, he looked at his cellphone contacts and dialed Melissa's number.

"This is Mel. We're not in right now. Leave a message."

"Mel, huh. Well, Mel, this is Travis. Just saying hi. Out of town for a couple days but I'll have my cellphone. Just that where I'm going, the reception is iffy. Later."

He hoped the "we" she spoke of wasn't a boyfriend or husband, but then she wouldn't have given him the number.

He cut over to Highway 69 off of 35 and headed south to Linn County. After a few miles he was used to the high frequency thrumming of the taped window, part of a soundscape that included Jim Rome Sports Talk alternating with a Jimmie Dale Gilmore CD. Selling Meachem

Hard Flooring LLC was a no-brainer, he thought, especially since he was just going to walk away from it, anyway. He was never meant to be a flooring tycoon. He fell into it. Cobb sold walnut and hedge trees to a lumber dealer who'd told him about a flooring business available for pennies on the dollar due to its owner's widow getting remarried. Travis jumped at it, tired of repo, bond work, and summons serving. He'd paid Cobb off for the initial investment, and made a few bucks even when the real estate market went south.

But it had become a grinding drudgery. Even though it was his own grinding drudgery. Bookkeeping, health insurance, taxes, employee turnover, complaints. He wouldn't miss it. The father and son team who were buying the company were both out of work and looking for something to invest their savings in that would provide them more security than most jobs were these days. He wished them luck. It was a living, but it was a bitch.

He turned off Highway 69 at LaCygne and aimed the Nova at Cobb's place. It wasn't far off the beaten path, but might as well be Timbuktu to county appraisers and the sheriff's department. A game warden had come up missing fifteen or twenty years ago, and no sign since, other than the trolling motor on Cobb's Lone Star with the serial number ground off it. Cobb had never seen him, and that was the story he was sticking to. Could be the guy had stumbled upon some of Cobb's LaCygne Green plants. Cobb didn't grow it in rows. It was here and there along fence lines where the planes would never spot it. In among patches of horse weed. Never a cultivated look. But Cobb knew where it was like the back of his hand, every plant. Cobb claimed it was the number two best marijuana in the world, due to the rot and peat of the marsh area.

A descendant of WWII hemp, it was even extolled in a

book of great marijuanas, right up there with Kush and Maui Wowee. Travis had no argument about that—it couch-locked him in the nicest possible way. He smiled to think about it. It was weekend stuff, that was for sure.

CHAPTER 6

Travis rattled across a small, one-lane, loose plank bridge with bolted steel-beam sides over a muddy creek. Despite the heat and the dry spell, rich greens and jungle-like vegetation rose up from the steep sides of the creek, a tributary of the Marais Des Cygne. He continued down a gravel road for a mile or more, then turned right, onto a dirt road that would be unnoticed by anyone not familiar with the area—barely a cut in the dark tall walnuts and piss elms. The canopy formed by hundreds of years of growth seemed as solid as a tunnel except where bits of light flashed through it where the sun found holes. Travis knew the road well, dust-dry or greasy-slippery. He'd been on it barefoot, on ATVs, dirt bikes, driving Cobb's big stake-side flatbed loaded with logs or hay, or the International tractor. They'd graveled parts of it from time to time, but the number nine rock just disappeared, as did the creosoted railroad ties they'd filled the ruts with. Nine miles of bad road was not just a figure of speech here. And Cobb liked it that way.

Travis slid to the right to negotiate a high-center, balancing the Nova's wheels precariously on the narrow shoulder and the road center itself, slipped back into the ruts when he'd passed that trick in the road. There were others. Only good friends and the very determined four-wheeler could make it in. Only good friends could make it out.

Vinita had never complained about her solitary life with Cobb. He took her to town and church doings as often as he could stand it. Then she began going by herself in the Toyota four-wheel drive Land Cruiser he bought her when LaCygne Green harvested well, or he sold more trees to the lumber processer. She'd blast through here like a demolition derby driver, head all the way to Kansas City, and get a fancy hairdo, a new bag at Saks, and steaks from a meat cutter on Ward Parkway.

He smiled. She had style. Vinita was her own woman. She'd threatened to get a day job, but Cobb talked her out of it, said he'd keep her in hairdos and city trips, just stay on the place and bitch at him to fix things. That was before Cobb began messing with the meth and speed, and Vinita had all her considerable faculties. Now the battery was out of the Toyota, and the light was often dim in her eyes. He wondered if she'd recognize him this time.

He rounded the curve and the road widened. The tree tunnel gave way to open land and sunshine. The late daylight was the color of lemonade, the shadows long and graceful on the mowed grounds. The main house was an inviting log structure with a full screened-in porch all the way around it. Cedars and pines formed a backdrop, and the lake was always a bit of a surprise to Travis. It sparkled like an Ozark resort. A dock ran out about a hundred fifty feet, and, bobbing next to it was an old johnboat and a 1940s Gar Wood speedboat. He pulled up alongside a dusty pickup as the hounds gathered, those who were interested enough to emerge from under the porch. There was some barking and baying, but it quit as he got out of his car. Some seemed to know him, others wanted a scent, all their long whippy tails going.

"Jack! Hey, Jack, and Jack, and Jack..." It bowled them over. A human who knew all their names. One or two remembered him.

"Watch them dogs. Them are trained attack dogs," Cobb said as he slipped up behind him, chopping the air around him in mock karate moves.

"Jesus, Cobb! You scared the shit outa me."

"Can't have. If I done that, you'd only be about a foot tall." Cobb squeezed the back of Travis's neck painfully and pounded him on the back. "Blue heron," he said, turning Travis toward the lake by his shoulders.

Travis watched the imposing bird take off from the bank in seeming slow motion, gain flight, and glide into the refuge. Across the lake was primordial wild country, everglades, marshes, and miles of waterways and growing vegetation. Cobb said there were catfish in there big as a man and bird species that hadn't been seen in this country since the late nineteenth century.

భుల

"Pete, oh, it's so good to see you! Tell us where you've been this time," Vinita said to Travis when he entered the kitchen. She was peeling apples. If she didn't lose her focus, there would be some delicious smells from that kitchen soon.

He kissed her, hugged her. She was so small, now. Frail. "Apple pan howdy!" he said, using his childhood name for it. "I'm here just in time, Vinita. You make the best in the west."

"West," she said, absentmindedly, and smoothed her shirt front hanging out of her jeans. "Yes. Maybe you boys go clean those fish."

Travis's mood dipped. She'd called him Pete, mistaking him for his old man. He knew it was irrational, but he found himself somehow impatient with her as though it was something she could control, allow or disallow like drugs, like when Cobb was on speed and all herky-jerky with shithead emotions. He felt heat in his face, thinking like this. He loved Vinita and Cobb, he just wanted them like they were. Cobb, alert, ready to kick ass or field-strip a windmill to get it going; Vinita, humorous and mildly mocking, sometimes a little disapproving of his latest choice of girlfriend, always urging food on him. She, alone, had kept up writing actual letters to him when he was overseas, newsy, encouraging, and loving.

Travis looked at Cobb. Cobb looked down, expressionless, slumped posture, arms at his sides. Then he was Cobb again, in charge. He opened the fridge, pulled out two Pabsts in one large hand, and dropped one into Travis's hand. "Porch," he said.

Big old-growth oaks, walnuts, and elms shaded the house, and the absence of air conditioning didn't bother Travis. Electricity came from natural gas generators and the natural gas came right out of the ground, so Cobb could have all the AC they wanted. He just didn't want it. He'd drilled for water wells and kept hitting natural gas. The water from the deep wells that did produce, brought water that was filtered pure through limestone and glacier layers a million years old. Fans buzzed all over the lodge-like house in the summertime providing a lazy lulling background noise that Travis often missed without knowing quite what it was that was absent.

The comfortable old wicker couch made squeeging sounds as Cobb settled into it. Travis chose the glider. A light breeze off the lake pushed through the screen, stirring a mobile that Vinita must have hung, a colorful thing with a small female figure flying among kite-like shapes. Travis wished her life could be as light and airy as that. They sat, each in his own thoughts. The cold beer was good after the drive. So was being there, but being there was changing.

"She's having a spell," Cobb said. "It'll pass."

"I'm sorry."

"Yeah, it's a piss-poor thing when someone like her gets off the track. I don't get it. Be worse if it was me, then it'd be hell on her. I wouldn't wish it on her. But I don't know what to do. She wanders out there, and I can't watch her all the time."

"Have you considered a place in town? Like a...facility?"

"Fuck that." Cobb finished the beer, crackled the can, got up. "Let's get us another one, go out to the truck for a second. See if that ol' binder'll start. Some of the boys are coming tomorrow. Coon hunt." He did a quick little dance and smiled. "Owoooooooo," he howled, quietly.

"Vinita be okay?"

"Yeah, she sleeps real good. Be back by morning, and, who knows, she might be okay by then."

The old four-wheel-drive flatbed started with a boost from Cobb's pickup. The dogs would sit, sway, and scrabble for purchase on the rusty safety tread of the open flatbed when they left for the coon hunt. Travis remembered the dusty interior and towel-covered baskets Vinita would send with them—fresh biscuits, sausage, fried eggs for sandwiches, melon slices, cookies. They might have to prepare their own this time, Travis thought. And the other staples—cooler full of beer, Cokes, water, and thermoses of strong coffee, bottles of whiskey. The toolbox, attached to the headache rack in back of the cab would contain pistol-grip lights, 30-30 lever actions in blankets, a pistol or two, tarps, and other gear.

Cobb wasn't big on shooting game he didn't need. Quite often, if the coon had given them a good go-round, he'd turn off the lights, whistle the dogs back, and leave, the coon perched in a perilous top branch, perhaps philo-sophically contemplating his brush with death.

"So who's coming to this shindig?" Travis said.

"Usual. Big Ray and Dammitt Ray. Your ol' favorite, Breeze. Harley Rankin. His boy. Joe Summers. Darrel and Duane from the feed store. Old Dan."

Michel Brouchard, aka Breeze, was a cousin, close as a brother, that Travis had grown up with when he'd lived with Cobb and Vinita, a reckless, daring boy back then who'd swung the farthest on the cliff rope over the deep water hole, and was the first to get laid in LaCygne. He'd sped around the back roads on an old Indian with bluedot taillights that disappeared from the sheriff's patrol cars like tracers from a machine gun. He was one of Cobb's marijuana, and now meth, network, running the Mexicans who'd started moving into the area. "It was kill 'em or hire 'em," Cobb had said. "They work hard, send good money home."

Cobb interrupted his reverie. "Okay, Travis. Out with it." He lit a Pall Mall filterless with his army Zippo, clanked it shut, and drew smoke like it might be taken away from him.

"Pete's gone. I guess you know."

"I know. I talked to him couple days before he done it."

"There won't be any service."

"She's sending the ashes. We'll take 'em to Tulsa, you and me. Or I will, you don't want to go."

"I'll go. What's the Glen Pool field?"

"We worked in the oil patch there. Had some good times." Cobb pronounced oil as *awl*. "Rose come from Tulsa. Vinita come from Vinita, Oklahoma. We both married Okies, Pete and me. The two best ones there were, I imagine."

"I hear that, Cobb. I sure do."

Travis drained his Pabst. "Cobb, he gave me something and it is one strange sonofabitch."

Cobb cocked his head at him in interest, pursed his lips.

Travis said, "What do you know about the JFK thing, the assassination?"

"Chickens one day, feathers the next. I know they meant business with that one round that blew his head off."

"Did you know what Reno had to do with it?"

"Oh, hell yes, Travis. Why do you want to get into that mess?"

"He put me there. You might say I inherited it."

"Well, that surprises me. Why would he do that?"

"He said I didn't have to, but if I did it right I could make a shitload of money."

"He'd know. But I'll tell you what, boy. It's a grizzly den." He looked around as if he was in earshot of someone.

"I'm selling the flooring outfit. I'm thinking about it. Doing the Reno Pete thing."

"You ain't Reno Pete, Travis."

"Meaning?"

"Well, he was honed, you know what I mean? He lived for it. Now don't go crazy on me, boy, but when your momma got killed, he went away, remember? What he did was, found the responsible parties and brought back their ears. Buried them in that same little old graveyard she's in. Their fucking *ears*. And he told me he kept 'em alive for two days. They begged to die. The rest of them JFK people left him alone after that. But you get to pokin' around, and they won't leave *you* alone."

"That truck bomb was meant for him. I found that out as a kid," Travis said.

"Nobody ever drove that truck but him. She just went

out to move it so old Ballou could get his backhoe out to the septic tank. Reno was on the river."

Travis massaged his temples. He'd known there was some mistake that his mother stepped into, but had never known it was anything to do with this JFK thing. Suddenly it was no longer an abstract and distant historical event. It had turned instantly personal. Those people were still around, some of them. He wanted to see fear and recognition in their eyes as they died. Yes, now it made sense. Money and retaliation. These fucks wouldn't know what hit them after all these years, but, yes, they would. He'd make sure of it.

Now, by god, maybe he'd bring some ears back, too. Throw them in with his old man's ashes. "There's some stuff in the yard of the old little house, Cobb. I got to do some digging out there."

"Not a good idea, Travis. We're sort of using that house and I don't want anyone out there making sparks and whatnot."

"I know what it is, Cobb. I'll be careful."

Cobb sighed, went behind his pickup, came out more animated, sniffing deeply, wiping his nose with the back of his hand. "I don't want no fuckin' smokin' out there, no picks, just a shovel, you hear me?"

"Uh-huh."

"I don't like you bringin' this shit back here. Don't like it a bit."

"Uh-huh." Travis went to his car to get his bag and the envelope.

Cobb spat on the ground. Travis knew he was suddenly on thin ice with him, but he wasn't sure how to get off it.

CHAPTER 7

They didn't want to catch us. If they would of caught us, say some ambitious out-of-the-loop cop had arrested us in the RR yard before we got away, they'd of figured out a way to cut us loose or kill us in a staged gun battle, but they wanted to avoid that. More likely we'd of been cut loose and the cop told to shut up or else. Shoot, I left muddy footprints all over the place. It was sloppy. All records would of disappeared. When they release the other stuff in 2039, won't be much there. I won't go into all that, but now for the stuff you need to know. First thing you need to know is this: if you're in, your all in. No walking away from this card game halfway through. You can do it. If in, do some digging.

The map of the yard was exact. The house was the center and all measurements were mapped off the house. Cobb gave Travis a tape measure and a squint-eyed look. He stood with his arms crossed under a huge cottonwood that Travis had always liked. Someone had told him it was over a hundred years old. There used to be a tire swing in it. He remembered his mother twirling in it, idly, reading a paperback book and smoking, while he threw baseballs at a blanket on the clothesline, practicing pitching. She wore a colorful print dress that day, but he couldn't quite conjure up the pattern. But he could see her clearly, smoking, reading, the tire twisting on its chain slightly.

The little house seemed more remote than ever now, in disrepair and tangled in brush and new weed trees that had grown up. Hedge and cedar. There was an ether smell from it that Travis figured had to do with the lab inside. He measured the first distance and began digging.

Once through the old grass and roots of new trees, the clay itself was tough and rocks were a factor as well. Sweating freely now, he went at it as though he'd be stopped at any moment, eyeing Cobb peripherally in the distance.

His uncle looked ready to cut a switch and chase him, as he did when he and Breeze got into his liquor when they were twelve. Travis began to laugh through his heavy breathing—digging in the yard of a fucking meth lab in the middle of nowhere for a cache of JFK assassination stuff. Was he just nuts or what? The world was, he already knew that, so maybe this made as much sense as anything else. Two feet down, he chunked into a PVC pipe or something like it. He began widening the hole around the pipe, which was buried on end, vertically. The top of the pipe was about eight or ten inches in diameter and he could see the threaded cap of it now. No telling how long the thing was.

"Cobb? Little help, please."

"Damn little," Cobb muttered, climbing over a storm-downed tree, kicking some brush out of his path. He looked down into the hole.

"I think if we just wiggle it around I won't have to dig all the way down," Travis said.

On their knees, they began to move the tube back and forth, loosening it enough to pull on it. It came up sur-

prisingly easily and was about four feet long. They
dropped it on its side and Travis was off to the next diagram.

"Ain't you going to open the sumbitch?"

"Why, Cobb, I didn't think you was interested,"
Travis said, noticing how he slipped back into the vernacular.

"Didn't say I wasn't interested. Just said I didn't like
it."

"Let me get the other tube up, then we'll look at 'em."

"Fine. I'll go get me another shovel. Sooner we get
outa this yard the better."

ぐうくう

Cobb openly snorted the powder now, shrieking it up
his nostrils from his one long fingernail. Travis ignored it
and kept digging. It was none of his business and it
smoothed old Cobb out some, even if it did make him
yammer like a woman.

When they had the other tube unearthed, Travis
watched Cobb stride to the dock. Tall, long-legged, moving deliberately, carrying one of the heavy PVC container
tubes across his arms like a piece of firewood. Cobb
strode, he didn't walk. Seven league boots. God, what
would the world be if Cobb got old. He wasn't young, but
he looked younger than his years, a boyish shock of salt-
and-pepper hair hanging over one eye, a two-day beard
on a grin-ready face. Travis played the Cobb game in his
head, the game that he and Breeze cooked up so many
years ago when they were kids.

If Cobb was a car, he'd be a super-blown 454 Trans-
Am with racing slicks, the color of red-hots and no muf-
flers at all, fire coming outa the headers. If Cobb
was…what?…a song, he'd be "Folsom Prison Blues" by

Johnny Cash *and* Merle *and* Lefty Frizzell, all at once with Chuck Berry guitar and that drummer from The Grateful Dead. The Cobb game got so wild, so over the top, that Breeze and he would yell over each other's descriptions and crazy Cobbisms until they would fall down in high-pitched laughing heaps, almost peeing their pants.

Cobb. He moved in gusts, nothing in his way when he was on his road, accomplishing, getting things done. Not skinny, but no fat on him, with ropy-veined thick forearms, feet in Red Wing work boots. They said, when he was a field superintendent at Massman Construction Company on the bridge jobs in Managua and Rio and Texas, that he ate standing up and shit a-walking. Travis always felt pride that Cobb was blood, even now with his uncle on crank, it was just a fact, a "deal with it" kind of thing. He was on it because of Vinita, the pain of her moving beyond his help, beyond his protection, it was pain medication and, if anyone had a problem with it, fuck 'em. When she wasn't having "spells," he tried hard to stay away from it. He'd get off it. Travis knew it was temporary. Cobb felt addictions were for people who couldn't deal with life straight on. But he was bewildered about Vinita. He couldn't get his big arms around that one.

Travis took the other PVC container they'd dug up, followed Cobb, emulating his walk like a kid would do, snorting with a little blow of secret laughter at that picture—long strides, seven league boots. "Watch out, Cobb coming. One fist of iron, the other of steel, if the left one don't getcha, then the right one will."

He thought back to when Reno was around. Cobb and Reno, man. He'd actually learned to be a little scared for people who crossed them. Even bad people. One of the Hoover boys accosted his mother in Self's Refuge Tavern near the turnoff to Cobb's. She and Travis were waiting

for Reno to meet them after the school bus on the last day
of school and drive them home. Hoovers were mean-bad
and you just didn't ever mess with them, but even the
head Hoover, the old man, Perf, would have told that one,
leave that woman alone, that's Reno Pete's old lady,
that's a death wish, boy. Perf Hoover's full name was
Perfect Venus Hoover and they say that's how he got so
mean, all the fights over his name. No one ever laughed
at his name after he'd turned about fifteen, except a depu-
ty sheriff in Fulton, Missouri. Perf had done hard time in
Jeff City over that one. Manslaughter.

Travis recalled his anger and his helplessness when
North Hoover—he had brothers named East, West,
South, among others—had tried to get his mother to
dance and hurt her arm jerking her out of her chair, spill-
ing her Seven Up.

"Leave her alone," Travis had shouted, throwing his
ten-year-old body at North Hoover, smelling the man's
acrid sweat, sawdust and booze aura on his rough denim.
Hoover smacked him aside, into a clatter of chairs and
empty tables.

Travis had a ringing in his ears, but he heard Hoover
say, "She don't want to be left alone, showin' her tits like
that in a T-shirt, her ass hangin' out a shorts. Fuck off,
boy."

"Hey, North," said one of the brothers. "Leave off.
Them are St. Cyrs." The barmaid came to the table and
said, quietly, "You best leave, hon, they're drunk." and
helped Travis up. Travis shook her off and they left,
Travis glaring over his shoulder at the Hoovers, his
mother holding back tears until they'd gotten to the road.
North made an obscene gesture with his mouth and wag-
gling tongue at Travis's mother.

Travis wanted to go back in, but she held his arm
tight, talking through clenched teeth, "No. *No.* You will

stay with me. And we won't say a word to your father, you hear me? Not a word. It's over."

His anger was such that red clouded his eyes and seeped through his thinking. He knew, at ten, what it meant to see red. And now he was seeing it again as her death became more clear to him.

It got out. News in the wildlife refuge traveled with the wind. Reno and Cobb acted nonchalant about it at home, but they left together, Cobb with the sawed-off twelve gauge. Travis saw him pull it out from the beam above the fireplace, in its soft, oiled wrap.

Days later, he got the story from Breeze, who'd heard it from the older boys. Cobb and Reno had entered the bar. Cobb, with the shotgun at waist level, advised patrons that anyone who wanted to leave should do it pretty quick. Chairs scooted on the board floor and barstools whirled. There weren't many there other than three Hoovers and a couple of their friends. The few others headed out, throwing gravel in the parking lot. Cobb told the owner, Bert Self, to sit down, hands on a table, if you please.

Reno walked briskly over to North, who jumped up and swung at him. Reno blocked it and punched him in the Adam's apple.

The others started to move but Cobb said, "This is him and North, boys. I got number five birdshot in here and I *will* pull the trigger. It don't make a shit to me."

Reno had decked North. Then he picked the man up by the belt and shirt collar, and, with an animal sound, he ran and whirled like those Scottish pole-throwers, and flung Hoover up into the lowered ceiling tiles.

The hole was there for years.

It wasn't physically possible. Hoover was maybe a mean scrapping hundred seventy five pounds. Reno Pete was not as tall as Cobb but about one eighty five and just under six foot, arms like tree stumps, but not enough heft to throw a man like he surely did. But Bert Self saw it ringside and sober.

When Hoover landed they thought he was dead. Reno, owing to his French ancestry they said, pulled a small but much sharpened bone-handled pocket knife from his jeans pocket, snicked it open deftly, and cut off the bottom part of Hoover's left ear, wrapped it in a bandanna.

"Ears bleed, looks worse than it is," he said. "I'd have taken it all but I want him to be able to hear me comin'." Then he smiled, still breathing heavy, and nodded to Self. "We'll talk about the damages."

Self, looking straight ahead, just fluttered one hand off the table, waved him away.

Reno walked out the door. Cobb backed out after him.

The hole in the ceiling tiles and the torn aluminum frames were eyed by many over the years, as they gazed up into the darkness beyond, thinking about powerfully focused anger. Another page in the St. Cyr legend.

That's when Travis began to fight in school. And when his mother died, it was hell on wheels. A bully once told him, "You think you're bad, don't you?" His answer was, "So bad that I'm going to make you look good."

He became a bully-hunter. If he couldn't beat them fair and square, he stalked them until he got them alone and he clubbed them. Cobb got him started in a boxing program at the Salvation Army gym in town, so he'd at least know what the rules were, channel the anger. Cobb didn't want him doing time unless he did it with a clear mind, not crazy rage.

ભ્ઓભ્

They'd brought the tubes to where Cobb cleaned fish, a small clearing by the dock, protected by shrubbery on three sides. They laid them on an old stainless steel table. Neither man said anything for a moment.

Cobb stood with a fist on each hip. "Well? What are you waiting for, dammit?"

"I don't know," said Travis. "These are like Pandora's box I think."

"Shoot, you opened that down in Daytona."

Travis had the largest tube in something like a head-lock in one arm, trying to open the threaded top with his other hand.

"Here, that ain't workin'. Hang onto it with both hands." Cobb pulled a pair of big channel lock pliers from a drawer in the table. He clamped them onto the square nut on top of the cap and twisted, the sinews in his large forearms bulging. It gave out a little creak. Then it began to move.

Cobb tossed the cap onto the table and waited for Travis to empty the contents.

The tube produced a cop's hat with DPD badge, the crown a little bowed from being stuffed in the smaller space. There was a mildewed uniform shirt with an insignia cut out of the sleeve. A badge, a heavy real one from DPD. A gun belt with a .357 magnum holstered on it. And more pictures with writing on the back in Reno's hand. One was in the direction of the street the limo was on, empty of traffic and people. Another was of the cars parked in the lot behind the fence. The notation said "Right before the parade." One was simply of the fence itself.

Travis felt a connection clicking into place somehow. He couldn't have explained it. Whereas the earlier envelope—full of historical. implicating items—was a small opening into a dark cave, this tube was the hoard in the cavern where light shone on it. It did have residual feeling, a perceptible, palpable life to it, as though his old man was handing each item to him and watching his reactions.

There was another gun in the tube. An XP-100 Remington bolt action pistol with a shoulder stock and a scope. A single shot weapon with a plastic-looking stock.

There was a booklet accompanying it and a note from Reno inside the booklet that said, *This is the most accurate pistol I ever fired. I'd of shot that sonofabitch for free. Youd understand if youd of been at The Bay of Pigs. Only got one shot but I made that one count. Half the shooters must of been winos and clowns. But the other half got the job done. (Oswald never pulled a trigger— they set him up from the word go). signed by me on this day, Reno Pete Meacham (St. Cyr). Nov. 24, 1963.*

Cobb took the gun, opened the bolt, and stuck his thumb in it so his nail would reflect sunlight. He looked down the bore, said, "Clean as a whistle. Must have oiled it up good before he buried it. We oughta take this out tonight, whaddya say?" He grinned at Travis, opened his eyes comically wide.

Travis snorted and shook his head. "You're somethin' else, Cobb."

"What? It ain't doin' anyone no good elsewise." He aimed it around the yard, making soft shooting sounds, the gun kicking as he swung it at imaginary targets.

"This here's a Fireball. Know what that is?" asked Cobb.

"Varmint gun, says here in the little brochure," Travis said.

"Remington Fireball wasn't even in production in 1963," Cobb said. "This here's a concept gun. They put a few out and the CIA picked it up because it was a kickass sniper weapon. Half pistol, half carbine. Pete had it out here, practicing. This very gun." He shook his head in wonder, handing it back to Travis. "He used special loads," Cobb said. "They seemed to explode when they hit something. Said they was frangible. Or breaching. Kill-for-sure rounds." He brought the baggie of white shit out, dipped his fingernail in it, and snuffed it into each nostril. Then he pulled his tin of Skoal from his back pocket, put a pinch in his gums. "Loud little sucker, as I recall."

He hunkered, elbows on knees, looking into the past. "He'd set up Vinita's melons and summer squash on logs about fifty yards away, overripe stuff she didn't want, blow 'em all to bits. Single shot. He'd eject and load and shoot, eject, load and shoot, just like that." He made the motions, the clicking sounds. His eyes glittered from the crank. "History." He sucked air through his teeth.

The other tube contained revelatory maps, drawings, papers, photos, lists. A long typewritten notarized signed statement by Reno. *Explosive stuff*, thought Travis. A list of names and phone numbers, last known addresses of people Travis was supposed to contact, from benign to dangerous, stars denoting levels of danger, five stars being the worst.

He put the contents back into the tubes, and buried them in the sand by the dock. Reno Pete was with them when they walked to the house.

CHAPTER 8

A silver dual-rear-wheeled Dodge Ram truck slid sideways in the gravel and a deep-voiced shout came from the settling cloud of dust. "Where's my favorite woman?" It was Big Ray. He pronounced it *woe-man.* "I come to fight her ol' man, kick his butt, and carry her off!"

"Bring a big lunch, dumbass. That ol' man you speak of is all action," Cobb said, striding toward the truck.

Travis smiled. Tonight and the next morning would be crazy. They called it a coon hunt but it was just little boys in big men's overalls drinking and dogging all night long and telling lies. At least one truck would be mired enough, it would require Cobb's old D-8 Caterpillar to get it out. Might be a fight. Some coons would be taken by the most serious hunters and cleaned by the dock, skins stretched on the old barn side to be picked up later.

Breakfast would be legendary. If Vinita was up to it. If not, Cobb and two or three of the others would cook steak and eggs, the sweet coon meat, catfish steaks, corn on the cob, and make gallons of iced tea and hot chicory coffee. Travis and Breeze would be relegated to the ice cream churns, whaling away until their arms ached. It was their chore since childhood.

Big Ray and Cobb bear-hugged and that turned into a wrestling match with both men grunting in the gravel. Dammit Ray broke them up, saying, "You old farts gone to have heart attacks." He'd been Dammit Ray ever since he was a child. Big Ray seemed to precede everything he said to Little Ray with "dammit." Big Ray and Cobb turned on him and chased him to the dock.

"Hot damn, you old man, my fuckin' cellphone." Dammit Ray tossed his phone at the bank as the two older men flung him into the lake. This was starting like all the other coon hunts Travis had seen. Despite his previously pensive mood, he joined in the laughter and hooting, knowing full well he was next. He tried strolling casually to the house, but noticed Cobb and Big Ray grinning and moving toward him.

Dammit Ray joined them, shaking himself like a dog. Then Breeze appeared, walking briskly to him with his arms open. "Gimme a hug big, boy," Breeze said.

It was all over now. Travis grabbed Breeze, flung him aside, laughing, running toward the house. He was blocked in. Instinctively, he fell into his boxer's stance.

"No fair punching, Meathead," warned Cobb and they had him.

Travis relaxed, watched the horizon turn sideways, and held his breath as he hit the lake, still cold in the warm spring afternoon. Briefly underwater, he opened his eyes and felt like a kid again, looking up at the sky through clear lake water. *Enjoy it*, his inner voice said. *Enjoy it all*.

And he was glad for the water because something broke inside him and he cried.

∽∾∽

Vinita emerged from the front porch, wiping her hands

on a towel. "Calm yourselves, you boys. Hear? You're gonna hurt someone. Stop that!"

She was herself this afternoon. Travis shook as much water off himself as he could and hurried over to her.

"Don't you dare hug me, boy, all wet like that. I'm not part of this, this—quit!" She swiped the towel at him, backing away, laughing.

"I needa Vinita," he growled as he hugged her, kissing her cheeks.

She was so small, getting smaller.

"Travis, Travis, why don't you come out more often? You can't be so busy you can't just drive out here—"

"I will, Vinita, I will."

"Now, look at me, I'm soaked." She tried to look put out with him.

By dusk, everyone had arrived. They drank sparingly, mostly iced tea and water, knowing they'd be overindulging later. One or two popped a beer from their coolers. Some revved their four-wheelers, sitting on flotation tires for marsh driving. Dogs were put back into cages in pickups after they'd stretched their legs and stiff-legged about the other strange dogs.

Vinita had prepared food baskets. As usual, pie and sausage smells issued from under the kitchen towels tucking them in. Her baskets were legend. Anything uneaten would be tossed. You didn't bring a basket back with even a piece of fruit in it. Cobb checked on her, made sure she had her TV programs, book and knitting handy, that she had eaten. She was tired and would sleep well, whether on the couch or in bed. A Harry Potter movie was flickering in the dark, the sound low.

The raccoons had been at Vinita's corn and other garden crops so Cobb wanted to start near the property and shoot a few, to rotate the leadership so the rest would stay away for a while. He looked at his dogs on the bed of the old truck. "You'll never see better than Jack and Jack over here, Travis. Jack ain't too bad either."

"What about Jack?" Travis asked.

The crank was making Cobb hyper, his pupils big and full of shit-for-brains.

"He's a registered Treeing Walker, he is. Pure blood. Beauty to watch and hear. Them others are damn good, but not purebreds. Jack's part Bluetick, Jack's mostly Redbone, Jack Dog and Jack Ford are Black and Tans. All got the way about 'em. They'll go head to head with anything out here."

Cobb started the truck, gunned it a couple times, watching the voltage meter. He was talking a mile a minute, the hunt and the crank fueling his excitement. He grinned at Travis. "Let the good times *roll*, boy!"

He headed out over open pastureland, Travis hanging onto the bench seat to keep from hitting his head on the roof. The others followed, bouncing in the twilight, throwing long shadows from the sinking red ball sun. Two dogs, Jack and Jack, went flying off the flatbed and ran alongside, baying.

"Listen," Cobb cocked his head. "That's ol' Jack, the Walker."

Travis started to answer but Cobb shushed him. The moon was coming up and a plaintive, hoarse-starting howl split the night, becoming insistent "Orffffs" that weren't barks but some other sound altogether.

Cobb grinned in the moonlight, pounded the dashboard. "Damn that's purty!"

Travis dreaded the eventual cliff like drop-off of Cobb's crystal high, though the drug seemed made for coon hunts.

He thought about his father and his uncle. Was it Vietnam that had made them like they were? Probably not. More likely, they'd made Vietnam like it was.

They neared the sound and Cobb shut off the ignition. They had to thrash through thickets and tangles to get a clear view. Travis saw the raccoon clinging to a topmost branch in a half-dead tree, no canopy of escape to adjoining trees. Cobb flicked on the battery-pack pistol-grip lamp and lit him up like a cop on a criminal. The coon looked away from the harsh light and waited, simply waited. Seconds after the shot, he relaxed his hold, plummeted some sixty feet, hitting a few branches on the way down. The dogs surged forward and Cobb called them off, praising the Treeing Walker for his job well done. The dog sniffed at the coon, whose eyes were beginning to cloud. They walked back to the truck. "Shoulda let you have that shot, wasn't even thinking," Cobb said.

"That's okay," Travis said. "I'm just along for the ambience."

"Do what?"

"Uhh, just along for the ride," he said, suddenly embarrassed.

"Get you a gun." Cobb indicated the tool box.

"In a bit," Travis said.

He didn't want to kill any coons. It was joyless execution. He wanted to tree some people on his old man's list. He popped the top on a Coors, thinking about the lake incident. He never cried, not even a month ago when he'd run the grinder wheel into his thumb and thumbnail, making a notch that squirted blood like a leak in a hose. What kind of boxer would he have been if he'd cried every time he got hurt? He smiled mentally, feeling the tension in his face melt away. A shit boxer, that's what. Which was what he'd been.

Cobb bungeed the coon to the headache rack back of the cab, and they climbed back into the truck. The next coon took over two hours. They had to abandon the truck and follow creek banks, crashing through thorn tree growth and high sawgrass in the open areas. The wily coon swam and dodged, doubled back, climbed trees, and somehow escaped them, leaving dogs to look up into coonless trees.

When they finally treed the big coon, Cobb shined his halogen lamp on him. The coon returned a blazing look of his own.

"Man, that coon is one mean sumbitch," he murmured. Then, "Let's go get a sandwich, Travis." He called the dogs who reacted with some disbelief and called them again, more sharply. "Jack! Get your asses back here. Now!"

They continued to look back over their shoulders. One had managed to climb some fifteen feet into the tree from adjoining brush. He tried to figure a way down and dropped with a yelp as he hit. Cobb turned the light back to where the coon had been. It was gone.

They found the truck after a couple of false turns. Travis applied more OFF, offered it to Cobb, who ignored it. They made quick, dry sandwiches from Vinita's biscuits and sausage, folding a fried egg into the two pieces of fragrant bread. Eating in silence, legs hanging off the flatbed, they watched the huge disc of a moon on its downward journey.

"I'd get off the crank, Travis, but why? I got a endless supply, I'm old, and it's a bitch to get off of it. Probly would kill me."

"Hey, Cobb, that's your deal."

"Yeah, I know. But Vinita don't like it. When she's…around."

In the distance, dogs bayed, fresh on a scent or a sighting. The dogs named Jack stirred and muttered. Cobb poured half a cup of coffee from the thermos, poured Jack Daniels into it from a pint bottle. "Your old man."

"Yeah?"

"He called me a couple days before you went down there. Said he was bailin'. Said it was bad and getting worse, that…well, I'm glad you went down there, bud. It meant a lot to him."

A shot carried across the marsh.

"What he left you is unfinished business. But the hell of it is, it'll never get finished. It's just the way things are."

Travis yawned. Then made himself a Jack coffee.

"You can do it. I was just jawin' when I said you wasn't no Reno Pete. I mean, you're different than him. But if he didn't think you was up to it, believe me he wouldn'a left you that stuff."

"I wonder, Cobb."

"Nope. He told me about it. Much as he could over the phone. You'll have help. Especially down in Louisiana. Family down there. Stone frogs and creoles." Cobb pronounced it *Loozianna*. "Let's go join the boys. Might be the last one a these ever."

Cobb tended to get a little theatrical on crank and jacked coffee too, Travis reflected. But he might be right.

They ran across Joe Summers and his little ATV loaded with raccoons. He and his dogs were on the way back. He pulled up next to the driver's side, the Kawasaki engine sputtering on low idle. "Ray and them got skunked. They treed some but both 'em too drunk to shoot." He laughed. "Michel got him some, give 'em to me as he knows I use 'em. Rest of 'em just playin' out there. Tellin' lies and braggin' on their dogs. Ol' Rankin's got a damn Beagle! But that little short-legged sumbitch is game, I tell you. It's Hazel's house dog. Getting a workout." He gunned the ATV and his dogs, having laid down panting, stood ready to go. "Be back out in a minute."

They left the truck when the woods got too thick. Jack Ford picked up a scent and the rest followed.

"You didn't bring you a gun," Cobb said.

"I'm doin' fine, just the dogs and you is enough for me," Travis said.

He took a swig from a water bottle and replaced the cap. Jack Ford's yodel changed to full blast treeing mode and they hurried to catch up.

⁕⁑⁕

Before dawn, they sat again on the flatbed. Cobb said, "Bone tard, Travis. Old, too. Vinita's checkin' out on life and with her shortin' out like that, I don't much care about the other stuff. I understand Reno callin' it a day, sure do, especially when he was dyin' anyway. He wanted me to make you understand something. He wasn't no psycho."

"Aw, Cobb, you don't have to—"

"Yes. Yes I do. Listen to me. Reno was at the Bay of Pigs. Know what that was? Anything about it?"

"Yeah, Cobb, I read about it. Not just the shit they have in school."

"Good. Anyway, he saw his friends cut to ribbons by Castro's men because JFK chickened out on giving them air support. Pulled it at the worst possible time. When they offered Reno big money to do it, he said *hell* yeah. Some a them cubes as he called 'em was his friends. Cuba would damn near be a state right now if Kennedy hadn't fucked the dog. Reno woulda done him for free. But he got mixed up with some freaks in doin' it. Those are the people you will be jackin' with."

His uncle poured the last of the coffee and Jack Daniels for them both. The dogs were asleep. Improbable visions of Robert Crumb comic book freaks walked through Travis's mind and he laughed out loud. Cobb didn't act like he thought that was inappropriate at all.

"Well, best get back to start cookin' for these coon-ass soonamagoons." He hopped down from the bed. "Worked up an appetite, I tell *you*."

෧෯෧

A pale and bashful first light showed that everything was ready when they got back. Outside grilles were smoking, picnic tables full of condiments, mismatched silverware, and stacks of clean shop towels for napkins. Vinita was not only herself, she was up to full speed.

Travis washed up at the hydrant near the dock, splashing cold water on his head and face. He looked back at the truck, saw Cobb doing a snootful from his baggie. Cobb beamed, pounded his chest with false energy, shouted, "Gawd all *mighty*, will you look at this? Vinita's been up and at 'em! You and me, boy, we coulda stayed out another two hours! I knew it! I just flat *knew* it!"

The birds were up. Joe Summers was snoring lightly in a hammock by the dock. Cobb upended him, dumping him out. They cleaned two coons and began grilling the parts, Joe muttering sleepily as they worked. Vinita was no-nonsense busy, filling iced tea pitchers and pitchers of lemonade in the morning sun. Coolers of ice sat by each picnic table. She'd bring hot coffee pots out last, set them on sterno heaters. She moved about in staccato gestures, her face set in almost angry concentration, forbidding any interruption.

Soon, they heard the gutter muffler of Harley Rankin's truck, and his dogs barking. Then the others began straggling in. Dammit Ray came alone. "Fuck him," he said when asked about Big Ray. "Let the sumbitch walk. Oohh, pardon my French." He grinned sheepishly hunch-ing his shoulders and covering his mouth when he saw Vinita shoot him a look.

No broken bones, no snakebites, nothing major showed up with the rest. One of Cobb's dogs was limping but that was it.

After they cleaned the few coons they'd brought, and washed up, they began picking food up at the stations, Cobb, Travis, and Joe grilling.

Big Ray came through a thicket at the other end of the lake, carrying a rifle and lights. All he said to Dammit Ray was, "You and me, bub. You wait."

Dammit Ray winked and grinned at the others as he spooned baked beans onto his plate.

Some strict owners kept dogs in cages, others fed theirs scraps from the table. Rankin's beagle rotated from table to table, a smile on his face and his tail whipping violently. Vinita, relaxed now, poured and replenished coffee and beamed at Big Ray's flirting and the compliments of the men. If this *was* the last coon hunt, thought Travis, it would be the best and the most fitting to remember.

The last vehicle and dog left by mid-afternoon. Cobb sat on the wicker couch and patted his knee when Vinita walked by carrying dishes. "Vinita, come here, take a break."

"It never gets done thataway. Maybe you could carry a few things inside your own self. Travis is helping."

Cobb crossed his eyes at Travis as he passed with an armload of dishes. "Trevis is hepping," he said in a falsetto voice. "Shit fire," he said softly.

"What was that?" Vinita called from the kitchen.

Cobb grimaced, stretched his back, went outside, and began picking up sterno heaters. One was still hot and he threw it in the grass, swearing. Travis saw it and began to smile.

Cobb glared at him. "Don't you laugh, dammit. I'll whip your ass."

"Someone needs a nap, I think," said Travis.

"Someone needs a ass whippin'."

"Little cranky, are you?" Travis realized how what he had just said could be taken wrong when he saw Cobb's murderous look. And even at its most innocent, he had crossed the line. "I didn't mean it like that, Cobb. I was kidding. And it was dumb, anyway."

Cobb's look softened. "Shoot, it ain't nothin'. What say we finish this and get some shuteye, go out and check trotlines tonight?"

Travis wasn't relishing the thought of being mosquito bait on the Marais Des Cygne, but it would be the chance he needed to talk to his uncle some more, alone, before he left.

Travis yawned. "Looking forward to it."

They slept from four in the afternoon to ten that night. At ten-fifteen, Cobb put a light blanket over Vinita who was asleep on the couch, turned the TV down, and shut the door softly.

❦❦❦

The mercury-vapor light atop the tall pole at the dock drew a cloud of bugs and reflected in the wavering black water. The aluminum boat had two motors attached to the transom, a small Johnson outboard and the smaller electric trolling motor. Cobb walked to the end of the dock, probably snorted a couple of blasts, though Travis didn't watch. He was busy applying OFF to any exposed areas on his body and around his waist. The nights on the Marais Des Cygne were time-honored rituals, his anointments a part of them over the years. Mosquitos never seemed to bother Cobb. Or Reno, either, back in the day.

Two of the dogs named Jack had followed them down to the dock. One lay down with a grunt, the other scratched fleas.

Travis opened the Styrofoam cooler and dropped the tube of repellent into it with the beer and ice. Sheet lightning flickered in the west and a barely discernible mumble of thunder rolled from that direction a minute later. Travis felt a little off center from shifting his sleep hours and the strangeness of what lay ahead of him in the coming days. A sharp call floated over the water, its edges softened by distance.

"Screech owl," said Cobb. "It's him and us up and about." He stepped into the boat, swaying with the movement he was causing. He sat on the bench by the motors. "You comin' or what?"

He pulled the rope and grasped the dock to steady the boat for Travis, who stepped in and sat facing Cobb. An inch or so of rain water sloshed around his feet. For lack of anything to do, he picked up a rusting French Market coffee can and bailed what he could.

"Brought a thermos of that." Cobb patted a soft plaid bag beside him. "Good strong chicory coffee and plenty of sugar." He grinned. Sugar was Jack Daniels.

Cobb choked the motor, started it, heading the boat parallel to the dock, then swung away from it in a smooth circling motion, its bow lifting. They were soon out of range of the dock light and Travis became used to the speed of the boat in darkness. The black water was smooth, so the little boat wasn't banging along jarring his teeth. After some twists and turns, Cobb slowed to negotiate through and around some tall grasses and shoots. The moon had emerged from clouds and Travis could see where they were going—into a funnel-like narrowing of water with growth on either side. Soon, it became a channel with banks and trees. Cobb slowed, cut the motor, and raised it. Then he started the electric trolling motor.

"Remember when me and you and Pete used to come in here?"

"Sure, I do."

"Little ways in here. There." Cobb pointed out a plastic milk jug marking a line.

"Yep."

"Deep lines for catfish. We'll check that when we come out."

The boat moved silently upstream. Travis was aware of bats, mosquitoes, the occasional splash of something sliding off the mud bank into the water ahead of them. The smell of combined rot, flowering plants, the primordial mud, and fish life was powerful perfume to Travis. He'd missed it.

"Where you gonna start on this Pete thing?"

"New Orleans. Most of it is there," Travis said.

"You know we got Brouchards there. Piccards. Couple St. Cyrs."

"Frog city."

"Old timey frogs. Keep to theyselves. Give 'em any shit, you end up in the bayou."

"Sounds like someone I know," Travis said.

Lightning flashed. The thunder came a few beats later, rolling through the tree-tunneled channel. The wind increased outside the more protected area of the creek, the trees overhead groaning and thrashing about.

Cobb pulled into a cove-like dent in the bank, turned off the trolling motor, and tossed a grappling hook anchor into the mud. "Wait out the storm here for a bit. Coffee?"

They sat in the boat, nursing their hot bourbon-laced coffees. The one line they'd checked had a couple of small bass and a turtle. They cut the turtle loose, and released the fish. Travis felt the boat rise and fall just a little. The lake and backwaters were choppy now, and the surge was affecting the creek. No mosquitos whined near his ears.

"Cobb, you think the old man had all his marbles when he...checked out?"

"Yep."

"How do you know he did it?"

"He said so. One night like this, by the mouth of the river."

"Who killed my momma? What were their names?" Travis asked it so softly he wasn't sure Cobb heard, or that he wanted him to. He saw her in the tire swing. Standing in the kitchen, forking sausages in an iron skillet, browning them.

"Guy named Morales, guy named Tinsley. Both CIA. Both dead and missin' their scalps and ears. He sent the scalps to their boss."

"Who's their boss?"

"Don't know. Might be in that letter to you. It's not like he sat up all night talking about it. He just told me and that was it."

Lightning cracked and a tree crashed upstream. The splash rocked the boat enough that Travis grabbed a side and sloshed coffee onto his leg.

"It always puzzled us that they knew where to go to wire his truck," Cobb said. "He never told anyone but me. The only thing we could figure is someone overheard it. You know how the sound carried last night at the coon hunt? Well, could have been like that. Like we heard Big Ray and Dammit Ray like they was settin' next to us. And they was across the slough. But then they wasn't exactly whispering neither."

Travis smiled. "They were hollering. Like always. But they were a ways off, all right."

Cobb pulled the anchor back and hung it on the transom, then backed out and headed upstream. They came around the bend and saw the tree that the lightning had struck. It was low across the water, fine for a little foot-bridge but impassable for their boat.

They tied up to it and climbed the muddy bank. Cobb lit the way with the coon light. The storm was moving east and the muffled thunder reminded Travis of boxcars bumping on a faraway train. The one trotline beyond the tree was empty.

The line closest to the mouth of the creek had two good-sized catfish which they kept. Cobb tied up again and they sat on the bank with their coffees. The mosqui-tos were back, Travis noted, but not as bad. The storm had left a fresh breeze and he could see whitecaps all over the lake.

"Need any money?" Cobb asked.

"Thanks, but I'll have a few grand from the sale of that company. Plus a grand a month coming in on that for a year. If they pay."

"You can stay with kin down there."

"Rather not, at least to start."

"Well, you need to meet them, anyway. They know everything goes on down there. Broussards are my deal-ers for LaCygne Green, you know that?"

Travis laughed. "They buy that ditchweed shit down there?"

"Ditchweed shit? Watch your mouth. They even want it down in Mexico to sell back to the *turistas*. We got Memphis and Nashville, too. Ditchweed my ass. Beats the shit outa that Maui bud you like so much."

"Yeah, well it did put me on my hands and knees that time. I thought maybe you laced it with something."

"You can save Breeze a trip down there when you go. We'll load you up in that Nova. They'll never give you a second look in that rust bucket."

CHAPTER 9

Cobb stood suddenly, dropping his coffee. He looked off across the choppy lake toward the house. "Shit!"

Travis stood, too. He could see a glow in the dark, some flames.

Cobb slid down the bank to the boat, choked the Johnson, killed it, finally started it. He'd have left without Travis if he'd gotten it started the first time. They slammed across the lake as fast as the little boat would go, banging the choppy waves. Travis held on with both hands.

Cobb made "unhh" sounds through clenched teeth as if he was making the boat go faster.

He bumped the dock hard and leaped out, leaving Travis to tie up. Travis tied to a cleat then jumped onto the dock from the bobbing boat.

The flames lit up the front drive and the vehicles there. The dogs were baying and running about. Cobb's silhouette disappeared into the front door.

A moment later Cobb reappeared carrying Vinita's limp form, her bare feet seeming to kick lazily as he ran with her. She looked small in Cobb's arms.

He kept saying "Awww, awww," as though to a hurt

child as he carried her down near the dock and laid her gently in a chaise there.

Travis remembered the big pump by the lakeside and ran to join hose lengths with their quick connectors. He ran back and started the pump, dropping its intake hose into the lake. He tried to reach the end of the hose before it whipped around from the pressure and had to chase it. Catching it, he dragged it uphill, and trained it on the roof where flames leapt, feeling the intense heat on his face and hands.

It was just a corner of the roof and screened-in porch that was afire, mostly outside stuff, and he had it under control in minutes. *Vinita couldn't have inhaled smoke from that, could she?* he thought. She had been in the far back of the house. Maybe she'd be okay.

"Awww, nawwww, naawwww," Cobb kept saying, a moan more than words.

He was kneeling by the chaise holding Vinita's hands. It raised the hairs on the back of Travis's neck. He'd never heard such a sound. Especially not from Cobb. It was total despair, awful pain. He let the hose whip and ran to throttle the pump down, hurried over to Cobb and Vinita.

"Jesus Christ," he said, when he saw what Cobb was moaning about.

Vinita's throat had been cut and there were bruises on her head and arms. He fell to his knees and retched coffee and whiskey. He stood when he could. He was no help, being this way, his head swimming. *Get ahold of your fucking self. Now.*

He couldn't pull Cobb away from her, maybe shouldn't. What could he do? He checked the smoldering front porch. It would keep for now. He'd have to call someone. Who? He noticed the gas can, then, near the porch. He moved it away from the smoking rubble and smelled gasoline on the porch, no doubt the accelerant used to start the fire. A dog pushed into his leg, wanting solace. Some dogs were sitting around Cobb and Vinita. One or two of them started to bay, heads skyward. Good God, what was going on?

He went inside. The gasoline smell was evident up and down the hallway. Someone had started this fire. He grabbed his cellphone from the bedroom he was using, looked up Big Ray in the string-hung kitchen notebook that served as their phone book.

"Huh?" said Big Ray. Travis looked at his watch. Two in the morning.

"It's Travis, Ray. Something awful has happened here."

After he explained what was going on, Big Ray sounded wide awake. "I'll be there in a couple minutes. Don't call anyone yet. You sure she's gone?"

"Yes." Travis's voice choked.

"I'll bring some morphine, hear? Don't let Cobb outa your sight. He's in bad shock, sounds like. *You* can't be. You hafta be cool, you fuckin' hear me?" Big Ray was louder now.

"I hear you."

Cobb was rocking back and forth, holding Vinita's hands, rocking her with him, silent now. The dogs were laying around him quietly. *Hound dogs*, thought Travis, *worthless as protection*. They might get their hackles up, but they just weren't very aggressive. What the hell had happened here? Had he brought this from Daytona? Another small shock wave hit him when he remembered Flame. He'd better call her as soon as he got the chance. Maybe he'd wake up and this would all be a nightmare fading in the morning sun.

Big Ray's silver pickup pulled up. He climbed down and walked slowly toward Travis and Cobb, taking in the scene.

"Where do you want it, arm, butt, where?" Travis said.

"Arm is fine. Don't need a vein. Just hang onto him." He pulled a syringe from a box, stuck it in a rubber-topped bottle, flicked it, and squirted a small amount in the air.

Travis and Big Ray tore Cobb's shirtsleeve open. Big Ray swabbed his bicep with alcohol, said "Bear hug him. Don't let him move."

Big Ray stuck Cobb and slowly emptied the contents. Cobb barely noticed.

Big Ray helped Cobb to another chaise, lying him down carefully. Travis got a clean sheet from the house and they laid it over Vinita.

Travis told him of the glow across the lake, the frantic trip.

"There was a car stuck in the road," Big Ray said. "You know how it gets when it's wet. Guy wanted a pull."

"Where is he?" asked Travis.

"Dammit Ray was behind me. We sorta told the guy we'd pull him out for twenty bucks. Then we detained him. Dammit Ray's got him."

Another Dodge pickup pulled into the drive. Dammit Ray got out and approached slowly, wiping his hands on his overalls. He and Big Ray talked quietly by the truck.

"Travis?" Big Ray called him over to where they stood.

In the bed of Dammit Ray's truck was a man, tied, and duct taped. He looked at them, and they at him. He was dressed in jeans, T-shirt, had a ponytail.

"The question I got is what was he doin' out here middle of the night. He says he was lost. A lost person don't turn down a dirt road after a rain, I wouldn't think. Had some blood on his T-shirt. Smells like gasoline. He got in all right but couldn't get out. He's catfish bait, I'm thinking. That might be a rental car. We'll have to figure out what to do with it."

"What do we do with him? Did he kill my aunt?" The overflow and ebb of adrenaline made Travis shaky, but he was calm, ignoring the jitters. He'd felt that in the provinces. Mostly just ready.

"Well, we cut him open, put a log chain in where his guts were, tie him shut with baling wire, slip him into the Marais Des Cygne. Or maybe he'll tell us what he was doin' here."

The man began rolling and making noises behind the duct tape. Big Ray looked at him like he was a curiosity then walked back over to where Cobb was. Dammit Ray stayed, facing the prone man, his arms on the truck bed side, wrists hanging limp with a cigarette in one hand.

"We got to think this over some. My best thought is, Vinita would like a good Christian burial, Travis. But we got to avoid the law."

"How do we do that?"

"Vance Funeral Home in LaCygne. He's a cousin. He'll do up a death certificate from Doc Wexler if he can sober him up enough to sign the sumbitch. He'll prepare Vinita. High lace collar. Purty as when she was a girl. Open casket. No questions," he paused then said, "Dammit," vehemently.

Travis looked at the ground. He felt sick again.

"What are y'all into here, Travis?"

"Can't say, Big Ray."

"Is it worth all this?"

"No. It sure as hell ain't."

"Poor Cobb. Poor Vinita. You gonna need us down the road, Travis? Help settle some stew?"

"Maybe. You're already helping a lot."

"I'd do anything for these people, Travis. Anything."

"I know."

そぶそ

Travis flinched as something darted by his face, but he relaxed when he saw it was just a large Monarch butterfly. He watched as it circled Vinita's body on the chaise, landing on her head. He started to wave it away, but something in its movement stopped him. The butterfly rose and circled Vinita, then lit on Travis's shoulder. He walked away from the chaise and the people in the pool of light from the house floodlights.

"Is that you, Vinita?" he said softly, feeling silly speaking to his shoulder.

He couldn't remember butterflies flying at night, but apparently they did. This one did. He was reminded of Vinita's mobile on the front porch, the female figure flying among kites, the feeling of freedom. She was free now. He looked at his shoulder. The Monarch was gone.

そぶそ

On the west coast of Africa off Sierra Leone, one of the crew of a Chinese fishing vessel marveled at the size of a monarch butterfly alighting on a brightly painted blue boat sitting tied to the dock. The large butterfly rose into the air, did some aerobatic pirouettes over the warm Atlantic water, and flew out to sea. A few minutes later the little blue boat began to bump and spin, pulling at its frayed rope. An airborne churn scared up some whitecaps in a widening circle a mile or so out in the Atlantic due to the disturbance above the eighty-degree water. Monarch butterflies flew in and out of the disturbed air, formed up in a small cloud, and headed for land. A diamond miner in the Bonthe district looked up to see a flock of very large monarchs diving and playing as they headed in toward New Guinea, and took it as a sign.

ℰℐℰℐ

At 12:30 the next day, Dallas Police Detective Ross Holt drove to Dealey Plaza with his bacon cheeseburger and an iced tea. He pulled up in the railroad yard behind the fence, where he could get some peace and quiet. He left the motor running for the air conditioning, opened the door, and got out. He stretched as he watched a couple of butterflies playing near the fence. Then he got back into the car and unwrapped the sandwich. *No more fast food after today,* he thought. *Why does food that's so bad for you taste so good?* He left the police radio on and ate while reading a book propped on the steering wheel. The book was Walt Brown's *Treachery in Dallas.*

ℰℐℰℐ

In New Orleans, a crime figure named Anthony Binaggio walked across Rampart Street to a small store-front private club, where he spent part of his day drinking demitasses of espresso coffee, heavily sugared, a habit he'd picked up from Carlos Marcello years before. A butterfly darted near his face and he swatted at it with the *Times-Picayune.* Even the fucking bugs were disrespecting him, he thought. One of his men had been shot on Mirabeau Street in Gentilly the night before, and no one had a clue about it. Some rival dealers, Blacks, were encroaching over there, but his guy had no business there.

Unless he was freelancing.

That bothered Binaggio. That and Rafferty warning him about some JFK-related shit that he could care less about. Rafferty. Guy lived in the past.

About the same time, also in New Orleans, at a private club in the World Trade Center, oilman Jerome Rafferty was shaking out a crisp napkin to place in his lap as his cellphone rang. A text from Brandi Binaggio. He'd get to her later. He had to figure out how to approach her husband again about some crazy goings-on in Kansas. Binaggio was off the reservation, it seemed, and a touch sensitive about it. Something about marijuana and unnecessary deaths causing the natives, apparently jackpine savages, to overreact. Kansas?

He noticed a stream of butterflies capering outside the window. He knew it was migration time, but hadn't realized they flew this high.

CHAPTER 10

The pallbearers were dressed in their best. Travis and Breeze were the ones who actually looked well-dressed in sport coats, ties, shined shoes, and regular pants. Big and Dammit wore white shirts buttoned at the neck and wrists with clean, pressed overalls. Harley Rankin suffered in a dark wool suit, the pants of which had several moth holes that showed white patches of skin until Breeze sat him down and colored the skin areas with a black Sharpie. The others wore pressed jeans and shirts. Cobb—shaved, hair trimmed—was glassy-eyed, his mind elsewhere, responding to comments with an absent-minded smile, holding the hand of each well-wisher in both his large paws. He wore a blazer of Travis's, pressed Wranglers, and a new white shirt open at the neck.

"She looks real purty," said a blue-haired town lady he didn't know. "She was a purty lady from out in Oklahoma, some Injun to her, I think, and she looks nice on the way to her Lord," the lady said, as if perhaps Cobb didn't know where Vinita was from, or who she was.

"Yes, yes," he said, patting her hand with both of his.

Travis wondered if Cobb felt like he did, wanting only to run off over the smoothly landscaped hill and keep running until he fell, his lungs shrieking for air, get up and run some more. Life, as they'd known it, was over, Cobb's grief unfathomable. Travis stood nearby, hands crossed in front of him, helpless.

"Was she your mother, son?" asked an old man with a very stooped back. It was an effort for him to look up at Travis.

"No, no sir. She's—she was, my aunt," he said, bending slightly at the knees to look the old man in the eyes. "They had no children," he added. *Oh shut up*, he thought. *None of this matters.*

"But you're a St. Cyr, aren't you?"

"Yes, sir." How could Cobb stand this?

The pastor had his say. A canned speech with a couple of Vinita mentions thrown in among platitudes. Cars and pickups were starting up and leaving. There was a reception at the Presbyterian church she had attended in LaCygne, then they could go home. To what? The dogs. The emptiness. He'd spring Cobb from the church thing early, take him back to the house. His friends had repaired the screened-in porch and roof from the aborted fire. The new wood and shingles stood out like scars.

Chances were Vinita would have lapsed into the dementia that was pursuing her anyway, Travis thought, with a flash of anger at himself for trying to mitigate the awfulness. There was no good side to any of this. The dementia would have been hell, too. His only hope was that she'd been anesthetized by it at the time of the murder.

A fog lifted within him. He gazed around at the small groups assembled, soon to disperse. He knew he would kill. Fuck the money, but might as well take that too.

Her killer was well into the wild and deep of the Marais Des Cygne, never to resurface. The rental car had been driven to Denver, wiped clean, left at the airport there at a long term parking lot, avoiding the sparsely placed cameras. They'd gotten what information they could from the man whose luck had run out. He was MK13, a Hispanic gang, and was supposed to kill everyone in the house, burn it if he had time, money up front. He couldn't connect his immediate boss to the JFK thing, or even to those trying to muscle in on Cobb's marijuana and meth sales. It was compartmentalized.

Breeze thought he'd seen him before, felt he was drug-related. His pony-tailed scalp and ears went to his boss through another gang member Breeze had dug up and taken to an abandoned quarry with a bag over his head. Big and Dammit Ray dumped him out there with the mementos. Travis now knew scalping was something like peeling a grapefruit. He was Reno Pete's son, after all.

Big Ray had said, "Naw, like this, peel it easy…" given the Spyderco knife back to Travis.

CHAPTER 11

"Hello?"

"Flame. It's me, Travis."

"Uh, hi."

"You all right?"

"Pretty much. What do you mean, exactly?"

"Anything odd going on?"

"Odd? No. Well, wait. I took Pete's ashes to Tulsa like he wanted. I hope you don't mind. I called you but got your machine, didn't have your cell number. Anyway, when I got back the place had been broken into. So yeah, that was odd."

"Did they take anything?

"No. Just tossed stuff around. We didn't have much of any value to burglars. I'd already given his guns to a friend of his. Creeped me out having them around."

"Yeah, I imagine. You might want to get just one back. For protection."

"Wh—why?"

"Just because. He was into some weird shit, you know that. There are people who might think you know where stuff is."

"You're scaring me."

"Good. You might think about moving, Flame. We

can help you. Reno wouldn't have wanted anything to happen to you."

"I—I'll think about it."

ᏆᎧᏆᎧ

Travis called his answering machine in Kansas City. Two hangups. One recorded message from a congress-woman. One recorded message from the Salvation Army. A message from the older member of the father/son team buying his business about floor sanders and the title to the truck and trailer.

And an unexpected message. "Mr. Meachem? This is Detective Holt at the Dallas Police Department. Need you to kindly give me a quick call at 214-555-4414. Thank you. He repeated the number, and said, "It's two p.m. Wednesday afternoon, June twenty-seventh." And he hung up.

"Detective Holt, please. Travis Meachem calling."

"Mr. Meachem. Thanks for returning my call. Did you know a Melissa Bradley, was an airline stewardess for Delta?

Travis was aware of bird calls, a faint splash from the lake. "Yes. Why is this in the past tense?"

"'Cause she is, Mr. Meachem. Very past tense. Throat cut in her apartment last week. How well did you know her?"

"God. I'm sorry to hear that." His forehead throbbed and his throat went dry. "Well, ahh, we had a date in KC. Went to dinner. I met her on the flight."

"That it, dinner?"

"Well, drinks later."

"And?"

"And what?"

"You know, Travis—may I call you Travis? We have

reason to believe you spent the night with her in KC."

"Okay."

"Now that's getting to know someone. Then you called her, left a message. You ever see her again?"

"No, Detective Holt, I didn't. I left KC the same day I got there, for my uncle's place in the Marais Des Cygne wildlife refuge. Still here. What were the circumstances of her...death?"

"Well, Travis, I'm not at liberty to say much about that now, maybe later. What were you doing night of June twenty first?" Holt's accent was rural Texas, a lot like Melissa's had been. Travis thought—in a vacant space between the incoming information and resistance to it—that it was a pleasant voice, a patient one.

"I was on a coon hunt."

"No shit? A real honest to goodness coon hunt? My old man used to have some dogs. What kinda dogs you hunt?"

"Black and Tans, Bluetick, a Treeing Walker, I think. My uncle's dogs."

"Damn. I know Walkers. That's a helluva alibi, Mr. Meachem. People see you on this here coon hunt?"

"About twenty people. All night. The previous evening, and pretty much all day the next day. They don't mess around when they do it. It's about a two day deal."

"No drinkin' I don't suppose?"

"A little," Travis said.

What sounded like a chuckle came back over the line. "Yeah, I recall some of that. Well, if you don't mind, I'd like to keep in touch with you while the investigation is ongoing. What's your cell number?"

Travis gave it to him. "But I'll be down South for a while."

"Where's that, Travis?"

"Louisiana. I'm checking out a new franchise. I'm

selling a flooring business and need to be looking at something else for income."

"Right. Well, I'll be in touch. Thanks for returning my call, sir. I'll call off the Overland Park people and the KCPD. For now. Coon hunting. I'll be damned." He made a sound like "huh," which could have been a short laugh, and hung up.

༄༅

Travis felt angry and hopeless at the same time. People close to him, old friends and new ones were being hurt, good people. The break-in at the parking lot in KC was part of this. Throats cut, two of them, were not random killings, but messages. *Don't pursue this.*

Fuck it, he was all in now. *All* in. Someone would pay, someone big, not just runners and errand people. He didn't care about the money. He cared about cutting a swath and leaving some ruins. But he couldn't half-ass it. That would make it too easy for them to kill him like a gnat.

Like Afghanistan, it would require clear-eyed planning to get these fucks.

They'd made it look like he was a suspect in one of these killings. They'd killed a beloved of his, and also a good lady he'd just met. Vinita's death might possibly have been drug fallout, until Melissa's killing. As little as he knew about Melissa's murder, the similarities told him all he needed to know. The car break-in, Flame's home being broken into—it was all related. The crewcut guy at the restaurant. He'd missed a bet there, he should have looked deeper into that guy, but he was too new to the game then.

"She come to me in a dream last night, Travis." Cobb's voice, close behind him, startled him. "Vinita, she come to me as if she was right here with us, plain as day."

Travis breathed out, came back to the present. "What'd she say, Cobb?" He had felt her aura in the house after the funeral, as if she was trying to say a proper goodbye. He'd spoken to her, in case it was her and not just his confused psyche. He'd told her he was awful sorry and she'd soothed him somehow and was gone. If any of that was real, it made sense she'd visit Cobb.

"She said she was all right, she was fine. Travis, it was like she was back with us," Cobb shook his head in wonder. "She said, well she didn't say it, she..."

"She conveyed it? She made it known?" Travis prompted.

"That's it. I mean I *knew* what she was saying. She said there had been no pain, she'd been somewhere else at the time in her head. She hadn't been frightened or hurt. And she was just fine now."

"Well, I'm glad to hear it. I sure am." Travis wondered what mechanism had clicked in Cobb's brain to keep him from going crazy, and if it was just neurons and chemistry, or did Vinita really visit him from The Other Side. He'd heard things all his life like that, especially back here in the refuge.

Cobb swallowed, looked out at the lake, and said, "I ain't gonna miss her no less, it ain't gonna hurt no less, but that's me, that's the living feeling sorry for theyselves, and they best get over it."

"We'll get to the other side of it, Cobb. But there's no way around it except through it. She was my mother for a lot of years, and you've always been the other half of that."

"She always said hate hurt the hater worse than the hated, but you know what I'm sayin'?"

"I do. I know. We'll take care of that part too. It's not

like we're gonna sit around and just take it. But Reno said you had to shed it to think correctly. I remember that. You told me he said that."

"He did. And we will. Like they say, the best revenge is kickin' ass. Effectively. We're gonna need some money. I'll take care of that directly. And that piece a shit Nova ain't goin' nowhere. Vinita's Land Cruiser will make damn good transportation. I'll get on that, too."

Travis needed his computer but he didn't want to go home and it was a desktop anyway. What he needed was a big-gig power Mac laptop with 4G. Breeze, he could get anything. Travis punched his number, thinking that very soon cell phones would have to be disposable. The people they'd be dealing with weren't flunkies.

"Yo, Breeze."

"Mofo. How's Cobb?"

"Pretty good actually. I need an Apple laptop, a 4G hot rod. Can you get me one?"

"Switch subjects much?"

"Sorry. We need some stuff and need to get moving. I can be nicey-nice later."

"No, you can't. I suppose you want it today."

"That would be good."

∽∾∾

Cobb was under the hood of the dusty Land Cruiser. New battery, new plugs, and wires. The interior was clean. Cobb had kept the mice out. The AC worked. Looked like they had a vehicle. Travis had removed some things that Vinita had left behind, some book tapes and CDs.

On the long drive to KC, she'd listened to Gershwin's Rhapsody in Blue, Frank Sinatra, Corinne Bailey Rae, Dwight Yoakam. A woman of varied tastes and interests.

And she chose Cobb, Travis mused. His two dads had married Okies. And violence had reigned. The love was strong. He'd seen that, but no match for the violence that came down like a rogue storm. Reaping what was sowed. Was that what it was? Was there something to that? Well, if so, then he intended to be part of the biblical hell that followed.

⧉⧉⧉

When he tried to pay for the Mac PowerBook, Breeze refused, palms out. "Just bring it back in decent shape. It's loaded up pretty good for whatever you might need."

The first thing Travis used it for was to check miles from KC to New Orleans—eight hundred, thirty-nine. Kansas plates on the Land Cruiser would stick out like a sore thumb, maybe they should rent cars. Cobb said no. When they got to New Orleans they would sell the vehicle, buy another one. Or simply switch plates.

"Don't worry about the little stuff, Travis. I ain't as dumb as I look. Are you?" Cobb swatted Travis on the side of the head. "Gawd, I hope not, for your sake."

Less than a week after the funeral and Cobb was showing flashes of himself again. He showed Travis a fat roll of twenties and hundreds after a LaCygne Green transaction and Breeze took a shipment of the meth crap off to the half-dead tire-stealing gap-toothed freaks who would take it to dreamland. Travis had to address that with Cobb. He'd put it off but now was good as any.

"Cobb, I don't want you down there. Not on crank."

"Shoot, Travis, if that bothers you I'll just kick it. But I'm goin'."

"You told me to always remember two things about an addict. One, they lie, and, two, they lie."

"I don't lie."

"Not when you're off crank, you don't."

"You best watch the way you talk to me, boy. I *will* ruin your fucking day, kin or no kin." His look was fearsome, but resignation was in his eyes. Vinita had been after him to quit.

It took Cobb a week. The meth hadn't yet damaged Cobb's nerves to the degree that the pain was unbearable, but one never knew about him. He either had an incredible threshold of pain or was just the toughest fucker Travis had ever seen, besides Reno. They needed the time anyway. Travis had to re-register the Toyota at DMV to get the plates up to date. He wanted Breeze to help him figure out the PowerBook's more arcane avenues and security issues.

Then Travis unearthed Reno's tubes to study the contents in depth. He found a spool of 8 mm film in an envelope also containing a DVD of the film. He slipped it into the player, taking note of a stack of Vinita's movies—old classics and a few newer ones. The Harry Potters had a stack of their own.

The first part of the black and white film swung wildly about as though the person holding the 8 mm camera hadn't operated one before. A shot directly into the sky, then the sun flashed and obliterated the scene before it settled on what looked like a three hundred sixty degree pan of the scene, with the person holding the camera at the center. This was the famed Grassy Knoll, or rather behind the fence bordering the knoll. Travis recognized the area from pictures he'd seen in a book by Charles Groden, a book full of photos of all aspects of the assassination.

The slightly shaking film showed parked cars, a background containing railroad cars and an observation tower of some kind, the tall fence of the type one sees around backyard swimming pools for privacy, trees, a Hertz rental car digital clock atop a building that read 12:07, more sky, then the operator walked toward the fence, pointed it over at what Travis recognized as Elm Street Extension, or Parkway, where the presidential motorcade had not yet appeared.

A few people were moving about across the street. It was all silent. There seemed to be a break in the film, then it showed cars parked in the railroad yard, zooming up on a white Chevrolet, about a 1961 model. The license plate was clearly shown: Visit Oklahoma 1963, XR-2486. There was a Wallace sticker on the bumper.

The camera swung back to behind the fence. A young Reno Pete in a policeman's uniform smiled at the camera, showed a two-piece weapon, applied the stock to the Fireball that Travis was now familiar with. He put the weapon to his shoulder, aimed around through the scope.

The cameraman fooled with the zoom bringing Reno close up then farther away. He zoomed to the gun, to Reno's badge, his hat, and the gun on his hip. It then went black for a second. When it resumed it showed Reno's back and the gun aiming over the fence. Reno had one foot on a lower two-by-four. There were two bullets standing on the top two-by-four. Travis assumed another one was in the single-shot Fireball's chamber.

Hatless now, Reno had his left shoulder forward to the fence. Another man moved into the scene, carrying a spotting scope which he rested atop the fence. Reno turned his head, said something to the man, who nodded, gestured to his left.

The camera swung to the Hertz time sign, 12:25, then back to Reno. *This beats the shit out of the Zapruder film,* Travis thought. *I wonder who's still alive to give four million bucks for it. Someone. Someone evil. Or maybe a whole carload of evils. And I'm gonna rattle their cage. All. To. Hell.*

A minute passed. Another. Film still rolling. They didn't want to miss this. The spotter said something. Reno's back moved as though relaxing. The camera operator raised the camera up to show both the street in front of the fence and Reno's head and shoulders. A puff of silent smoke framed his old man's head, Reno still looking through his scope. The spotter turned, said something. Reno reached for the two bullets standing on the fence rail, but before he touched them it all went black.

Travis hit the replay, backed it up to right before the silent shot. It was pretty clear. As the open limousine pulled alongside the fence, Reno's shot was the one that undeniably killed the president. Some anomaly in the zoom lens made it look like the limo was only ten feet away from the fence, when it was actually more like fifty. The president's head appeared almost as large as Reno's and the spotter's, when it blew into a haloed mist. Travis hit the stop button on the remote. There it was. Reno, smoke, the president's head coming apart in the gritty still picture before him, brain matter in the air.

Travis took a deep breath, realizing he'd been so shallow in his breathing that he was lightheaded. There was no doubt his old man had done what he'd said. Jesus. And he'd walked away.

They had gotten into cars as though they were leaving a luncheonette, drove away unhindered. The setup pigeon, Lee Oswald, had survived, so they'd had to send Jack Ruby in to execute him on worldwide TV. You couldn't make shit like this up. Who would believe it. Oswald was supposed to be dead by a cop's bullet in West Oak, but he'd smelled the deal, figured it out. The cops didn't know what to do with him. They were falling all over each other like blind pups in a meat house. Hang him in his cell? Fake an escape attempt? No, have Ruby shoot him on the pretext he loved the prez and didn't

want the first lady to go through a trial. He wondered
which mental giant came up with that crap. Un-fucking-
real. What was real was Reno's part in it. That was doc-
umentary real.

*And I was in Afghanistan, but not for God and Coun-
try*, thought Travis. *At least I wasn't fodder for these
same assholes.* He knew that, on some level, all during
his tours, but people still needed killing, and he per-
formed with excellence. He was there, like Reno Pete
was in Vietnam. No, not like Reno Pete. More like a
high-priced chauffeur with a flak jacket and an M-16.
Reno knew what was happening and he was "advising."
He didn't give a shit about all the Washington flimflam,
the flag waving, the rake-offs and the hog-skimming. He
had his own clear-eyed motives. Part of him was a patriot, like Colonel Wood in 1776, the ancestor whose name
he took from time to time. Part of him was pure merc.
He'd been at the Bay of Pigs because he believed in it,
but he was well-paid, too.

He killed JFK because he was the man who'd hung
him out to dry in Cuba. He was the man who'd gotten a
lot of good men killed. Reno made it back to Miami after
hiding in the Zapata swamps rather than heading for the
Escambray Mountains, as did the remnants of the bri-
gade. It was no more hostile than the Marais des Cygne to
him, and he could have lived there for months. He haunt-
ed the beaches at night and found a small tattered sailboat
some invaders had tried to rig for escape. He was picked
up, dehydrated and drifting, by a charter fishing boat
halfway to Miami. He knew he'd lived for a reason.

Travis looked back at the tableau. He framed it forward a little at a time. The camera operator had focused
on the people in the car. The first lady's mouth formed an
O. JFK was now almost out of sight, having slumped to
the seat and his wife's side. Connelly was looking at his

own bloody shirt, then he was on the floor as he was hit again. The driver's demeanor was oddly calm. The car had hardly moved forward during this time. It appeared to have stopped, or slowed almost to a standstill.

Travis advanced the video. Mrs. Kennedy was climbing onto the deck of the trunk and a secret service man appeared from the rear, apparently to push her back into the car, then he climbed in. It looked like she had retrieved a piece of the president's head. Yes, that's what she was on the trunk to do. What had been in her mind? Get the pieces and repair him? She had to be in shock.

Travis was viewing something no one else in the world had seen. There had been witnesses who had seen the smoke from the shot. Witnesses who'd even seen Reno and sworn a cop was behind the fence. They'd been shined on by the Warren Commission. No one wanted to hear their testimony. Some had even died, trying to get their story out. Travis clicked the remote to off. He needed to think, take this in. He needed to be aware of his surroundings again, like in Kandahar. There was no peace there, even when it was quiet. There could be no peace now. He would adapt, as he'd adapted there, but he needed to quicken the pace, he needed to see things that weren't there again, or things that were minutely out of place, things that telegraphed, fired a synapse that was a microsecond faster than his enemy's thinking.

And he'd have to get in shape. Jesus he was soft. He grasped the roll at his middle. Pinch an inch my ass, this is pinch a handful.

He thought about Reno disappearing into the Marais de Cygne for days on end with only a knife, so he'd come out ready, senses sharpened, cleansed. Kurtz Territory, Travis had called it, explaining the Conrad novel, *Heart of Darkness*, to Cobb. After that, their own language included that.

"Kurtz sighting," Cobb would say after looking for a lost calf on his four-wheeler off in one of the refuges.

Or fishing way back in the river, Travis had caught a glimpse of something in the vine-tangled trees.

"Kurtz?" Cobb had asked.

"Maybe," Travis had said, spooked.

CHAPTER 12

A bench and weights from Travis's college days sat rusted and cobwebbed in one of the sheds. His speed-bag, a heavy punching bag, and gloves were back in the storm cellar under the main house. He would run daily. Start slow, not try to get it all back in a week. Like he had a fight in a month, yes, get ready for a month away. He could do it. Sit-ups, pull-ups, push-ups, running, reflex work. Make a list, follow it for a couple days until it was solid in his brain. Cut to two beers a day. He didn't smoke, that was a plus. Other than LaCygne Green, but that could wait until he was in shape.

He got up from the sofa, ejected the disc, slipped a Harry Potter out of its box, and inserted the JFK disc. Tossed it on the floor. In his room, he unpacked a pair of jersey sweat shorts, running shoes, then changed and headed out into the bright, still air.

The Gar Wood was gone from the dock. He guessed Cobb was out on the sparkling water clearing his head, if such was possible. Travis listened for the powerful Packard marine engine but heard nothing, saw nothing, shading his eyes with a palm, scanning the lake's visible horizon.

There were plenty of places on the big lake not visible

from here; Cobb was probably tied up in an inlet, thinking.

Travis stretched, attempted to touch his toes—no go—did some jumping jacks, twisted at the waist, bent over backward. Then he began to jog down the gravel drive to the hard packed dirt, into the darkness of the tree-tunneled road. His eyes adjusted as he kicked it up from a jog to a run, and he forced himself to be aware of all sounds, motion at the sides of the road, in the trees, his own breathing.

Sunny patches on the road flashed by. He would run to where the 1948 Chevy pickup was, with the tree growing up through its rusted bed. That was roughly two miles from the house. Slow jog back. Widen the distance daily until he could do the whole road distance.

His own sweat cooled him in the dark tunnel. The fruity smell of the bog, the rot of soil-enriching underbrush, fresh mint, skunk cabbage—a mixture he didn't realize he'd missed until it filled his nostrils, flowed to his lungs, became a part of him, whirled him back to childhood. It was the exact opposite of Afghanistan's acrid anxiety-laden shit-and-cordite smell, and nowhere in the cities came close. Refuge.

He slowed at the rusty Chevrolet, visible through the new saplings nearest the road, waiting for its own version of eternity in its camouflage of patchy sunlight and darks and lights of the forest. He turned, stopped, bent over, his hands on his knees as he breathed deeply half a dozen times. Then he straightened and stretched, began the jog back, punching as he jogged, eliciting "oof" sounds, and affecting his balance. *I'm coming, you motherfuckers. It's time.*

He came out of the road into the open again, squinting at the bright shards of chop on the lake. The wind was up and from the north. It felt good, but he shouldn't cool down too quickly. He slowed to a brisk walk.

He heard it from the north and it gave him goose bumps. Just once. A scream like a big cat. He'd heard one before in rural California, outside Santa Maria, and it was imprinted on his consciousness. Not a human sound, though this seemed a cross between human and some big cat like a mountain lion, a panther. The sound carried in the wind from across the lake. There were no big cats in Kansas. At least, he'd never seen or heard one in the refuges, though they were certainly wild enough to be home to such a creature.

Then he heard the big Packard marine engine start up from a distance, heard the Gar Wood moving beyond the marsh grass and trees that framed the lake a half mile away. Cobb was pushing it. Travis could sense the redline being approached on the tachometer, heard the protest in the whine. Then he saw the classic speedboat round the curve of the inlet, throwing a high white rooster tail of spray, and laying over too far on its side as it barely carved the water, losing purchase. Cobb was going to flip the sonofabitch!

Then the whine died down some and the boat sank back into the lake, still throwing white water, still bow up, but like a calendar picture, where a Rhonda Fleming-like beauty in a one-piece swimsuit from the '40s would be sitting above the seat, smiling, head back in the wind, hair streaming behind.

Travis breathed again. Cobb never pushed the Gar Wood. He babied it, pulling it out of the water at the first sign of weather. He'd talked of building a boathouse at the end of the dock. Sensing a calamity averted, Travis continued his brisk walk up to, and on, the gravel drive, ending up on the dock. He pivoted at the waist, touching right hand to left foot, or nearly doing so. He knew what the hair-raising sound had been.

The boat rumbled up to the dock, sounding like a '49 Mercury custom Reno Pete had once brought home, probably won in a card game. Cobb tied up where bumpers would save the boat sides from being scuffed, and climbed out. "Working out are you?" he said to Travis.

"Figured it wouldn't hurt."

"Never does. Reminds me of your canvasback days," Cobb said.

"Yeah, it didn't help me much then, did it?"

"Aw, you just got cocky is all. You come outa golden gloves all flush with winning."

"I wasn't cocky. I was fighting damn good boxers who were hungry."

Cobb looked at him, sucked air through his teeth, then reached for his Skoal can. "Tell me something, Travis. And tell me the truth." He turned and looked back toward the lake as he put some in his gum line, moved his tongue over it.

"Do my best."

"You think that dream about Vinita was just me wishin', or do you think it was her?"

"I think it was her. You know how full of life and strong she was. She couldn't just leave."

Cobb nodded, stuck the Skoal can in his back pocket. It settled into the faded circular imprint of a hundred cans before it. Then he walked back to the house.

Travis dropped to the deck, and started doing pushups.

CHAPTER 13

The next day, after running and working out until his gray sweatshirt was dark with sweat, Travis showered and took another look at the JFK film.

Reno was far from alone in wanting JFK dead. But he'd been paid, and paid well, judging from all the bank statements, thirty or more, where he'd deposited eight grand in CDs and one grand in savings. The reason for that amount, Travis had learned, was that the fed tracked any deposit over ten grand.

The film left no doubt that there was a conspiracy. The president had been hit twice before the head shot. Connelly was hit before that shot and afterward as well. Other bullets went astray. Arlen Specter's "magic bullet" theory was even more ridiculous after viewing this film. That Warren Commission wasn't investigating anything. It was covering a lot of tracks, and not very well. Arrogantly.

The plastic tubes contained names, dates, and people to see. They had to have been buried in Cobb's meth lab yard within the last couple of years.

The envelope contained four copies of the DVD, and a note that a fifth was in a safe deposit box in a Tulsa bank, the key in the envelope.

Guy who shot this was killed in Costa Rica. He didn't give a shit about it one way or the other, thought it was funny. He was a soldier of fortune from the word go, but didn't want any part of the blowback on the jfk thing. These are the only copies, I know that for a fact—we (me and Wayne Ruzinsky) broke into a production house in South KC and transferred the old film to DVD in 2004. Good thing, too, as WR said the old film was about to go to hell from time damage, exposure to ozone, and the like. Wayne, of course, saw the footage in transfer, but he has since gone on to his reward. Not by my hand either.

He was shot in a botched (sp?) jewelry store hiest in St. Louis. And he didn't say jack about it because he was scared shitless. I made sure he saw the list of dead witnesses over the years. Wayne was a good man, but all of us know how to talk at the wrong time for whatever reason. You can put these DVDs In safe places. And there are ways to make new ones now that are pretty easy I understand, where no one else has to see them being made. Look into that. I'd make 100 of the s.o.b.s. And build a way into it to spring them all should you get sideways in this thing. I know of a good lawyer in KC who knows how to keep his mouth shut and who could spring these on 50 different news outlets if need be. Know about Facebook? YouTube? I am laughing right now thinking about this "airing" as Wayne used to say. Your old man, a YouTube sensation. Going viral, haha, like the flu. Well, make sure that can happen, and make sure they know it can happen if anything happens to you. That's your insurance policy, but its not foolproof. That and my noterized signed statement. Make copies of that to, and keep the original.

All the stuff in the tubes is good evidence. Trouble is, some law enforcement agencies wont help. Lawyer's name is Montgomery Webb, he's downtown KC, 816-555-3341. Tell him Reno sent you. He'll work with you and you can trust him. Only person I trust more is Cobb.

Start by sending them pictures of the badge. Copy of picture of me. Picture of the DPD insignea cut from the uniform. Those will get there attention!!!"

Travis put the papers down and pushed the replay. Reno killed the president again, calmly reached for the two bullets on the fence, and it went black. Travis wondered what Reno Pete was feeling at that time. It wasn't like Reno was political, although he was dead-set against communism. Would he have taken the job if it was someone else? Maybe not. Had JFK sent in air support at the Bay of Pigs, he wouldn't have done it, no matter how that had turned out. Even if Reno had spent years in Castro's prisons, he would have chalked it up to his luck running out.

Travis was still having a hard time believing it all. The evidence was incontrovertible. Incontestable. But his old man being pivotal in the most important event of the twentieth century—he just couldn't quite allow it to form as reality in his mind.

He'd have to, of course. Something his old man had said surfaced in his consciousness. "Fuck 'em, all but eight, six to carry you and two to pull the wagon."

And in the end, no one was there to carry him, there was no wagon. The pallbearers, who would have carried him, carried Vinita instead. And his mother. He wondered how Melissa was ushered out. Her mom was still living, in Waxahachie. He thought she'd said that. That must have been tough on her. Melissa had friends. There would have been a funeral.

A "celebration of life," as they tried to spin it nowadays. People laughing through their tears as they told stories about her. Pictures of good days pinned up on a board, maybe a Powerpoint slide presentation. Fuck 'em all but eight.

Vinita, his mother, Melissa—they died by the violence the others lived by. Innocents. Well, chickens were coming home soon, finally, to roost, if he had anything to say about it.

But was that an end to it, or just more violence sown to be reaped again and again?

Maybe Cobb was right. Maybe there was no end to it.

~∞~

"Cobb? You all right?" Travis called into the hallway near the closed door.

"Yeah," Cobb said, groggy sounding.

About par, thought Travis. It was a bitch getting off that shit, but it had to be done. And Cobb was motivated.

Cobb came out of the room, unshaven, T-shirt and jeans, barefoot. He yawned, scratched, said "I think I can eat somethin'."

Vinita had always fixed him snacks and meals when she was able. He'd learned to fend for himself during her spells. It was a good sign he was hungry.

"What do you want?" Travis asked.

"Oh mebbe eggs, grits, like that. I'll get it."

"Let me whip up something for you. Cobb. I'm not too bad at it. Bachelor and all."

"Izzat what they call it. I thought you was just gay."

Travis pulled a frying pan off the overhead rack. Sounded like Cobb was coming around. "Wonders never cease. The Cobb is becoming politically correct. You used to say faggot."

"That too." He sent a tired smile in Travis's direction. "Vinita would like it, me gettin' off the stuff."

"Yes she would."

~∞~

The next day Travis asked Cobb, "You ready to hit the road, old man?"

Cobb did a shuffling soft shoe, arms outstretched, sang, "Getcher hat and getcher coat, leave your worries on the doorstep, and just direct yore feet…"

"To the sunny side of the street," Travis joined in.

"We are going to kick some ass, Travis. Smoke and broken glass wherever we go, okay? Dicks in the dirt."

"That's the plan, Dan. But with finesse." Travis wondered if they were up to this, giddy and silly as they were being.

Would they drive to New Orleans just to die? Is that what they were planning? And was giddiness just the other side of depression? A scary side of Cobb's withdrawal and Travis's quixotic ride into the unknown to kill the bogey man? Fuck it. Whatever awaited, they'd meet it head on. Or maybe sneak up on it with a club like he used to do with bullies he couldn't quite handle.

೧಄೧

"Man this Land Cruiser is a luxury car compared to my old beater," Travis said to Cobb well on the way to Oklahoma.

"It's what she needed for that nine-mile driveway of ours. Slap that mother in four wheel drive and it'll pull stumps."

"Moves right along."

"Ain't no Cadillac, though." Cobb's five-year old Cadillac was an out-of-character vehicle, like the Gar Wood, but Travis chalked it up to a kind of drug dealer mentality. He was glad they hadn't taken it on this trip, though either car would be lost in the carnival that New Orleans was fast becoming once more, after Katrina.

Cobb was on the phone now to Breeze, "Don't feed

'em nothing—that's why they call it *pasture*, dammit. Just make sure that gravity water tank don't stop up. Well, if it does, call me. Or get Big Ray to look at it. No it probly won't." He put the phone down. "I don't know about Breeze stayin' there. Sometimes he don't act like he's got good sense."

"Don't those cows have a pond or two?"

"Yes. Scummed over. And they foul 'em by shittin' in 'em. But they water at that tank, anyway. It's always worked. Now he's got me worried it'll stop working. Dang."

Travis was glad to see Cobb engaged again in every-day problems. "Shoot, Cobb, you know Harley and those guys will take care of things."

"Hmmph." Cobb lit a cigarette, rolling his window down.

Vinita hadn't liked him to smoke in her Land Cruiser, but grudgingly allowed it with the window down. Travis turned the CD player up. Jimmie Dale Gilmore sang "Dallas is a rich man with a death wish in his eyes..." in his familiar twang.

Travis felt a goose walk over his grave.

⚬⚬⚬

They shared a double room in Dallas the first night, but Cobb's bad dreams kept Travis awake, and he felt groggy in the morning. The lawman, Holt, had asked him to call when they came through Dallas, so he did that in the lobby after exchanging their double room for two sin-gles.

He poured a coffee from the "continental breakfast" setup, sat down with his phone, and dialed the number he had for him.

"Detective Holt."

"Travis Meachem. You asked that I call when coming through—"

"Travis. Right. You in town?"

"Yes. Not for long, though."

Holt asked where he was and suggested they meet at a nearby IHOP. Travis hadn't wanted to meet him, just let him know when he came through, as requested. But that was folly. Of course he'd want to meet, look him over, check out his instincts about him. And that was almost a favor on Holt's part as he could have made it uncomfortable for Travis. He said sure, finished his coffee, scanned the lobby and the grounds through the picture windows. Sunny day. Travelers ranging from business people to families.

He eyed a young woman in a short skirt who was checking some charts on a laptop, obviously on her way to a presentation of some sort with two older men. He looked at her legs then felt her eyes. He smiled a sort of "busted" smile and she laughed, smiled back. Another day and he'd have asked her if she came there often or some stupid thing to get the flow started. He went back to the room.

⌀⌀⌀

"I'm going to meet that detective, the DPD guy I told you about, then I think I want to stop by Dealey Plaza, poke around over there. I could come pick you up after I see Holt."

"I got no interest in all that. You a suspect?" asked Cobb.

"No. I think he just wants to dot all the i's, be complete. He used to hunt Treeing Walkers, I tell you that?"

"Can't be all bad. You go on. I'll find plenty to do."

❦❦❦

He parked outside the busy IHOP, waiting for a bit—whether for another car to come which might have been following him, or just to get a sense of his surroundings, he didn't know. He had shifted back into a gut mode in the last few days. It had been on days like this, no danger being broadcast, that bad things had happened in the Kandahar region. He thought about Reno, how he would have adapted to that whole deal. He'd have ghosted about, become an Arab legend, a bogeyman to them, not quite human, certainly not predictable. He'd have driven them batshit. And he'd have returned with no stories, no long stares, no trauma at all, quick to smile and change the subject to Travis's grades at KU, or Vinita's tomato patch.

Two teenaged girls with pierced eyebrows and nostrils, wearing torn up fishnet hose and coloring in their hair, passed by his passenger window, smoking and acting tough. He watched them flip their cigarettes into the bushes and enter the IHOP. One wore a tight miniskirt, the other had short shorts wedged up her butt. They talked in that Texas drawl about someone named Frank who thought his shit didn't stink. They'd be soccer moms someday, or cashiers at an all-night convenience store.

He checked his rearview mirror, looked through the IHOP windows, thought he located Holt in a booth—wavy gray hair, chunky dude in a seersucker jacket, open collar white shirt, and a loose tie. The only guy alone that he could see.

Travis entered the cool air zone, decided he liked it better outside. Holt waved to him, the guy he'd speculated was him. How did Holt know who he was? Driver's license picture and PSC ID, he imagined. Travis raised his chin at him.

He had a sudden sense of déjà vu when he looked at the ketchup bottles on the tables. Travis slid into the seat across from the solid-looking man.

"Well, you don't act real guilty driving all the way down here to see me, Travis. Can I call you Travis?"

"Sure. I'm *not* guilty. Of that, anyway."

Melissa's face smiled at him from the recent past. He closed his eyes, rubbed them, and shook her off.

Holt laughed. "Relax. Security cam showed a messkin-looking dude sneakin' around about that time. We're pretty sure he's the one. Plus you was at a damn coon hunt."

The waitress came then, swiped at their table with a wet rag, leaving trails. She laid down another set of silverware and a napkin. Travis ordered breakfast while Holt got another coffee, raising his eyebrows at Travis's rather large order.

"I'm buying, Detective Holt," Travis said.

"Call me Ross."

"So, Ross. How are things going on that case?"

Holt told him in general terms and Travis decided he didn't know any more than before. Holt asked him to sign a statement he'd prepared and passed it over to him.

Travis read it. It just outlined what he'd told Holt over the phone. He signed and dated it, slid it back to him. His breakfast came and he spent more time eating and listening than talking.

The detective talked about his father's dogs and some hunting incidents. "...this was before tracking collars, couldn't afford them anyway, and one walker was missing. She was one who wouldn't holler, pure coon hunter, that was what set her off, nothing else, there she was, not saying a thing, top fell through in a septic in this abandoned farmyard." Holt took a sip of his coffee.

"Yeah?" Travis said, spearing a sausage.

"Well, it's not really a story to tell a man while he's eating. It'll keep. So what are you going to do while you're in Big D?"

"Mostly leave. I kind of always wanted to see Dealey Plaza though. Can you point me there?"

"It's on my way, five minutes from here. When we leave, just follow me, I'll show you. You one a them conspiracy people?" Holt smiled, moving a toothpick side to side in his mouth.

"Well, I've read some books, got some opinions. What do you think about it?"

"Well, since our own government admits it was probably a conspiracy, I tend to think Oswald was set up. And the gun. A Carcano? Well, an Eyetalian wouldn't even fire the damn thing less it blow up on 'em."

Travis reflected on the irony of a DPD detective taking him to where Reno Pete had committed the crime of the century in a DPD uniform. He decided he liked this Detective Holt. But he wouldn't want to get on the wrong side of him. His eyes belied his country talk and friendly nature. Cop eyes. He couldn't help it after too many years of seeing what he saw every day.

CHAPTER 14

Holt parked the unmarked car in the railroad yard behind the fence and waved Travis over. "This is a national monument now, so pretty much the whole thing is as it was in '63. Three acres of it anyway. This area is parking for DPD. That's where the station is." He pointed toward a five or six story building. "And the railroad tracks have been paved over but that just moves the railroad area back a ways. It used to come up to where that little wall is." He pointed across Travis. "This is where that white Chevy was supposed to be," Holt said. "You know about that?"

"Yeah. Someone with a walkie talkie driving it?"

"Uh huh. And here was where a cop and another guy supposedly were." Holt walked to the fence, took up Reno's position in the film, aimed an imaginary rifle across the fence pointing at Elm, across the way. "And there was someone else, depending on who they talked to, maybe with a camera, right over there." He pointed to an area right behind them.

Travis felt a frisson of chill down his spine as he imagined his father aiming from this spot right here where Holt was standing, nearly a half century ago. The shot that changed the world and set the stage for everything since. Did it satisfy Reno Pete? He doubted it. His old man wasn't a simple person.

"Travis? You haven't heard a word I've said, have you?" It was Holt, next to him now. "Man, you're in a trance."

"No, yeah—it's just, you know, history. Someone here, about here, shot Kennedy. It's a little overwhelming—I mean I can *feel* it."

"It's what some guys on the force call psychic leftovers. There's something about crime scenes that you can feel. Battle scenes, too. Like civil war battles? You can go there and feel the thing. Unsettled, like. Guess I'm used to it."

"Why would someone kill Melissa? Melissa Bradley. Was it robbery or what?" asked Travis.

"Didn't appear to be. We picked up the guy's rental car in Denver. Trail ends there. It was more like a…well, I shouldn't discuss it, actually. It's still active."

They walked back to the car. Railroad tracks crossed Elm on an overpass, Travis noted. That overpass. All those cops around, Travis thought, and no one bothered Reno and those guys behind the fence. Of course, they didn't hang around, either. They probably hauled ass. Everyone saw the smoke, heard the shot, but no cops reacted to it other than the motorcycle cop from the escort, and he turned back. Even with what Travis now knew, there was so much unexplained. No one would ever know the full truth.

History was like that. Reno said, in the tube letters, they went to a safe house in Fort Worth, stayed there for three days, were flown to Mexico. He flew back to KC from there, drove to LaCygne. Pass go, collect the other half of $300,000. Bank it. All over the country. Nowadays you'd just have them send it to the Caymans.

Holt's presence at the fence, possibly on the exact spot

his father had occupied, made Travis nervous. Cop eyes. Reno'd had the same look. Sometimes his eyes didn't smile when his mouth did.

They shook hands in the parking lot.

"Good luck on your business deal in New Orleans," Holt said.

"Oh, I'll need that, Ross. Thanks. Don't let the psychic leftovers get you down."

Holt removed the toothpick. "You think of anything on this Melissa deal, anything you might a forgot, call me."

He was standing by his car, still watching as Travis looked in his rearview mirror.

⸺ ❧❧❧ ⸺

Cobb was in the coffee shop when Travis returned to the motel. He had another cup of coffee while his uncle devoured a short stack, eggs, sausage, and grits. They decided to take off by one, head for Shreveport, maybe even New Orleans by ten or so that night. There was no real schedule, and Travis no longer felt in a hurry. Life was totally different now.

"I figure we ought to split up in New Orleans," Travis said. "I'm gonna be pullin' some folks' chains down there and we're better off not being a pair. We can get some cheapie prepaid cellphones to keep in touch."

"Okay by me. I need to look up the kinfolk. I'm stayin' with Broussards. You need to meet some a these people too. Could be a big help."

"Could be. Well, we can take this car over there and you can drop me off later, keep it over in Algiers. I booked us at a place called Maisson de Vries in the French Quarter for now. Fancy but real private."

The countryside was far different than mainstream

Kansas but still reminded Travis of the Marais Des Cygne refuge with its sloughs and backwaters. No Kudzu in Kansas. Yet. They devised a code word system while they drove—use 'business' in a conversation or message, and that means extreme caution. Use 'shot' and that would mean 'No.' Use 'miles' and that means 'Yes.'

It seemed little boy clubhouse but it was deadly serious.

They pulled into the French Quarter at eleven-thirty that night. Travis was a little surprised to find it lit up and rocking, couples strolling with drinks in their hands, cops here and there, strip show hawkers describing the delights inside the dark doorways, and music issuing from most buildings. The last time he'd been here, The Big Easy had been The Big Muddy. The stench of death permeated everything and Travis had carried an M-16 to protect the elite.

Cobb pulled up by the Maisson de Vries. "I'll wait here. Find out where I can park this thing, okay?"

Travis rang a doorbell and was greeted by the night manager who politely asked to see his ID. He was given a parking pass and two keys and shown on a diagram where everything was. The rooms adjoined a private courtyard. For what they were paying, the courtyard should be paved in gold and full of dancing girls, Travis thought. Featherbeds, it had said online. He was ready to sink into something like that, all right, after a hot shower and a stiff bourbon.

The trip was the best thing in the world for Cobb, he reflected, even if it was a trip into some unknown hell, later. He was recovering from a double whammy, grief and speed at the same time.

A knock on the door after a shower brought him fully alert. "Yeah?"

"Me, Cobb."

Travis pulled on a pair of old jersey workout shorts and a T-shirt, opened the door. Nobody there. He peered out into the hallway and was suddenly spun around and helpless in a come-along and a headlock. Released immediately, he fell back against the doorjamb.

Cobb pushed him into the room and shut the door. "Just keepin' yuh sharp, big boy."

"Cobb, this ain't the fuckin' Pink Panther."

"Do what?"

"Nothin'. What was that all about?"

"Well we supposed to be on our toes here, right?"

"Yeah, but I don't think it starts right this minute."

"You didn't see that Escalade that was about ten cars behind us all the way from Shreesport?"

"No. Are you kidding?"

"Yes, but I been keeping my eyes open." Cobb looked at him owlishly, eyes wide, tongue out the side of his mouth.

Travis knew he was right, however light he made it seem. He needed to get wired tighter. Later. He could smell the pungent LaCygne Green. "You're a joker and a smoker and a midnight toker. I could do with some LaCygne Green, pardner."

Cobb produced a baggie. "I give up Gonzales, but I still smoke and drink, and this here will always be around. My *main* product." He waggled the bag at Travis. "Primo," he said.

೧೨೧

They split up in the morning. Cobb took off for Algiers, and Travis found a small coffee shop nearby. He bought a paper, a beignet, and coffee and sat out on the sidewalk patio at a small table. He watched the street movement from behind his paper and his shades, feeling like a tourist, but with overtones of paranoia, grief, and nervous anticipation all twitching and playing with him. He had booked the room for ten days. After that he'd move around. If he was still alive. Cobb had paid and checked out, telling Travis, "For that kinda money, I'd expect two Playboy bunnies and Elvis hisself."

☙☙

Travis returned to the room, sat in the connected private courtyard, and Googled the names on his father's list. He played the DVD of the killing shot once then stuck it in a George Thorogood Greatest Hits plastic CD case, tossing it in a careless pile of CDs he'd brought with a boom box. He then checked out banks near the French Quarter and found one within walking distance. He duct-taped the gun, an old snubnosed Smith & Wesson .38, model 10, to the top of a cord-hung lamp in the middle of the bathroom, changing its balance a few times until the lamp dangled correctly. He could get to it quickly there, by standing on the old clawfooted bathtub rim and no one would see it in plain view unless they were seven feet tall. Judging from the layer of dust and grime on top of the porcelainized metal shade, housekeeping would never see it, even when changing the bulb.

He packed up the rest of the DVDs and some copies of the tube contents and set out for the Hancock Bank to rent a safe deposit box and start a checking account. As he walked, he felt the relative comfort of his old Middle-East anxiety about death and imminent physical danger settle in to his awareness, a familiar old friend. It was always with him over there, to some degree, and he never tried to compartmentalize it or squelch it. It wasn't fear, but was another sense. He would notice things that others didn't. The fresh crumbled dirt scattered to disguise where an IED lay buried. Fresh camel shit. A glance from a bazaar booth to a building behind him. Or just a wrong stillness in the too-bright air. He got that from Reno Pete, he felt, much as he tried not to be like him.

Once, he'd stopped the embassy convoy from nearing an abandoned Toyota because the bed was covered with a plywood panel but not bungeed or fastened, and the windows weren't broken out yet. It didn't look right. Nor did it feel right. To Travis, there was a palpable air of anticipation.

They did some door-to-door, moving farther back all the time, making it look like practice, and he found an entryway where he could observe without being seen. He waited forty minutes and, in the time-lapse photography of his mind, everyone and everything changed several times except one person, a beggar sitting half a block away. The sitting man shifted nervously and glanced at the truck one too many times. Travis cleared the area and ordered the man around the corner, shook him down, and the cellphone fell from his robes igniting the Toyota bed full of explosives. He didn't shoot the man, but took him in and turned him over to regular army. It was a fruitful intelligence find. Unlike many security service contractors, he had no problem working with the army and CIA as well.

His time-lapse view of the French Quarter was feeding him information now, but the light was not arid-bright. It was drenched the color of absinthe, and it sat heavier, somehow, without wavering on you like the road mirages in the other gulf. He'd been here before, during the Katrina catastrophe.

What most Americans didn't know was that Blackwater and other PSCs were all over New Orleans before, during, and after Katrina, to guard the wealthy sectors and dispatch looters. They worked for Homeland Security and the Governor of Louisiana as "Hurricane Relief."

Working CONUS, or continental United States, was weird for Travis and most of the others. They'd rather have been on foreign soil. No law applied there. None really applied in New Orleans at that time, but they'd felt a need to work in a more back-alley fashion. Some news media picked up that they were there but it was largely ignored. Black Escalades and Suburbans, bearing various PSC insignia, patrolled fairly openly toward the end and worked with NOPD. Travis's company, AdvanceGroup, worked alone. When they left, they had no casualties. The "enemy" count was dismissed as flood deaths. It was then that he had discovered the hard-to-find, little advertised Maisson de Vries.

On the way back from the bank, he stopped in a convenience store to pick up some toothpaste and other items he'd neglected to pack. The only other people in the store were a very old obese Black lady and a stunning girl he could hardly pry his eyes away from. She was in her mid-twenties, wild electric frazzle of black hair shooting in all directions, long eyelashes, prominent cheekbones accenting her beautiful face, voodoo-like silver bones on hoops for earrings. Her skin was light cocoa, and she looked like a product of some fortunate racial mixtures he'd seen before. Creole, sure, he thought. Wow. This girl was gorgeous. He felt physically shocked, as though with a mild stun gun. Nerves, he thought, and the LaCygne Green from last night fucking with his chemistry.

Her looks and the way she was dressed made it hard for him to concentrate on the simple items he was putting in his basket. He'd dropped several ladies deodorants in, which he now replaced on the shelf. She was dressed simply but remarkably. A mini-skirt-length V-necked white T-shirt at first seemed her only clothing, but showing beneath it were a pair of lavender shorts, and the outline of a white running bra. Her shoes were white Nike low cuts with little puff balls at the back attached to low socks. Dancer's legs. She was slim but nicely filled out. And she was kind. She had helped the Black lady with her debit card at the counter, smiling and talking to her, showing her how to swipe her card and sign the awkward screen board.

"Yeah," she was saying, "you can practically just put an X on there, the way these things mess up your signature. That looks fine."

The large Black lady smiled at her, thanked her. "You sure are a pretty thing, hon. I love your earrings," she reached to touch one, and the girl inclined her head toward the lady's hand.

"I got 'em at Madame Lola's. You should drop in there. The prices are really good."

"I will. I'll just do that, girl. You take care, now." The Black lady patted the girl's shoulder and headed for the street, hoisting her colorful mu-mu above her feet.

The Creole girl took some dollar bills from a wallet, concluded her business, being just as nice to the high-school-aged counter girl, her smile genuine and radiant. Then she was gone.

Entranced, Travis wanted to say something to her just to slow her departure, see that smile some more. He sighed ruefully. She's got some dumbass hulk of a boy-friend who probably goes into a frenzy when she even so much as looks at another guy. Probably a fucking bouncer with a shaved head and sleeve tattoos. He paid for his items, took the bag from the clerk, remembering to smile and say thanks. Women like the one he'd seen made things better for everyone around them.

Back at the room he left the French doors to the court-yard open, enjoying the breeze that stirred the sheer white curtains. Orchid-like blossoms fell from the catawba tree in the courtyard, and Travis felt at peace, at least for now. He poured a cup of chicory coffee from the room service wheeled tray and opened up the sheaf of notes from Reno Pete.

Be careful. Even with innocent appearing circum- stances and youll survive. Your instincts will begin to re- gain the sensativity they were supposed to have. Never give them a trail, a licence plate, a phone no, a friends name, a watch you own that can be traced, a shirt with laundry mark. These are smart bad people. You, dead, solves a problem. Once you start this, no way out but thru. Be a chickenshit when you need to. Square off against them = a sure way to die. You may have to kill. Do it with a clear head and do it quick. Do not hesitate. Fuck morals, these people need to be dead. But it puts more people on your trail. Cobb has contacts in NO, use them.

The first guy on the list is J. Weeks. Wrote a book called "Plant" about how they framed Oswald. He got some stuff right but missed a lot to. But he was so close he had to have inside info. So he was watched, maybe burgled, maybe thretened. They may still be watching him. That mean's you cant meet face to face. Now this might sound corny but you have to disguise. Get used to it. And if Weeks has been turned, he'll be an obstacle. He could help if he's clean but you never know. If he gets to insistant about a meet, back off. Give him a tidbit, like you know there was a sewer shooter, mention his weapon as a .22 Ruger long barrel pistol, no more, see what that brings out.

Some of these writers have been turned. There's a 1000 bucks in here. That should get you started. Sorry I couldn't finance the whole deal. And if you decide not to do this, keep it and burn the rest of the stuff, or bury it again. Might be best. This is no reflection on you Travis, it's the truth. You decide if you're up to it. I know *you are. If there's anything to life after death I'm behind you and smiling at you all the way.*

I always loved you. Believe me I'd of taken your mom's place if I could of. I know that was our sticking point. It was crazy hard to go on after that. Crazy hard. Revenge didn't even make a little dent in it. It hurt us all to see you, what it did. If you do this you will sure enough ruin some days, and the money will set you up. I think you can do it or I'd never put it out there for you. You're a little different then I was, more like Cobb maybe.

Remember how you played that bigass catfish? Took you half the day. That took patience, strategy, smarts, and stamina. Especially for a little boy your size and age then. That's when I knew you'd be good in the world. Little light line (5lb test?) big fish 14lbs. Remember how good that was on the grill? We could see you were proud, deserved to be, we were to. Your mom thought that was the best catfish we ever had. Salt, pepper, lemon. Those were good days. Get em while you can. I know you don't think so right now but good days will be there for you again.

Sorry to bail the way I have by now. (If your reading this I have.) Fucking drs keep you going like the battery bunny. Keeps their paychecks coming. Well, that's it. You only need to read more if you're going for it. If you do, play it like a 14lb catfish on 5lb test. Carefully. Patiently. Use violence only if you have to (you'll know) and then quickly and out. It's a tool. Use it when they balk or lie or try to play you. Also use it to piss them off. When someone is angry they don't think right. Pistol whip a man and you'll piss him off but you'll scare him to, he will know your for real. Be sneaky and chickenshit, not frontal assault. I know you guys bulled your way in middle east, but sneaky pays off.

Travis folded the papers—blue-lined notebook paper torn from a wire bound school type notebook—and poured the rest of the coffee. Damn. Reno remembered that catfish. It *had* taken half a day to land that sucker. Travis was not about to lose it. It bent the light pan-fish rod double at times. He'd been only dimly aware that his father was there the whole time, now and then offering quiet advice, but not getting in the way. That night they'd cooked catfish steaks. Cobb and Vinita were there. His mom and dad. Some friends of theirs with kids his age. It had been a good time. A relaxed time.

A perfume-like fragrance drifted in from the court-yard. What was he doing inside? He took the laptop and papers out to a stone bench in the shade of the catawba tree. A couple of hummingbirds darted and played around blossoms in a vine covered wall where the scent came from. He began to calculate how much the room cost him by the hour, then muttered to himself the mantra Breeze and he used when they'd spent too much on a night in Kansas City, "Fuck it, it's just chips."

He looked up Weeks online. *Johnathan Weeks, JFK conspiracy theory author. His book* The Plant *made a case for Lee Harvey Oswald impersonators and imposters setting Oswald up, by planting the Mannlicher-Carcano rifle and cartridges in the "sniper's nest" and hiding the Mauser, which was one of the guns purportedly used, on top of the building by the clock. Weeks died of a massive heart attack June 18, 2010. He was working on a second book that revisited the subject matter of the first, but his notes have not been located. The publisher, Scharff Co., has not responded at this time.*

Well, check that guy off, he thought. He was iffy anyway, Reno'd said. Travis might get his book, see what he wrote about it. He seemed closer to Reno now than ever. Funny. The man had never spoken of love, not to

Travis anyway, but there it was in his letter. Had his pen hand hesitated before that declaration? How hard had it been for him? Reno wasn't glib. It wasn't something he'd simply toss off and continue from there without some thought.

He must have had some notion of his health problems a while back. The tube with the guns and first letter could have been buried for 30 years. The second tube, probably last year when Reno showed up for a visit.

Travis had met him in Kansas City for beers and barbecue on Southwest Boulevard. He'd looked a little drawn then but Travis attributed it to age, hadn't thought about it much. Reno must have known then. The room phone rang, a regular old-fashioned telephone sound, his reverie disappearing like cigarette smoke. It was Cobb.

ꝗꙅꝗ

Cobb picked him up, took him to Algiers to meet some of the Broussard clan. Travis had put it off for no reason, other than he felt it counter-productive. But he relaxed now. He'd take a break, meet some family. They pulled up to a compound, the front of which was surrounded by high chain link fence and surfaced with gravel. The high gate whirred open, sliding to one side, and they entered. Travis could hear laughter and shouting from the house.

Three dogs circled the Land Cruiser silently, until a chunky, balding middle-aged man in a New Orleans Saints T-shirt whistled from the iron-barred front door. The dogs retired to an open garage where someone was welding, the intense blue light flickering on and off. Vehicles were parked around the house, one a car hauler that had *Arnaud's EZ-Tow* painted on the doors in gaudy metallic script.

Inside, Travis's senses were assailed by the aromas of cooking, chaotic noise from what sounded like a police radio, Cajun talk, accordion-heavy music, some building sounds, hammering and sawing cacophony, and children arguing. "Toin on de fans, dammit, the meat's boining!" a male voice yelled in a Brooklynese accent, which Travis recognized as pure New Orleans.

A female voice answered, "You let me do the cooking, go outside or something."

Sheets of plastic covered one wall open to the outside, and some workmen were framing in another room or addition to what might have been a patio. It was like a party at a construction site.

Cobb said, "Get yourself a drink, Travis. Ain't nobody goin' to serve you here. It's like home, but another planet, too."

A pugnacious child holding a game screen looked up at him. "Who are you? What are you doing here?"

Which earned the little smartass a slap on the head, from his mother, Travis assumed. She was a nice-looking olive-skinned woman in slacks and a low cut top which displayed ample cleavage.

She smiled and repeated, "Who *are* you? What *are* you doing here?" Her sparkling eyes smiled along with her mouth.

"I'm Travis. He's my uncle," he said, nodding toward Cobb. "And I have no idea what I'm doing here."

They both laughed.

"You the Meachem boy," she said. "Really a St. Cyr, though. Your daddy changed the name around now and then. But you a St. Cyr sho 'nuff." She looked him up and down, then hugged him. He returned the hug, inhaling her perfumed warmth. She pointed to some framed pictures on the wall leading upstairs. "This here's Reno before he was Reno."

The picture was obviously taken in New Orleans in front of a filigreed iron railed building. There were several young people in it, his father in his teens, a flat-topped ducktail haircut, Levis, and a short-sleeved shirt with the sleeves rolled up a notch or two in the fashion of the day for hoodlums and hot rodders. A cigarette hung from his lips, a sardonic half smile on them. He stood with one loafered foot against the building, thumbs in his jeans pockets, looking a little like James Dean. The other kids ranged from teens to smaller children. The Dallas picture would have been maybe five or six years after that, he thought.

He looked into his dad's eyes. Cool. Colorless in the faded photo. Same as the Dallas look. What would have appealed to his mother's gentle nature about a guy like this? He looked like his very next act would be to hot-wire a car.

A roar of approval went up from another room where a baseball game was in progress.

"What's the occasion?" Travis asked his uncle

"Far as I can tell, it's just Saturday at the Broussards. Big family. Plus they working on some kind of addition."

In that moment, a girl slipped down the hall and into a bathroom, but the quick glimpse of wild black hair and long white T-shirt told him it was the girl from the convenience store. What was she doing here? He lost focus. He was aware of Cobb talking but he was waiting for the bathroom door to open, show him it was just an illusion, some memory trick. He flashed back on the girl's smile, her voice, and the wild hair, looking somehow both fashionable and disheveled.

"You listening to me, boy?" Cobb's voice broke through.

"Huh? Sure I am—"

"Well, I just said your damn phone is ringing, or doing

something anyway." Cobb tilted his bottle of NOLA Blonde microbrew back to finish it.

Sure enough, the phone was playing his ringtone, a truncated siren whoop. He looked at the number. It was local. When he answered, a voice said,

"Travis Meachem? AKA St. Cyr? AKA a number of other last names?"

"Who is this?" He put his finger to his opposite ear against the noise. He looked back at the bathroom door, it was now open, but no one was there. Damn!

"You will never know that. But my identity is neither here nor there." It was a cultured southern voice, a pleasant voice. Effeminate. "We will, however, meet."

"I don't think so," Travis said. Had he imagined the girl? He tried to concentrate on the unusual phone call. He felt off-balance, gut-punched.

"Oh, what you think doesn't matter in the slightest. We will meet, and very soon. Sounds like you are at a party. Those Broussards. They are a lively crew."

"I'm hanging up now."

"I wouldn't."

Travis was aware of a bead of sweat running down his side, his breath coming short. How could this happen? How could anyone know his phone number? He supposed it was possible, had to be, but wouldn't it require a law enforcement agency or something?

"Okay."

"Now we're talking. I believe my proposition will be of great interest to you. And I know it will be of great value. What I don't know is if you're smart enough to accept it. Did you know your father had an exceptionally high IQ?"

"He was smart," Travis answered, feeling awkward and foolish saying anything at all. This wasn't some crank call or a wrong number. It was someone who was well informed, someone confident in his advantage. What's more, the caller knew exactly where he was at the moment and knew something of the Broussards. Travis turned, checking to see if anyone was talking on a cellphone, walked into the dining room, looked about. No one on a phone. This wasn't a joke.

If the caller meant harm, chances were it would have occurred by now. His eyes flicked to the window he was standing near. Outside it was innocuous enough, nowhere to fire from, really. Which didn't mean squat. They could have his coordinates and rocket-firing drones for all he knew.

The voice went on. "Exceptionally high. He blew the tops off the standard tests we gave him. And more advanced ones. It was like he enjoyed doing it. Hiding behind his street language and poor grammar. So if you have a quarter of his brainpower, you're a bright boy indeed." There was a pause.

Travis said nothing.

The voice continued. "Now, about our meeting. You'll come to the Effigy Gallery off Bourbon Street, two hundred block, today just before closing time, which is 4:30 sharp. It's an art gallery. We will meet for about one half hour. Tell no one. Bring no one. Unarmed of course. Come in and browse the inner gallery away from the street windows at 4:25. Marie will lock up and leave at 4:30. You'll stay. I'll pop in about then. Got that?"

"Yes. How do I know I can trust you?"

"Oh, that. You don't. But if you don't show up, oh my, that would be catastrophic for you. And yours." He hung up.

Travis's first meet, and far from any terms he'd have come up with. This wasn't going well. What would his old man do? The person obviously knew Reno from a long time back. One of the bad guys? Maybe not. He said he had a proposition. The threat was if he didn't show up. He looked at his watch, 3:15 p.m.

"Problem?" Cobb asked. He was twisting the cap off another fancy looking NOLA microbrew.

"It's started. Can you run me over to the French Quarter at four or so?"

Cobb handed him the keys. "They're putting me up here and it's kind of like when I'm at the compound in Marais Des Cygne. I get home, I don't want to leave. What do you mean, it's started?"

"You'll be a big help when things get hairy. Just remember this, if I don't call you at six p.m. Effigy. It's a gallery in Vieux Carre, and I have a meeting. I can't say anything else yet."

"Want me along?" Cobb was suddenly attentive. He set the beer down.

"Not this time. Cobb, who is that?" Travis asked, pointing.

The girl was in sight again, hunkered down talking to a gaggle of kids who were clamoring around her. She had one little boy by the shoulders and was admonishing him about something, probably aggravating a girl standing nearby, sniffling and trying not to cry. Then she talked to the little girl and had her laughing through her tears. Travis was charmed at the scene.

"That's Emilie. A shirt-tail cousin. Briard I think. Somethin,' ain't she?"

She straightened up from her child-talking position and stretched. Travis noted the tendons in back of her knees, the dancer's calves. She waved at someone and walked in that direction, smiling.

"She quit college over to LSU, was stayin' with a relative, but he was puttin' his hands on 'er. Guy got caught by his ol' lady and she's on the street now. Somethin' like that."

She was standing now, talking to the woman who had first welcomed him. Emilie glanced at him as they talked. Then the other lady caught his eye, smiled, and gestured to him to come over.

"Emilie, this is Travis St. Cyr, visiting from Kansas City. Travis, Emilie Briard."

They stood, smiles frozen as an awkward silence grew between them.

Travis looked at his watch. "I have to go, Bourbon Street, appointment…" He reddened, unaccountably.

"Oh, could I get a ride with you?" Emilie said. "I'm sorry, that was forward wasn't it? I'm sort of lacking manners, but I do need a ride."

"Of course! Sure! How do we get past the dogs?"

"They're all show. Come on!" She took his hand and they were shouldering through some people to the front door. She waved to the woman who'd introduced them.

Cobb looked over at them as they left. "Six on the dot," he said, tapping his wristwatch.

Travis nodded. He opened the passenger side door for her, the dogs just standing there, bored.

"Don't ever pat them," she said. "They'll never leave you alone after that."

❧❧❧

It was hard not to look at her on the drive over. She pointed out a park she'd grown up playing in and nearby homes of childhood friends.

"We moved to Montreal for years. It was like the other side of the world to here. Colder than a polar bear's butt too. I came back to go to LSU but that was going nowhere and I was older than most students. All my friends were gone, married, doing stuff everyone does."

She watched the passing neighborhood, silent now.

Travis looked at his watch. 4:15. "How far is the French Quarter?"

"Just a little ways, five minutes."

"I think I'm going to have to ask you to take the car, pick me up later, is that all right?"

"Sure. Where are you going?"

"Effigy? It's a gallery on Jackson, I think, just off Bourbon Street, 200 block."

"I know where it is. How long you going to be?"

"Maybe half hour, hour."

"How about I meet you at Napoleon House?" she asked.

He pulled into the curb in a no-parking zone.

Somehow it was like they'd known one another before, or for a long time. He watched her adjust the seat, put the Land Cruiser into gear, concentrating. Then she flashed him a smile, as she pulled out, causing a passing car to swerve and honk. She laughed, waved, and was gone.

CHAPTER 15

The Effigy was obviously an upscale gallery and not merely a tourist attraction. The polished wood floors and old trim were pre-Katrina, but somehow Travis didn't think these had seen any flood waters. New-old maybe. The place was vintage New Orleans, quietly elegant.

The art was spaciously arranged, not crowded. A large nude hung on the opposite wall, a weird Mardi Gras look to her, holding a bird mask on a stick to her face. She was life-sized and overly voluptuous, lips parted. In the shadows behind her were men dressed in business suits. The painting had a menacing, compelling feel. On a pedestal in the middle of the room was a coffin-like structure with a stuffed vulture inside it. The piece stood on end like a shrine, vertically, and was ornate with gold leaf and stained glass jewels all around it. A filigreed cross topped it off. Other walls held wild, fiery abstracts of what looked like molten lava.

Travis walked cautiously into one of several interior rooms away from the street windows. He was conscious of the noise his footsteps made on the gleaming hardwood floor and he admired the workmanship, though the very thought of laying it made him queasy. The Effigy was utterly silent. He was uncomfortably aware of his own breathing, and a twitch in one eyelid. He was defenseless, he knew, but what choice did he have? This could be the end before he'd even begun. No one knew where he was except Cobb and Emilie. He could disappear without a trace. Would they risk that? Would he be interrogated? He stifled the impulse to slip out the front door and into the crowd. He had no idea what was in store for him here, but he vowed to exercise much more care in the future. If he had a future.

He turned at the sound of smartly clicking footsteps, high heels, in the main front room. A woman, older, handsome in a green jacket and skirt, was turning off some lights. Her gray-streaked hair was cut fashionably short, longer on one side, and expensive green and gold earrings flashed with her movements. The front room darkened, even with the soft light of late afternoon filtering in from the street. It was clouding up outside. She left track lighting spots on the buzzard and the nude.

Oddly, she patted the vulture's head—as though it was something she did whenever she closed up—picked up a green patent-leather tote and a ring of keys. Without looking back, she exited to the street, locking the door behind her, dropping the keys into her bag. He couldn't tell if she had set any alarms or not. She had seen him, he knew that, though she had not conveyed any kind of emotion, just a glance, perhaps a slight nod. Attractive lady. If Cobb had seen her he'd say, "I'd like to git *her* agin. Agin a brick wall. Agin a tree."

Travis smiled slightly, then the hair on his neck moved as he realized another presence was near him—a squeak of soft-soled shoes on the polished wood floor.

A young man ran a metal detector over him. "Arms out, please."

Travis complied, almost relieved that whatever would

take place was starting. He could smell the young man's aftershave—bay rum mixed with the smell of cigarette smoke on his suit. The device sounded, and he was asked to remove all pocket change, rings, watch, as if at an airport. Then he was quickly frisked, and his things returned to him.

"Follow me, please."

The man was neutral, like a mannerly pit bull. Well-dressed, solid, large neck, sloping shoulders. *I'm not in that shape yet*, Travis thought, *but close*. This guy looked built for trouble.

The young man opened the door of a large office and indicated a chair facing a handsome, curved, glass-topped desk of burled wood. Obviously quite expensive, some trend from years past. Travis couldn't place it, Eames maybe. The guest chairs were leather and chrome, sleek yet comfortable-looking, a classic design from the '50s, Travis recognized from his college art history classes.

"Be seated. He'll be with you momentarily," the pit bull said.

"Who will?" Travis asked.

No answer, a side door closed softly. He eased into one of the chairs. *This could be it*, he thought. They knew he was unarmed. What would Reno have done? Shit, these were Reno's people. But Reno didn't trust them. Or had he? Travis hoped these weren't the ones who'd ruin his day.

The room was dimly lit, with track spots illuminating paintings on walls and a light emanating from a Degas ballet sculpture on the desk. The bronze piece was about twenty inches high and was turning slowly. A light above it shone down directly on it. Travis reached out to touch it and his hand went through it. It wasn't there. It was a hologram or something like it. The clearing of a throat sounded and Travis tensed involuntarily. There was someone in the room, behind the sculpture. *If my heart was weak, I'd be flopping around on the floor by now.*

"Some collectors prefer to have the original in a vault somewhere," said the cultured voice he'd heard on the phone. "We make these up for them so they can appreciate the piece with no reservations about it being damaged or stolen." He was on the opposite side of the Degas.

Travis started to rise so he could see the person.

"Stay where you are. I'm sorry, but I will remain en camera as they say. In shadow. Rather like the men in the painting in the front room, no? By the way, you must know, you are closely watched. Any rash move will be met with immediate consequences. Now that that unpleasantness is out of the way, would you like a drink?"

Travis started to speak, but his voice caught on the first word. He coughed and tried again. "Actually, yes, thanks. A bourbon, rocks." He hated being at such a disadvantage. *Won't let this happen again.* His eyes darted about, and he felt the itch of perspiration on his forehead. Where was he being watched from? Fuck it, he'd just get through it. He had a crazy impulse to overturn the desk. Hugely inappropriate, like laughing at a funeral. Only it would be his funeral. *Relax*, he ordered himself. *Go with it. Choices are limited.*

"Reno's favorite. I'll have one with you."

The side door the pit bull had used opened and a man with a tray appeared. He poured the two drinks at a wet bar, using silver tongs for the ice cubes. He placed the glasses on the tray and brought it to Travis, then to the man behind the Degas. Then he was gone.

"Ever wonder how Reno got his name?"

"I guess I never thought about it. He spent some time there, I know that."

Reno hadn't been a man who invited a lot of questions.

The man, the *Gallery Ghost* in Travis's mind now, took a drink. Travis could hear the ice shift in the glass across from him. The Degas holograph turned. He glanced down at his chest half expecting to see a red dot wavering there, or five of them. No dots.

"It had to do with payment for various services. Back in the early days. He'd sit in on a high stakes poker game in Reno, or roulette, craps, have the most *amazing* luck. We'd make sure he won a predetermined amount, and the taxes to cover it. Then he'd cash in. Big wins, taxes paid, everyone happy. We did it in Vegas too. We have properties there."

"Why did someone try to kill him?" He'd asked the question without really thinking it through. But it needed asking, even though he half knew the answer.

"Ah. That was unfortunate. Rogue element as they say. Rogues among the rogues. There was a small faction who decided to get rid of the sniper trail to the assassination. They were arrogant and sloppy though. They vastly underestimated their targets. That was their biggest problem. You see, they had killed witnesses and gotten away with it. Needless killing. All it did was call attention to itself as witnesses died suspiciously."

Gallery Ghost set his drink on the glass desktop with a faint click.

"Anyway, they decided to kill the killers. Big mistake. The snipers were all carefully vetted pros. Reno knew they were on his home ground. He never would have started that truck they wired. Your mother did, by pure chance, before he could get word to anyone."

Travis's hands gripped the chrome arms of the chair. His jaw clenched painfully. Some of those people were still alive. Was Gallery Ghost one? Travis saw his mother swinging in the tire under the old cottonwood, reading. He couldn't tamp down the visceral emotion he was experiencing as he tried to shut out the recurring movie in his mind, the whump of the explosion, the truck lifting in the air, the fireball. *Collateral damage*. He exhaled through his mouth, slowly.

"They learned a valuable lesson about loyalties in the few hours they had left," the Gallery Ghost continued. "Though it seemed an eternity, I'm sure, once he got hold of them. We almost lost Reno's trust, those of us who valued it. Indeed there was always distance after that. His wife, your mother. It was terrible. My sincere condolences are as fresh today, as then. I do hope you believe that."

Travis didn't know what to believe. Blowback had killed his mother. Maybe Vinita. Melissa in Dallas. Someone was still out there.

"It surprised me when you called me. How did you get my number?"

"I don't wish to be rude but I won't be answering many questions, Travis. I will ask a few, however."

"Well, you said come. Here I am. Now what?" *Oops, another question, fuck him.*

"I see Reno in you. To that point, you're not in New Orleans for the nightlife. You're here because you know some things. You have something to sell. I know the buyers. I know them quite well. How much are you asking?"

Travis sighed. What difference did it make? "Four million."

"Make it five. Plus expenses. Say a hundred thousand. We'll stake you."

"I don't get it. What's this about? I'm asking questions again, I know, but this is hard to understand…—"

"Slow down, Travis. Cool your jets as Reno used to say." Gallery Ghost chuckled. "A million for the gallery. A front like this is expensive to maintain, even with legitimate sales. But the money is really nothing. Let's call it refurbishing. I just don't want to spend it out of my own pocket. Plus it's convenient that you'll be doing the heavy lifting."

"I don't get it. Why wouldn't you just go after it yourself? Why stake me?" Travis shook some ice loose in the glass and sucked on a dwindling cube. He didn't want to push his luck, but wanted to understand *some* motives here.

As if they could be understood in this hall of smoke and mirrors he'd entered.

"Again, I needn't explain myself but I will, somewhat. Let's just say I enjoy the game. I want to see a little more justice done before I shuffle off. It's very convoluted, Travis. Justice *was* done when JFK was dealt with. Don't think it wasn't. He was an ego out of control. He actually believed he was president. Dangerous, dangerous man, worse than his father. But what you need to know is that you can pursue your objective with some actual prospect of success, with our help. We owe it to Reno, believe that or not. Five million is pocket change to the people you'll be up against. But I want to see them afraid. There needs to be some house cleaning as well. They sense this. They are already scuttling about, striking out blindly."

"I'm inclined to say no and walk," Travis said. "I've got reasons other than the money."

"Travis, Travis, you're acting as though you have choices," the Gallery Ghost said in mock exasperation, almost effeminately. "I don't have many audiences with people. Howard Hughes was a gregarious partying fool compared to me. You should pay rapt attention here, Travis. You can walk. But not far. When you're no longer whinnying with the herd it won't cause a ripple, believe me."

Travis was finding solid ground, he felt. The Gallery Ghost was powerful, but he didn't know everything. The threats were signs of that.

"I have safeguards against that no-ripple shit. It may not be a tsunami, but it will sure as hell cause some damage."

"Aha. Reno lives. And just what might these safeguards consist of?"

"No deal."

"Oh my. And if I say, we have ways…"

Travis peered into the turning Degas between him and the Gallery Ghost. It was kind of crazy, but this meeting was starting to take on a normalcy of sorts. Though like the ballet figure, it could make you dizzy if you watched it closely. "I'm sure you do. Okay," he said, placing his glass on the desktop, "I would have been asking four mil. Now it's five mil plus change with your involvement. What are the chances?"

"That they'll pay? Oh, quite good. Five is nothing to them. They are manipulating trillions as we speak. They're tricky, though. They'll salt it with counterfeit bills. Do things to trip you up. My part will be to get you clean money and out of their clutches. To that end, I've someone for you to meet. Elsie? Come in please."

Being continually off balance was like an inner ear disease or the fucking flu. Elsie? What was he talking about?

A compact Black man entered the office from the side door on the balls of his feet, jauntily. He wore Converse lo-cuts, a T-shirt with the face of Malcolm X silk screened on it, black jeans. His hair was dreadlocked. He had a couple of plastic bracelets on one wrist, an ornate chromed watch on the other. He stopped at the chair next to Travis and brushed the dreadlocks to one side before sitting. He turned a bit toward Travis. "This my man?" His voice was confident, humorous.

"It is. The man of the hour," said Gallery Ghost. "Travis, this is Elsie. Not LC for initials, but Elsie, the girl's name. His mother wanted a girl and pre-named him. To his credit, he kept it. He's a very unusual person, and we're giving him to you for the duration of your quest. You'll find him of great value."

Travis was alarmed. He wasn't a fucking corporation, he wasn't a team. He and Cobb would handle this. "I'd rather work alone," he said.

A sigh came from behind the Degas. "Again, much of what you want is a non-factor to me. Elsie will prove, as I said, to be of great value. He knows New Orleans, and he knows ways, avenues, corridors of power, and the wiring of the machines. He knows how to avoid danger, how to zig when zagging is not in the best interests."

Elsie grinned at Travis. He put out a fist for a bump. Travis reciprocated in a resigned way. "My man!" Elsie laughed. "We gone have some fun."

Travis's eyes narrowed as he thought ahead to negotiating the meaner streets of New Orleans with this character. Instinctively, he liked him already, but as a beer drinking companion at a sports bar, not in a complex game where death was a constant threat.

"He loves adventure," said Gallery Ghost. "And interesting assignments. And money. Elsie's a find. You'll see."

Elsie leaned forward and drifted his hand through the Degas two or three times, shaking his head in amazement. "Looks so real, you know I'm sayin'? He looked at Travis. "Just like a lot of things. Shit will fool you, dog. We has to find out what's real and what's not." He grinned as though he'd imparted an object lesson in a particularly clever way.

Travis looked into the Degas. "I have a couple reservations—"

"Oh he long gone," Elsie said. "He through with us. Thing about him is, he gives you what you need, then he

gone like the wild goose in winter." He laughed. "Me too,
pretty quick here. You need anything, I be around. You
don't come to the gallery unless called. I'll be giving you
ways to get ahold of me. No phones. No pagers. It'll
work, you'll see."

He held his fist out, bump, clasp, elbow to elbow, a fi-
nal hand slap.

Travis kept up with him.

"You pretty White, Travis, but you okay, you know?"

Travis laughed, in spite of himself.

CHAPTER 16

Y ou're late," Emilie said.

Travis liked the accusatory feel of that. It was as if they were paired.

"I had a meeting. Went longer than I'd expected." When Travis had entered Napoleon House, Emilie was at the bar with a man on either side of her, intent on buying her drinks, but she was nursing a Dr. Pepper and gracefully not accepting. They melted back into the crowd when Travis showed up and Emilie greeted him with her blame and a smile.

"I'm kidding. I found a rare parking space right outside and I was so proud. I wanted to show it off, but it was only an hour so I had to move it. Parking tickets are a bitch here."

Travis ordered a bourbon and water and looked at Emilie.

"My drinking day begins officially," she said. "Salty Dog, please."

They took their drinks to the hostess and got a booth. Outside, a passing Elsie gave him a thumbs up from the street through the window, moved on. *Surreal*, Travis thought.

"Who was that?"

"A new best friend," he said.

"Looks pretty street. How long you been in New Orleans?"

"Couple days."

"Wow, meetings at high-end galleries. Rasta guys. You get around. Did you buy any art? Any hash?"

"No and no. You a cop?"

She looked suddenly contrite, peered at her drink. "I'm sorry. I'm so nosy."

"Now, *I'm* kidding. Ask me anything."

She brightened. "Where are you from?"

He told her about the Marais Des Cygne, his French ancestry, relation to the Broussards, Kansas City, and that he and his uncle decided to get away after Vinita had passed away from Alzheimer complications. She seemed mesmerized, watching him with a little smile as he talked, nodding, and drinking. He ordered another.

"What about you?"

"I'm homeless. Got kicked out of a place when a cousin tried to nail me, even with his own wife at home. The son of a bitch. She figured I led him on, which no such a thing. I didn't like it there, anyway, just a temporary thing until I get a job. Another LSU dropout cruising New Orleans."

"You can stay with me at Maisson de Vries. I have plenty of room." He felt his face heat up as she looked up at him, cocking her head. What the hell possessed him to say that? Two drinks? The strange afternoon?

She grinned. "Wow. Maisson de Vries. What do I have to do?"

"Nothing."

"You know, I believe you. And you know what else? I dig the *shit* out of you."

Travis laughed, surprised. "No one's ever told me that. Not in those words."

"*Tres eloquente, oui?*"

"*Mais oui.* And that's about all the French I know. That and *voulez vous avec* etcetera and some other inappropriate stuff."

"My bag and things are back at Arnaud's. Not that he had room for me, he doesn't. If you don't mind my asking, how long are you staying at Maisson?"

"Week or two. Longer. I dunno, yet."

"Well, you're not sleeping on the sofa."

He raised his eyebrows as he took a drink.

"I am," she said, returning his raised eyebrow look with a grin. She held her drink out and he clinked it with his.

"I have a quick call to make," he said, pulling out his phone.

☙❧

The crowd had thinned at Arnaud Broussard's but the hammering and circle-saw sounds were still going. As the gate slid open, another car hauler pulled up behind them, loaded with a motorcycle and a Nissan sports car. Repos, Travis thought. He didn't miss those times. Some guys lived for repo, liked the rush. The mean, efficient ones made money.

The same dogs stood at the driver's side door and stared at Travis. He stared back. They were a rot mix, hard to tell what they were thinking. Tow-yard dogs were generally not very social. Arnaud himself swung down from the truck, a short muscular man with a wide face, shaved head.

The dogs abandoned Travis and clustered around their boss as he approached the Land Cruiser.

He shifted a cigar butt in his mouth. "Travis. Emilie. Whuddup, peoples?"

"I came back for my bags. Found a place to stay for a while. Arnaud, don't look so relieved," she said.

"Hon, you always welcome at Broussard's. You know dat. We even got a no-paw de pretty girls policy enforced by de chief."

The chief, Travis knew, was Mrs. Broussard, the woman who had greeted him on his first visit. "Just no room right now wid de remodeling and guests—"

"I know, sweetie," she said, getting out of the Land Cruiser. The dogs ran to her side and jostled for attention as she went inside.

Travis got out and walked inside with Arnaud. Cobb was at the TV, watching a Royals game, but he didn't miss Emilie bustling by, and he smiled archly at Travis.

"Man you moved pretty quick on that one," Cobb said.

"Don't be a dickhead."

"I come from a long line of dickheads. That makes you—" He paused. "—a dickhead!" He brightened as though the equation was sudden and satisfying. "Beer?"

"We have to be going. What I didn't say in the phone call was I had a meeting with someone I need to talk to you about. We're in the shit now. Be careful."

"Whoa, wait a minute, you ain't goin' nowhere without you fill me in." Cobb stood and motioned him outside.

Travis told him about the call and the meeting as Arnaud helped Emilie load the Land Cruiser.

"Fuck's a hologram?" Cobb asked.

"It's a three dimensional picture of something that's not really there," Travis tried to explain.

"You sure you're not on LaCygne Green?"

"The important thing is, this guy, whoever he is, is on top of it. He's smart and he's way up the ladder on this. He knew Reno pretty well. He might be a big help, he might be our downfall."

"Where you taking her?" Cobb head-pointed at Emilie as he dug for his Skoal can.

Travis sighed. "I'm so fucking stupid, Cobb."

"Ain't no pill for that, but what made you figure it out?"

"She's staying with me."

Cobb almost choked on the Skoal. "Ho, *shit*!"

"I know."

Cobb moved his tongue around over the chew, replaced the tin. He said "Hmph." Then he said, "You know, Reno didn't want Rose involved with that business back then, but he wanted her more than he didn't want her involved." He paused. "Know what I mean? It was just as sudden and just as damn inconvenient."

"Doesn't make it right."

"No. I'll say this though. If it's just sex, cut her loose."

"That's not it. I can't explain it," Travis said, glancing over at her, as she settled inside the Toyota.

"Travis, no use worryin' about it. This happens to St. Cyr men at the least convenient time. It's the one thing you get in this life that's good. Enjoy it for the short time you can. Might be a month, might be thirty years, but, by god, it'll be short, or seem thataway."

"But dammit, Cobb, why right now? This is crazy. Why not when this thing is over and done and I meet her in the Fiji Islands or some damn place. I wish..." He trailed off.

"Mm-hmm. Wish. And if frogs had wings they wouldn't bump they ass a-hoppin, now would they?"

Cobb's eyes were wide, his mouth pursed, just like he'd always looked before grabbing Travis as a boy and tickling him until he gasped for breath.

"Don't do this shit, Cobb. Not out here, not in front of her." He backed away, then whirled, evading Cobb's grasp. He was laughing when he got into the Toyota.

"What was that all about?" she asked, half-smiling, eyebrows drawn toward her nose, causing a small dent in her forehead. She had one arm along the seatback, legs tucked under her. He felt he would see her in this posture, this place, all his life.

"My damn uncle, horsing around. He's just a big kid."

"We all should be."

"I know."

ᗫᔕᗫᔕ

At Maisson de Vries, he felt somehow conspiratorial, as though they had to sneak past a fraternity house mother or something. He also felt this hooking up was completely counter to what he was doing in New Orleans, and dangerous. Travis was older than her father probably was, as well. Talk about drawing attention. But damn.

What he was feeling for her surely had much to do with hormones and chemicals, but there was something else there as well. No explaining the strong desire to protect her or the pure comfort just being around her.

And she confused the issue, the reason he was here. If he thought she was so great, he should cut her loose, roughly, get her the hell away from it. Or be selfish, reckless, put her in danger and himself in more danger and compromise. *Fuck this*, he thought. *Some things you don't question. I'll deal with it. Nobody expects me to be a couple except maybe Gallery Ghost who appears to know everything. It might even be an advantage. Yeah, right, and rocks grow.*

She emerged from the steamy bathroom, adjusting an earring. Good god, she was beautiful—in a black short bare-shoulder cocktail dress and very little else. Her springy comic book hair was sleeked back on her head and drawn into some kind of collection in back. Her cheekbones were more pronounced by this effect, and her eyes were made up in a way that made them longer, hard to avoid, but then why avoid such beauty—like looking into the eclipse without a shield.

She sat down to put on her heels then leaned back in the loveseat, arms spread along the back, crossed her legs, looked at him. "You going like that?" she asked with a half laugh.

It seemed like they'd been together for years.

He was still in baggy shorts, chucks, shirt hanging out. "I thought we'd pick up a pizza."

She smiled. "That's fine. I just like to play dress-up sometimes."

He showered and changed into a blazer and jeans.

When they entered the restaurant, men looked at her, then him, back to her, thinking their sugar daddy thoughts and wishing unspeakable things.

Over dinner, Travis learned that Emilie's father disappeared early in her life. She didn't remember him, only knew he was Creole, half Black. Her mother, she told him, was poor, worked two jobs. She herself had been on her own since early teens. She dabbled in, then escaped, drug use, applied herself, got a scholarship to LSU. Then she simply got tired and quit. She'd worked as a stripper and dancer in New Orleans, but never as a prostitute though she'd considered it, knew some. She modeled for a photographers' consortium and that had brought some good money her way, plus some TV commercial work with the possibility of feature film parts. He could see her in films, easily. He didn't know about her acting chops but she'd certainly dress up the scenery.

"I'd be good at it," she broke into his thoughts.

"What? Acting?"

"Prostitution. It's a form of acting. Basically."

"Basic, yeah."

"What would you pay me?" She was enjoying this turn of conversation, even though it was making him uncomfortable. Probably *because* it was making him uncomfortable. She was enjoying being a center of male attention in her small black dress, but not in a vain way, more in a girlish, teasing way. "Well, do you think I'd be successful? Drive a fancy car? Have a little book full of congressmen and bigwigs?"

"Oh, sure. All of that. No doubt in my mind. But there's a price for that."

"There's a price for everything."

"You're right, there." His thoughts drifted to Vinita, his mother, Melissa the stew. He so disliked his train of thought, he excused himself brusquely and went to the rest room. He splashed cold water on his face and accepted a fresh towel from none other than Elsie.

"Dat yo daughter, mahnn?" He drew those words out and laughed softly. "Yo accomplice?" Those words were fast and comic.

"Elsie. Jeez, Towels?"

"Nahh, man. De towel guy, he takin' a break. I never take a break. Don' boddah wid de tip, I catch you later."

When Travis looked in the mirror again, Elsie was gone.

He returned to the table, but it was empty. He looked around, half suspecting that she would be with some man at the bar but she wasn't. He sat down, spread his napkin back in his lap. The waiter arrived with the entrees just as she turned the corner from the ladies room in the other hallway.

ℰↃℰↄ

As they walked back to the Maisson, the night was humid, yet fresh-feeling, with condensation running on the windows of the bars and restaurants they passed. She stopped him at a narrow alley and took his lapels in her hands. Somewhere, a Nat King Cole song floated from an upstairs balcony window, "…and touched two lips that lied."

"Oh, not here. Believe me, not here," he said. *Deja fucking vu*, he thought, as Melissa's face in the alley in KC floated to mind, then flashed away.

She urged him into the alley. "Yes, here dammit"

They kissed in the darkness, but his eyes were open and darting from side to side. Then he got into it. *Screw it*. They were a single unit, their hands sliding and feeling cloth and skin, tongues touching, rolling. A couple passed, laughing, murmuring to one another, and they moved deeper into the shadows.

"I dig the shit outa you," he said and they both laughed into one another's mouth, expanding their cheeks, making them laugh again.

She unzipped his jeans and exposed him to the New Orleans air, crouched low in the alley. He came almost immediately, summoning the trinity, arching his back, his knees weak, and he kept coming as she continued to work her mouth and tongue on him. Soft explosions of light were going off behind his tightly closed eyelids. When he'd finished, she stood and replaced his cock in his pants.

He zipped up, shakily, and she patted his still prominent lump. This was definitely not part of his planned regimen of being aware of his surroundings.

He could only breathe, inhaling, exhaling deeply.

Her dimples showed in a passing slice of headlight. She took his arm. "Walk me home."

୧୬୨

They smoked LaCygne Green, watched late night shows, ate leftover cupcakes, and drank wine. Then she made good on the promise to "fuck your wheels off, bubba from the Marais Des Cygne."

CHAPTER 17

The morning sun streamed through the breezy curtains from the open French doors. The catawba tree dropped a blossom or two as the jasmine perfume danced in the door with the sun but Travis awoke to an empty bed.

Emilie was in the courtyard doing yoga in a brief outfit, and he noticed she could stand on her hands with her feet hooked behind her head. He would have to accelerate his workouts. His once-hard pecs had become nascent man-boobs and he was conscious of his spare tire, though it was diminishing. She told him she loved it all, he was not to change, but it wouldn't hurt for him to accelerate his running and resistance training she had intimated.

"I will be your personal trainer," she'd said. "*Very* personal."

Travis brushed his teeth, threw on a sweatshirt and shorts, began doing pushups in the room. Soon he was aware of Emilie's legs near him. He looked up.

"Want to go running?" she asked.

"Sure. But nothing real fast. I'm getting back into it."

She wore shorts over her yoga outfit, donned her white Nikes.

The morning had already warmed up to noon-like

temperatures. They took off on St. Peter, off Bourbon Street, then down Burgundy. Thunder rumbled overhead and rain fell intermittently amidst the sunshine. After warming up, she sped up, calling over her shoulder, "Meet you back there. I need to *run*, run."

He watched as she ran on ahead, becoming smaller. He stopped to catch his breath, head down, hands on his knees. When he looked up, she was gone. But that was impossible. Unless she'd turned mid-block? But there was only an alley mid-block. He ran, saying "Oh shit, oh shit" until he realized it wasn't making him any faster.

When he got to the narrow alley, he turned in fast and regained his balance by grabbing onto a drainpipe that pulled loose and rattled as he rounded the corner. That noise got the attention of a long haired gaunt individual with sunken eyes and bad teeth holding a knife. Another similarly scary looking dude hauled ass around a small rusted truck with a camper box, and squirted out the other side, running out the alley entrance and up the street. The alley was a dead end. The truck sat idling with about a foot clearance on either side. Travis looked wildly about for a weapon, but found none. He stood aside as the freak with the knife came bursting out of the alleyway and headed the same direction as his companion.

Travis looked into the passenger side of the small truck. Empty. He noticed the ignition was popped, the truck obviously stolen. He raised the rickety back window of the camper box and there lay Emilie, still as death, duct taped, eyes shut.

He pulled her by the ankles to the open tailgate. Someone appeared behind him. He whirled, ready to go at it, knife or no knife, and was relieved to see it was Elsie. He had a little Ruger LC9 with a silencer on it in one hand and was looking around, no humor in his eyes or demeanor this time. The suppressor, Travis knew, wouldn't silence the gun, merely disguise the sound, making it difficult to ascertain what, exactly, it was, and where it was being fired from. Elsie was a pro.

"I was lax, man. Shoulda been here."

"Why, what happened?" Travis was trying to get the tape off of Emilie's mouth without damaging her. He smelled something strong that made his eyes water, ether or chloroform, that's what it was. The rag was up by her head. He pulled her farther out of the camper shell and ripped the tape from her ankles. Elsie produced a knife that snapped open on its own and cut the tape on her wrists. The tape over her mouth hung on but her mouth was free. She moaned.

"Had a call. Witness said two meth types were watching her run, pulled in ahead of her, and jumped her. They never even saw you—you were two blocks back. I'm thinking it's a crime of opportunity. Not part of your deal. But I don't know that. These guys are pretty scuzzy for contract work but you never know." Elsie's lazy vernacular had gone along with his humorous demeanor. He had concealed his weapon after making sure the alley was empty.

"Let's get her outa here, fast. Help me get her up front," Elsie said. "I'll drive. Don't touch anything."

Elsie wore gloves now. Travis didn't even want Emilie in the shitty truck again, in the freak aura and sweat smell, but they got her in the middle of the bench seat and backed out into the street. By the time they reached the Maisson turnoff, a false alley, she had come to in a limp, woozy way. They waited until no one was around and helped her inside. Then Elsie roared away in the little truck.

Cobb called within half an hour. "Heard you had a scrape."

"How the hell did you—"

"Arnaud. His boys picked up the truck for impounding. And he's got a line on the dirtballs. How? Who knows? Anyway, how's...she? What's her name?"

Travis resented that just a little, but that was Cobb. "She's going to be okay, some scrapes, bruises. Fuckers chloroformed her."

"Dang. You want 'em?"

"What would I do with them?"

"I dunno. Ruin their fucking day? You're gonna have to start uppin' the ante sometime instead a just jackin' around and having fun."

"I don't know that they're part of it."

"Don't matter. Everybody is part of it now, if they get in our chili. The way you gotta look at it. You want me to get 'em?"

"Yes."

"Call you back. Bring me that Land Cruiser sometime."

❧❧❧

When she was awake, she showed an icy meanness. "Damn right I want 'em dead. Motherfuckers." Her mouth was tight and white around the edges. It showed where it would pucker when she was old. The rest of her complexion was the color of wet cement. The adrenaline had coursed through her and she was shaking but not with fear.

"They may not have been part of our...problem."

"They'd have killed me. After about a week. You know that. Filthy fucking freaks." She paused. "What do you mean, our *problem?*"

"They might be a part of something else I have to tell you about. Or they might just be coincidental. Whatever they are, they're dead meat. But we're going to find out as soon as they get corralled somewhere we can…uh… talk to them."

"What something else?"

"You know anything about the JFK assassination?"

"The JFK—at LSU I had a history course that covered it. The professor was into it bigtime. Yeah, I know some things about it."

"Everything kind of hinges on what you believe about it, whether I tell you anything or not. Like do you think Oswald was a lone nut killer?"

"Yeah. And pigs flew out of his ass. And the government never lies."

"You okay to go get some coffee?"

⌘⌘⌘

"Wow. I mean big, *big* wow," she said. They were in Café Du Monde. She got up, limped to the coffee bar and got a refill of her café au lait, and limped back. "So, Gallery Ghost, what's his next move, do you think? Are we—you—waiting for some word or what?"

"Well, here's the deal. Since I met you, I haven't been doing anything. I half felt like backing off."

"Why? Shit, Travis, you can't back off. You're in it. Especially if the freaks were sent by them. I'm in danger, so are you, so's Cobb. We're already in it. Something one of the freak brothers said—one of those smelly pukes said. 'She's gotta be alive.' And the other said, 'That don't plug her hole.' Really. Believe me I don't like repeating it, but doesn't that tell you something?"

He remembered the ponytailed freak whose luck ran out in the Marais Des Cygne, Big Ray saying, "It's kinda like peeling a grapefruit, here gimme that knife…" Travis knew now there was no turning back, and she knew it too. No way were they going to get to this woman. He'd make sure of that. He was going to have to take it to them, and escalate like a crazy man. But without anger, like his old man said. It was the only way. No more waiting. He'd have to contact Elsie and the Gallery Ghost.

"Okay, we're in. Do you trust me enough to know that I'll take care of you at the end? I mean money."

"Let's just get there, Travis. In one piece. We'll sort it out then."

He nodded thoughtfully, slowly. The old mixture of fear and exaltation began to rise in him, the bully-hunter, waiting in the woods with an axe handle.

The mixture that had been his companion in the provinces.

❧❧❧

"I left that Ranger over on the causeway like it broke down," Elsie said. "Arnaud's Tow picked it up and it's impounded. I checked it out real good for anything that might be helpful but it was just a stolen junker. One freak gave up the other one. We have them both but it's a pain in the ass to keep them. You want them?" Elsie was checking out the surrounding area as they talked.

"What do they know?" Travis asked.

"Zip. They low level, shitbums, do anything for a fix. They were contacted on the street. Their heads are working on about three brain cells. Nothing of value. Believe me, they'd spill it if they had anything."

"What does Gallery Ghost say?"

"He don't say shit. What do you mean?"

"Well, what's the next step?"

"Fuck, man. How you ever gone get anything done? This yo deal, man."

"Cancel their ticket. Do the world a favor," Travis said.

"Now we talkin' They swamp gas. But you gots to do the canceling. Let's go, funky White boy."

Outside a cab pulled up. Much faster than any cab he'd ever hailed. They were taken to an area under the Huey P. Long Bridge where they transferred to a ramshackle graffiti tagged van. Elsie drove the van about three blocks to an industrial park full of *For Lease* signs. They pulled up to an outside storage unit. Elsie unlocked it. Inside the hot, airless container were two forms, bound and gagged.

Only one moved. Elsie backed the van up to the doorway then opened the back doors. He motioned to Travis as he dragged one form to the van. Travis helped lift the limp, deadweight form into it. They carried the other one. He struggled and tried to communicate through the tape over his mouth, eyes wild. He was sweating and smelled of defecation. They dumped him into the van and Elsie checked around the storage container then locked it.

As he drove, Elsie handed Travis the automatic with the suppressor on it. "Ticket puncher." He frowned at Travis's questioning look. "You the conductor on this train, dog." They drove toward the causeway in silence. Once, when the animated one in back made some noises, Elsie said, "Shut the fuck up."

Near Metairie, they pulled onto a secondary road, then a dirt road, and into some posted land. Bayou country. Elsie pointed to a crudely lettered sign that said *If U can read this U R within range*, and laughed softly.

They pulled up near a backwater canopied over with branches. Elsie unceremoniously dumped both bodies out near an upside down aluminum johnboat. "Do 'em here. Get 'em to the gators in that little boat. This takin' out the trash ain't easy, my man. It's better when you can just leave 'em somewhere in the city. But the man says swamp the fuckers."

ↄ⁄ↄↄ⁄ↄ

Travis held the pistol at his side, its muzzle pointing at the ground. His thoughts were all over the map but the recurring one was, "That don't plug her hole." He looked in the eyes of the one still conscious. He knew if he did this, he was over another threshold. He wanted to kill this asshole, and that's what made his throat dry, not the killing itself. Reno wouldn't have overthought it. He'd have done it by now, and forgotten it, or at least compartmentalized it.

At that moment, the conscious one had a seizure of some kind and he bounced on the ground in a stiffened, arched way.

Then he collapsed, his eyes clouding over and he was quiet.

"Save on ammo," Elsie said. "Tweaker trash just do theyselves in, mothafuckin' dumbasses. Start draggin."

They rolled them into the johnboat, up to their ankles in muck. Elsie pointed to the oars. "You get one, I get the other. It ain't far. Man, I hate this shit. I paid two hundred dollars for these shoes, waste 'em on these honky drughead trash. You lucky I been told to help your ass."

Travis said nothing. They rowed to an open area that looked deep. Plenty of tree cover above and around them. They rolled the two over the sides.

"What happens if they float to the top?"

"Buzzards, gators, bigass fish. They be gone pretty soon. Where's my piece?"

Travis pulled it out of his belt and handed it over.

They left the van under the bridge with the keys in the ignition. Elsie had called ahead for the same cabbie. When Travis got out at the Maisson, Elsie said, "You did all right. It'll be good." He said "aaight" for all right.

The cab shot into the evening, the sky turning reds and

blues like a spectacular bruise on a mugged and beaten day.

∽✄∽

Emilie was sleeping. He watched her for a minute. She showed some concern on her forehead but otherwise she was sleeping soundly. Elsie had told him she'd be thirsty but the chloroform after effects on a person her age would be negligible. He fixed a drink, picked up his laptop, and quietly opened the doors to the courtyard.

He looked up Effigy, found a professionally designed gallery site conspicuously missing any hard information about the owner or owners, merely stating it was owned by a New Orleans cooperative of arts patrons who wished to further the arts in the South.

He toggled through pictures of various functions at the gallery—Mardi Gras, a New Year's Eve party, a Friday arts tour gala, but none had anything of interest, just the usual pretty girls with their heads together posing for snapshots as though they wouldn't fit in the photo if they just stood naturally, groups of drinkers, costumed revelers, one aping the nude in the big painting, standing with a stick bird mask in front of her face in a skimpy outfit, the painting in the background.

He also found an Effigy II in Santa Fe that was possibly affiliated. One in Dallas. And an Effigea store in New Orleans that might be a part of the group. It sold fashions and accessories, plus items like soaps, candles, bath items. All were sketchy as to ownership.

Travis leaned back against the catawba tree, inhaling its perfumed blossoms, its scent blending with jacaranda and jasmine. Many of the same smells were in the bayou they'd left, but they mixed with ominous feelings there and were anything but pleasant. Would he have done it?

Yes, he knew that, for a fact. And even without having to, he was guilty of it. He'd be guilty of more before he was done. How many souls had his old man dispatched? Cobb, how many there? Breeze? Big Ray and Dammit Ray? Not your normal bunch of friends and family. None of them were bloodthirsty by any stretch of the imagination. But they found themselves in situations, and they were simply damned sure they'd come out on top. How many had he, himself killed over the years? It didn't pay to think about it.

Could he just take Emilie and go? Forget this? Find a way to make a living, even if it was a Cobb-endorsed enterprise. Live happily ever after. He'd never been happier—and he'd never been more anxiety-filled. At least he knew he was alive.

His phone buzzed.

"Hey Cobb."

"Them two dirtballs. They were connected but they didn't know who to or why. Just someone paid 'em to get you and her, or one or the other. Bring whoever they got to an address. We got the address. Then your guy got them. Or you did. They gone?"

"Like summer wages."

"Address won't do much good. But we do know it's them. I'd say it was time to go in like the Fifth."

He was referring to the Fifth Cav choppers in Apocalypse Now. He loved that movie like Vinita had loved her Harry Potters. He had been in C Company in Vietnam but the movie was better, he said. He never said anything about his time in Vietnam, but not because of shame or guilt or trauma. It was because he felt they weren't allowed to win it. He hated that.

"Why won't the address help?"

"Hell you think it's their summer home or something? Like they go there all the time? It's just a place. For sale, you know, one a them old factories that pigeons live in. Flood property."

"Thanks, Cobb. Talk at you later."

e∞o

Emilie had showered and cleaned her scrapes with alcohol and aloe lotion Travis picked up at the drugstore. She was back at her yoga and workouts.

"I'm going to talk to the Ghost, Em. Back in an hour."

He wandered around the gallery until the attractive woman approached him. Cartier gold glasses on a chain, librarian style. Diamond stud earrings. A beige silk blouse and black skirt showed off her well-kept figure. She interlaced her fingers in front of the skirt.

"See anything you're particularly interested in?" she asked.

No irony, or at least none that he could detect in her green eyes and slight smile, barely lifted chin. She could be fifty, he thought, but a better kept fifty than Daytona Flame.

Both were sexy in their own ways. *Call Flame* he noted to himself, *see if she's okay*.

"I was looking for a Degas, actually. The ballet figure."

"I'll make a call."

e∞o

"It's time to move on these people," he said, talking at the Degas.

"Would you like me to change the sculpture? Perhaps a Rodin? Or something more contemporary?"

"I said—"

"I heard what you said. Yes, it's time. It was time a

week ago. They very nearly killed you. You're sloppy. Are you just going to hang around the Maisson de Vries until they find you? That could be in an hour or a day."

"Okay, I need to go on the offensive, I know that. Right now I can only react. I know that's not good. And there's the girl. I can't have her in danger."

"Then you should have kept your lust at bay. She is in danger. An unnecessary barnacle on your keel my boy. You have Reno's list?"

"In my head."

Elsie slid into the chair beside him.

"Elsie, you think you can work with this character?"

"He ain't too bad."

"Travis, that's high praise coming from Elsie. Who's next on the list? Wait, let me hazard a guess. An oilman? Rafferty?"

"That's the name."

"Scoundrel, but charming. More money than H.L. Hunt. By the way, Gallery Ghost, I like that. It's rather fun."

Travis wondered what Gallery Ghost looked like. Fastidious in an Ivy League suit, he imagined, silver hair, sardonic half smile, polished. He would be wrapped in manners and wouldn't project in any way how thoroughly dangerous he was.

∽∾∽

"I'm sorry but Mr. Rafferty is unavailable." Icy. Barely tolerant.

"Tell him Reno Pete has reached out to him. He'll talk to me."

"Hello? Who am I talking to here?" Deep southern accent, whiskey voice.

"A friend of Reno's."

"Reno's out of the herd. He sho' was somethin', wadn't he?"

"You can cut the fucking cornpone act. You pissed me off."

"How's that?"

"When can we meet?"

"Aw, any old time. I don't do anything except hammer them sheikhs and fuck with oil prices. You know, just—"

Travis cut him off. "I really am gonna cut through the shit with you. This is not a game. You try to make it one and I *will* ruin your fucking day."

"Reno *is* reaching out. I'd recognize him anywhere. Hey, I'm having a do at the house. How 'bout you come by and we'll talk there over jerk chicken and fun drinks with loose women runnin' around. Sound good? You like women, don't you? If not, we got some a them funny boys too."

"Call you back." Travis hung up.

He was going to let this guy stew for a while, call him from a payphone or a throwaway. He'd immediately call in his cronies or his security people or whatever, but Travis would let this go a day or two, get the next one on the list. But no warning, no call. He'd just sneak in and get this one.

∽∾∽

Emilie helped him apply a Harley-Davidson tattoo with a South Boston location on his forearm. He wanted it seen and noted by the asshole he was going to kidnap. Elsie and Emilie were a big help with street theatre, both being actors.

A scraggly auburn ponytail wig and a porkpie hat from Goodwill, stomach padding, and a goatee. Emilie added eye shading to make his eyes look sunken, clear wire-rimmed specs, and a mole on one cheek. Good to go.

Cobb didn't recognize him when Emilie drove the Land Cruiser back to him. Cobb looked at this character Emilie had brought with his usual stinkeye toward strangers. He took the keys from Emilie without a word then said in a low voice, "Who's this jasper?"

Emilie started laughing and Travis said, "Fuck's it to you, old man?" Cobb moved forward and Travis said, "It's me, Cobb, cool them jets."

"Shit. Travis. I thought she was two-timing you with a, a...I don't know what. What the hell are you supposed to be, anyway?"

"Just some person that'll make a police sketch artist crazy. If it comes to that. At any rate, a wild goose chase runaround."

"Man, that's good. Looks real. Some street freak." He shook his head, lit a Pall Mall with his clinking Zippo. "I think it's your calling."

೮⁄ᗧ⁄ᗞ

The third name on the list was Anthony Binaggio.

This guy was New Orleans Mafia boss Carlos Marcello's right hand man back in the '60s. Young dude back then and didn't have a hell of a lot to do with JFK but he inherited the Marcello rule, and Marcello did have plenty to do with the JFK and the RFK killings. Thing is the deal was much bigger than anyone ever figured, even the conspiracy writers and people who tried to crack it. Jack Ruby said it when he tried to get the Warren Comission to move him out of Dallas—he was ready to give up what he knew, not a lot, but he told that dipshit Warren a whole new form of govt was going to take over, and they just laughed at him. Well, it happened. He also told them

they wouldn't see him alive again and guess what. Doro-
thy Killgallon (sp?) a journalist met with him and noised
it around she had something big and she bit the dust right
away to. Lot of "suicides" back then. Suicide was shoot-
ing off your mouth if you knew anything at all. And this
thing was so big, a lot of people knew things. Its still big.
That's why you'll get your money. And it's why they'll
finally leave you alone when they figure out what you
have on them. They'd rather pay out tax dollars than risk
riots in the street. And what your asking is pocket change
to these people.

Binaggio. He understands control. You need to. When
he's lost control and you have it, then he'll listen. But
you'll have to hurt him to get it. Never lose control once
you have it. Put him in the hospital if you have to. Tie him
up and pistol-whip him. That's control. He has a grand-
daughter. Make him think you'll damage her. He'll think
twice then, but he's dangerous."

Back at Maisson, Travis downloaded a photo of
Binaggio's granddaughter from Facebook, from Elsie's
information. He hated using tactics like this but the guy
was, at least, indirectly, responsible for deaths of those
close to him. The gloves were off. This fucker would
soon realize someone was bringing it on, fast and direct.
Then, on his phone, he loaded a recording of a girl
screaming from a distance "Please, don't!" then dissolv-
ing into shrieks and snot-crying. Elsie and Emilie again.

Elsie brought him a car, left it on the street. A disposable maroon Buick Skylark, older and beat up but it ran
well. Arnaud's boys would pick it up and have it crushed
never to be seen again.

Travis was calm yet anticipatory. He realized he was
in the thick of it now, no mistakes, clear thinking, he'd
win this sonofabitch. *Reno, you and me. Revenge is*
sweet, money is sweeter. He was tight, getting the jitters

again, but he knew they'd dissipate once it was on and he was doing it, like in Afghanistan. The New Orleans light was fresh lime, the air was electric. Things seemed the right shape as he scanned the street. Three lady tourists noticed him and crossed to the other side of the street.

CHAPTER 18

Cobb gave him the go ahead by crossing the street diagonally. Travis pulled out into traffic and the target limo ahead of him turned left. Travis followed five or six car-lengths behind in traffic. When traffic thinned, he dropped even farther behind, keeping the black Lincoln in sight a block or two ahead just to make sure the route was the same as before.

They had surveilled the trip for days. Binaggio always took the same route to his office, stopping at an industrial park where the chauffeur would get out, unlock a small *For Lease* building, and, after disappearing inside, he'd emerge with a package. This would be where they would waylay the chauffeur and pick up Binaggio.

They passed the Lincoln and pulled into the industrial park, out of view, parked in the alleyway behind the building.

Elsie picked the lock quickly and expertly, motioned to Travis. Travis entered the back door of the building, let his eyes adjust to the darkened interior of the musty-smelling small office. Then he found the cubicle where the package was waiting. He took up a position in the next cubicle.

Gallery Ghost had given them information on the

chauffeur—mob connected, martial arts educated to a degree. Nothing spectacular, a few moves, a soldier not a leader, a competent driver, well-paid by Binaggio, probably lax and casual, possibly even resentful of his stagnant position with nowhere else to go.

Travis heard the key in the lock and the door opening, low whistling from the chauffeur, confident walk into the cube holding the package. When the man turned to leave the cube, looking at the package, inattentive, Travis approached him from behind, swung a nightstick to the side of the chauffeur's head, the resounding Thok! letting him know he probably wouldn't need another blow. The man went down like a sack of grain. One moan, then nothing.

Travis tied and duct taped him securely after removing his trousers and coat. Took the package. Put the man's trousers on over his cargo shorts, shrugged his jacket on over his white shirt, and buttoned it at the neck. Then he walked quickly to the limo with his head down. He opened the door and ordered Binaggio out with the snubnose .38, frisked the protesting mobster, and told him to get behind the wheel and drive. He had Binaggio drive around to the back where Elsie had parked, the .38 jammed against the man's ear.

"Out," Travis said.

"You are really fucking up," Binaggio said. "You don't know how much."

"No, you fucked up. But I'm gonna let you live because you're gonna find me the money." He purposely broadened his A's so his accent might be construed as Boston.

"I'm gonna find you a grave, asshole."

Travis smacked him with the side of the pistol, and Binaggio went down on one knee, started to rise, holding his face. Travis hit him again. This time he stayed down groaning.

"More?" Travis said, raising his gun hand quickly.

"No, no," Binaggio said, holding one hand palm out to Travis, the other at his face. Then he said, "Jesus, are you nuts?"

Travis hit him again.

"Okay, okay, no more, I got it, I got it."

"Good. You people are so fucking arrogant. Kill the prez, make billions, think you got it made. I don't give a shit about your games. All we want is our share. Move!" Travis fast-walked him inside, pulling him along by his coat collar, the gun muzzle at his bloodied temple. The man stumbled as he walked.

Elsie was inside, a hood over his face. They tied and duct-taped Binaggio.

"Want you to see something," Travis said, showing him the download from Facebook of his granddaughter. This caused Binaggio to struggle and make noises. Travis raised the .38 again, and Binaggio was still, eyes wide. "Now I want you to hear something." He held the cellphone next to Binaggio's ear.

Binaggio struggled when he heard what sounded like a girl being hurt in some way. Travis shut it off. Then he knelt and talked quietly into Binaggio's ear, "We'll kill your dumbass Jersey wife, your sons and daughters, and their families and their fucking cooks, and their cooks' kids and their fucking gerbils, no matter how well you guard them. This idiot fuck that drives your car? He goes first. Next week. If you balk at all. At all, hear me? Nod if you hear me."

Binaggio nodded.

"He goes, then your granddaughter. No games, just facts. We. Don't. Care. We just want money and we're gone. Now I want to show you something else."

Elsie moved the stolen flat screen in place then inserted the DVD in the player. Travis sat Binaggio up, and wiped the blood out of his eyes. He pushed the On button making sure the chauffeur's coat sleeve rode up his arm revealing the Harley tattoo with the Southie identification.

When it was over, Travis took the DVD out, put it in a protective case and they left. Travis shed the chauffeur's jacket and pants in the alley, called Binaggio's office, told the receptionist where her boss and his driver were. They walked to the old Buick.

As Elsie drove, Travis wiped the surfaces down. Then he called Cobb.

"Take it to 'em?" asked Cobb.

"Took it to 'em," said Travis.

They parked the car in a no-parking zone in the Vieux Carre.

Elsie raised his hand, little finger and index finger extended. "Proud of the boy," he said.

"Who you callin' boy, boy?" Travis said.

This time he got the whole fist bump, exploding hand, and thug hug treatment.

∾∾∾

Travis was suddenly very tired. He knew they'd kill him, in any case, after they'd made him suffer. Now they'd just do it with a little more glee. More people in the audience.

At the Maisson, Emilie showed him how to remove the tattoo without scrubbing, using cleansing cream and theatrical makeup remover.

"So how'd it go?"

"You wouldn't want to know. You'd think way less of me," he said.

"You're wrong about that. The history prof who taught the JFK thing? He was ex-Department of Justice.

He told us stuff that would curl your hair. They're all scum, the mob, the feds who helped cover up the conspiracy, the DOJ, the FBI, the CIA, the—"

"They can't all be bad." Travis lay on the bed.

She straddled him so she could work on his face, daubing his sunken eye makeup, peeling away his mustache carefully. "Yeah they can. I hope you beat the shit out of him."

"You're psycho bloodlust. I like that in a person."

Her face was close to his. She stuck his mustache on her upper lip, kissed him.

"Ugh. Take that thing off," he said, "That's like making out with Tom Selleck."

❦❦❦

The hologram had changed. No longer the coltish grace of the Degas young ballerina, it was a Modigliani head sculpture, long and almost oriental looking.

"You like it? I own it. It would auction at forty million or more. So, you ask, what do I need with your paltry million? Expenses. Pocket change. As I near death I need so little. Art. A few dollars. Wine. A good book."

"Same here. Wine, a book, a classic Bugatti or two."

"You're cynical. Reno's son. Ah well. Elsie tells me you kicked dago ass, in his colorful vernacular. You did the unthinkable, Travis. Why the uptick?"

"Nobody's taking it seriously."

"Oh, you're wrong there. But, in a way, you did get their attention in a much accelerated fashion. Possibly unnecessary, but effective, I admit. So what forces do you think are now unleashed?"

"Big, badass clouds of Herculean proportion I imagine. The same ones that were unleashed when they got a whiff of the story in the first place."

"Well, at least you don't underestimate anyone. What is your strategy behind rattling these kinds of cages?"

"They'll run into each other. Keystone cop time. If I played it right, they're seriously knocking heads in the south Boston area."

"Boston?"

"I gave them a couple of clues. Misleading ones."

"That won't last. These people aren't dummies. Organized crime is still quite well organized. And the oilman you referred to as cornpone, he's been asking around as well."

"Cornpone is next."

"Well, don't rough him up too badly. He's old. Vicious, but old. Still has the touch, however. I lost a couple hundred thousand to him in a card game some months ago. Brilliant poker player. These fools out there now with their dark glasses and ball caps, next to the real thing, they are slobbering morons." He chuckled then sighed. "It's become a nation of poseurs and tweeters. No character whatever. No wonder we're floundering."

Chalk that up to your new form of government. You brought it on, you and god knows who all else.

⌘⌘⌘

They met at the room in the Maisson, Cobb, Elsie, Emilie, and Travis. Travis brought up pages on the laptop as they sat around the big glass coffee table strewn with the aftermath of slabbed ribs, salads, iced tea, and beer.

"This is our next guy." He slid the MacBook around so they could see the oilman's picture. "I figure once we roust him, we wait for the payoff. Of course, they will resist that because the old blackmail rule-of-thumb persists. Kill the blackmailers and make sure you have the materials. I needn't remind anyone here that we're in deep shit now. The people they're in league with invented interrogation torture. That's why none of you know where the stuff is. And that's even worse, because they'll keep you alive longer."

"Shudder," Emilie said.

"It's no joke, Em," Travis said.

"I know. I fucking mean 'shudder.' I'm doing it." And she did.

"I'm thinking, Cobb, that we send Em to your place, keep her safe."

"Like Vinita? I don't think so. And Breeze is a hound dog, you know that. Your best friend would sell you out in a heartbeat for this here..." He trailed off, sliding a look at Emilie.

Travis smiled. "This here?"

"This here purty little thang. Besides, she's got sand. She can do this."

"Okay. Cornpone's having a party. We're going."

"Mistah Travis, may I say somep'n, please suh?"

They all looked at Elsie.

"I be's servin' at the mistuh Cawnpone's party. I will be a mothafuckin' Oncle Tom gray hair old bobble head-ed grinning simpleton to the man, okay? You will not ra-re back in recognition and say 'Izzat you, Elsie?' as my nametag will say Chester. I will be yo suhvah and my name is Chestah, capische, Whitey? Workin' on getting Em here a catering gig."

ᴄ⁄ᴈᴄ⁄ᴈ

"Arnaud called," Cobb said. "Bikers are being rousted all over the place. By the mob, but, get this, also by the cops. Bruno says Binaggio didn't make like a formal complaint, but he's got cop friends. So that whole deal got his attention bigtime. Once we get Cornpone's cage rattled, then we go for the money."

"Just so you know, Cobb, you get a cut after I take care of Ghost's pay."

"Aw, hell, I ain't worried, bub. By the way, it's time to quit using our names, know what I'm sayin'?"

"I do, Bertram."

"I ain't no fucking Bertram."

"How about John?"

"John it is, Junior."

"We carry ID that Elsie gets us, John. We buy throw-away phones. We use cars provided by Arnaud."

∽∾∽

The party was in high gear when Travis pulled into the circle drive in a chauffeured limo. The limo would disappear in a few minutes. The theme for the party was beach, so Emilie had dressed Travis in a Hawaiian aloha shirt, surfer shorts, and flip-flops. He liked it. Comfortable.

He also had an American Express Gold Card in the name of Junior Wells, and some other credit cards and ID. His driver's license said he was from Monroe, Louisiana. A police check, if initiated, would give him a history there, though no one would specifically remember him. Junior Wells. Also known as JK Wells. Just a guy. Born in Fayetteville, Arkansas. Sold drilling equipment out of Tulsa.

The credit cards worked, for real, but someone else paid the bills. It would go on his tab. He used the cards with something approaching abandon now. If he didn't get the big payoff, he'd be dead, so it only made sense. When he did get the score, he'd pay Gallery Ghost from some villa in Tuscany, maybe a glass house in Cabo. Who knew?

He entered Rafferty's home through the pillared front. A servant led him to some French doors opening off to the side of the impressive foyer with its *Gone With The Wind* staircase and gestured to a brick walk leading to the pool area.

Junior Wells's flip-flops slapped the blue tiles at Rafferty's poolside and he accepted a glass of champagne from a passing server. Cornpone lived quite well. The crowd was a merry bunch, dressed for fun—some of the men wore tux coats and swim trunks, boat shoes. The women wore bikinis and heels, colorful coverups, flowing silks, garden hats.

A live band played Beach Boys and Jan & Dean surfer favorites while a runway built right over the more-than-Olympic sized pool featured actual models in swimsuits and crazy-looking high heeled shoes. The water from swimmers splashed onto the temporary deck and the blasé models paid no attention. They just looked pissed off. Like runway models. He guessed it was a model thing. One or two of the girls wore transparent tops and bottoms, one unfastened her top and swung it around as her breasts jiggled nicely to the music and her stiff, fast gait in her improbable-looking extremely high-heeled thick-soled shoes.

He looked around him as a voice announced the suit and shoes of each girl over the music: "Natalia is wearing a yummy little Nanette Lepore Cote d'Azure Cherry-print bikini, her shoes are Manolo Blahnik chain-maille snake sandals, less than two thousand dollars for the whole outfit…"

Oohs and ahhs echoed. Someone yelled "Show us your tits!"

The model showed no signs of hearing any of it. She stopped, did an impatient little move to show the suit and shoes to both sides of the gallery, hand on an angular hip, sashayed away, her buttocks working overtime. *Two grand*, Travis thought. *Shitfire*. None of that stuff covered more than six square inches of skin, all told. Maybe you got the girl with it.

He set his champagne glass down on a table after barely a sip, picked up a tiny sandwich, and ate it in one bite. Across the blue-tiled patio, by a serene reflective pool, he saw Elsie serving drinks by a tent with tri-cornered flags fluttering from its pointed top. He was Uncle Tomming all right, smiling, yassuh yassuh, cocking his head in deference to an overweight rich redneck in an epauletted safari shorts outfit and Abercrombie & Fitch-looking hiking boots. The guy sported a boonie hat like the one Travis used to wear in Afghanistan.

He'd like to transplant the asshole, stick him on the Pakistan border in that outfit.

The models had retired for a change in fashion and a hairy round little man was mincing along the deck in a Speedo to jeers from his buddies. He cannonballed off the runway, splashing a group of colorfully dressed older guests.

ⅇↄⅇↄ

Cobb pulled up on the street in an unobtrusive late model Acura, parked, and walked through the open side gate toward the music coming from the swimming pool area behind the big porticoed house. There was no security that he could see. He wore white slacks, a silk aloha shirt, no socks, and Topsiders. With this outfit and his Gar Wood, he'd fit right into a spread of *Town & Country*, though he didn't know it from *Popular Mechanics*. He heard the music and laughter and would have liked Vinita on his arm.

By the time he'd gotten to the pool and ogled his third

topless wet girl, he'd revised that. She wouldn't have taken to this bunch.

One nude young lady was body-painted with a beach scene complete with palm trees and a sun artfully disguising one nipple. *Like to git her agin*, Cobb thought.

He saw Travis on the far side of the pool. He didn't look like Travis—dark glasses, mustache and soul patch, porkpie hat, aloha shirt hanging out over beefed up, pillowed gut, unkempt long hair pulled back in a ponytail, and another Southie Harley tattoo which he would display to Rafferty when the time came.

He was talking to two women and, when Emilie walked by with a tray of hors d'euvres, he reached out and patted her ass. Emilie turned and glared at him, and the two women tittered over their umbrella drinks. Travis grinned and touched the brim of his hat at her and she stalked off, actually quite pissed-looking. *Nice*, thought Cobb.

She was wearing a wig, but it would take a makeup genius to make her look dumpy. *Like to git her agin*, Cobb mused a bit guiltily. But not very. He turned his attention to the crowd, taking in the details, distances, people who might be security, found a couple.

Cobb wandered to the main bar and asked the bartender next to Elsie for a Southpaw Beer, but they had none. He settled for an expensive New Orleans microbrew, tipped it, ignoring Elsie who was grinning like a fool at an older Colonel type who was telling him, "...now take your Jews, they just as good as White folks, and now, so are y'all."

Elsie was all yassuh and mm-hmmm and white teethed laughter at this anachronism, probably wondering how the old fuck had lived so long.

꧁꧂

Travis saw Cornpone then. There was a spattering of applause and good-natured cat-calling as Rafferty walked through the pool area, raising his hand in a sort of dictator's salute, the back of his hand toward the crowd, smiling broadly. He was dressed in long surfer shorts, a white pleated tux shirt hanging out, Teva sandals, Tom Ford shades. He appeared quite comfortable in his skin no matter what he wore, a man in his seventies and fit for his age, sporting a little bit of a pot belly he made no effort to hide.

Travis edged closer to him, then next to him, taking his elbow to steer him away from a snorkel-wearing colleague bent on talking to him, and facing him toward the back lawn so Travis could put the next ploy into motion.

He brushed at Rafferty's white shirt. "What's that on you? Oh my gosh." He brushed at it again.

Cornpone looked down, then back at Travis. A red dot from a laser sight was wavering about on his white shirt. A rifleman was in the trees by the street.

"What is this?" Cornpone said.

"I guess it's what it looks like, a fucking near-death experience."

"What do you want?"

"Five mil and change. Then me and my people are gone like Hoffa."

"We—I—can do that."

"Then do it." Travis knew wherever the older man was, people would congregate. Some were beginning to come toward them now. "Let's go somewhere private, or some bad shit will rain down on you and your loved ones. Got any of those? We're all set to rain on them."

"Sho do. Don't we all?" Cornpone smiled. "You, too. Am I right?"

"Somewhere private. We don't jack around."

"So I heard. No need for any of that, son. Follow me."

On the way to the older man's study, they passed bunches of partiers and cliques, handshakes and back slaps, through several sets of quad French doors, to a back, quieter part of the mansion.

They passed trophy kills and race car parts on the wall, into a large study where one wall was a blown up photo of a gusher well.

Elsie had told him to keep Rafferty away from the working side of his desk where buttons connected him to security people, alarms, and weapons.

As Rafferty started around to sit at his desk Travis directed him to a large comfortable leather chair instead.

"Cain't write a check here, son."

"Don't want one." Travis shut the door softly, then sat in a chair opposite the older man. He pulled out his phone and, keying the JFK movie, pressed start, handed it to him.

Rafferty watched, pursing his lips from time to time, then asked, "How much did it cost to set that up?"

"Oh, Mr. Rafferty, I think you know it's real. It can all be authenticated, well beyond doubt. The super eight is still available. And datable. Everything in the film has abundant provenance, believe me. Lots more, too. You guys can buy it all for a cool five million and it's over with."

"Why would I be interested?"

Travis rose from his chair. "Games, huh?"

"Aw, hail, son, worth a try. Shoot, five million is no problem. But blackmail is a never-ending deal. How do we know it ends there?"

"After five or six years of waiting for that shoe to drop, you'll relax."

"Afraid of that. Well, let's get on with it. You know, we're not bad people. Not like you. I have a feeling you're bad people. Us, we more like patriots."

Travis smiled. His eyes didn't.

"Well, you don't know any background. Me and Hunt, we were upstate here, meeting, and a rest home caught fire. Me and ol' Harrelson Lamar Hunt packed them oldsters outa that home like Jenny get the mail, got 'em all safe and then had to scoot. Wouldn't do for us to be found somewhere we shouldn't ought to be. See? Nobody knows stuff like that. Real life heroes we were. Called it mystery heroes in the paper."

"Then you blew the president's head off and killed fifty or sixty persistent witnesses. I'd say your karma bank is in negative funds."

Rafferty's voice took on a plaintive whine. "They was all warned. None of it was my doing." He crossed his bare legs and put his hands on the chair arms, sighing theatrically.

"Well, Mr. Rafferty, I still have to guarantee my people five million dollars. Cash. Twenties and hundreds. Gold fucking Kruggerrands if you want. But it's gotta be quick and it's gotta be real. Any counterfeit bills and people die."

"Oh, hail, son, there's gonna be counterfeit in there, cash, some anyway. It's not like we'd plant it."

"Nope. Each bill clean. Period. Any technology attached, people die."

"Technology? You mean like chips? GPS? That kinda thing?"

"You're not as dumb as you look. Neither am I by the way," Travis said.

"You say your people. How many people we talking about?"

"No questions," Travis said.

"Well, if it's like our deal back in '62, everyone and their grammaw talked."

"It's not like that."

"This is it? No Bobby? No Martin? No Malcolm X?"

"You guys really got after it, didn't you? Nope. Just JFK."

"Okay. All right. You get five big ones. Shit, that low-IQ CEO walked away from Merrill Lynch after wrecking that train, and he got over a quarter of a *billion*. Just for quitting! You in the wrong game, boy. I could set you up in the speculation business, just oil. Talk about a dinosaur, its day is done, and I could make you money that that gent would just slobber and crawl for." Then he leaned forward. "And if we want? We can crush your lame ass, boy, *and* your team, *and* your people and stub out any sign you'd ever walked on the *earth*. You can't kill us all. Too damn many of us. Bad as Muslims. Worse. We smarter. We know they ain't any seventy-two virgins slickin' up their goodies for us when we take that dirt dance. We got to do it all right here. You see that girl in the paint bikini? Savin' it for ol' me. Ol' turkey neck, pot-gut, shit-lookin' me. She be all over me like Hoover on Tolson soon as you out the door—and she does tricks that are against the law in Boy's Town, Mehico. I can get you that and more every day with your breakfast burrito. Five million, sheeeeyittt. Five *billion*."

Travis looked at him, pulled a .22 out of his waistband, placed a silencer on the barrel, and screwed it tight.

"Twenty-two huh. I'da thought rookies like you would carry 357s or tech-nines or some dumbass thing. Reno Pete woulda used a .22. Know who he is? He's the lead in your little movie show. Was anyway. We used to tell him go get so and so. He'd say, ruin their day? That meant terminal. Funny thing, he'da done JFK for free. He was somethin' else. Some kinda SEAL or somethin' worse."

Travis laid the gun across his lap. "Something on your shirt."

Elsie opened the door a crack and shined a laser pointer in on Rafferty's shirt. Then shut the door after the older man had looked down and seen the red dot dancing on the ruffles of his tux shirt.

"I get it. Don't worry, I get it." Cornpone held both hands palm out in front of him. "I'm dead meat if I don't come across somehow pretty quick. But I gotta whiz or do I just pee my pants?"

Travis noted where the bathroom was in the study "Leave the door open."

Cornpone did and, after he finished, washed his hands, took a drink of water from a glass on the sink. "Okay. I didn't kill anyone. Mechanics did that. Some good, some useless. Reno was the best. I was a money man. The groups were the mob, the Cubans who wanted back in to Cuba, the CIA, big business blue chips, the bankers, the oil business, and the military. Old boy racked up some serious opposition. He actually believed he was president." Rafferty laughed, shook his head.

Another time and place, Travis was afraid he would like this man. *Whoa*, he told himself, *this ol' boy is just North Hoover with education and power.*

"Get me a ceegar outa that box on the desk, would you? All cubes, by the way."

Travis rolled a tube out of the box, recalling how his old man had called the Cubans cubes and handed it to Cornpone. He'd let him talk a little more then take off. Rafferty was playing for time but it wouldn't help him. Travis was still within his set time limit.

"Get one or a handful for yourself. Can't beat 'em. No one ever will."

He took one for Cobb, put it in his shirt pocket.

"Gimme a bourbon, if you would, please."

The old man wasn't screwing around, Travis sensed, just getting comfortable. But time was an element here. He gave him a bourbon rocks from the wet bar, looked at his watch. "Two minutes, Mr. Rafferty." As he looked up he saw Rafferty eye the tattoo. Then Travis took a bottled water for himself.

"Call me Jerry. Anyway, JFK was two, no, three things that nobody could deal with. One, he was idealistic; two, he was un-bribable, being so damned rich; and three, I already said, he believed he was president. He may have been an intellectual but he was a dumbass, nevertheless. Hoover hated his rich ass. So did Lyndon. That's some power for a start. Add in about nine-tenths of the power structure out there, wheeee doggies, you got some enemies. I'm tellin' you this so you know there was a crowd involved. Line formed at the rear. You know I think ol' Bobby actually thought it was a lone nut gunman until the microsecond before he got drilled. And not by Sirhan, no sir. One shot from behind." He nodded at the gun in Travis's lap. "Little ol' .22. But that's a whole 'nother story, and you ain't got any movie shows of that. Least I don't think you do."

Travis cleared his throat. Cornpone held up his drink. "The point, yes. The point is some a them big power-dogs is dead and buried." He paused, raised his glass to Travis. "Some ain't. And there's a whole...how you say?...cadre of young power-dogs out there. MBAs. But they ain't as dumb as *they* look, just like you and me." He tossed off the drink. "And that's the point."

Travis rose. "You'll hear from me. We got cross-hairs here and there. Red dots on some folks."

"Oh, I don't doubt it. Five million coming up. You sure you wouldn't like to have some inside info ever now and then and be a speculator? One who never lost? There's a whole shitload more than a nickel in that. Just fuckin' around in the oil patch will make you Ay-rab rich."

"No thanks." Travis closed the door and hurried out

the French doors to the quiet hallway. He had no illusions that he was top dog in this dealing. It had gone according to plan, but it could go south a hundred ways from here.

∽∾∽

He slipped the cigar into Cobb's aloha shirt pocket, as he passed him, said "Let's went, old feller."

Elsie stayed to continue his charade, see what he could pick up. Emilie went back with Cobb, after feigning illness and drifting out a side door. Travis's limo picked him up in the circle drive but bore no license plate for the eyes that were certainly on him by now.

He was let off at a Walmart and picked up at the loading dock in back by a Broussard employee in a stolen truck, dropped off at the causeway entrance. He walked into a thicket and a waiting prop-boat took him across the bayou and dumped him on land where a four-wheel-drive Hummer picked him up and dropped him in a warehouse doorway, which shut after he entered.

He shed his costume—changing his look to that of a homeless man—pushed a pre-loaded shopping cart down Elysian Fields Avenue and into an alley, where he changed into khakis and emerged from the other end on a Kawasaki motorcycle that he'd left on the street ten blocks from Maisson's false alley.

He walked a circuitous path that took over an hour, two coffees at a Starbucks, and plenty of watching before he felt it was safe to head back. He had Elsie to thank for the trip which he felt was partly Elsie's practical joke and partly for real.

But it sure as hell would flush out anyone following him.

∽∾∽

"Some party that old letch threw," said Emilie.

"Yeah. Money talks, and money has fun. We're gonna find out about all that."

"He pinched my ass."

"Good taste." Travis looked at Emilie, and a small, cold spike of fear intruded into his thoughts. Suddenly he thought of Vinita, Melissa, his mom, and now he had brought this girl into the same dangerous circle, because of his own needs and something the movie people called love, but was it? Or just what The Gallery Ghost had said. Lust. No, it was deeper than that. But should he have walked away much earlier? Of course. Was he strong enough to do that? Obviously not.

"What's the matter, Travis?"

"Nothing. Why?"

"You looked so serious. Pensive."

"Well, we're in the soup, Em. I should have kept you out of it."

"There wasn't any way to do that, Travis. Not if we're what I think we are."

"We are, Emilie. It's gone way past 'I dig the shit outa you.'"

"It has, hasn't it?"

"We have to move out of this place. It's gotten too comfortable."

"I know. But I love it." She faced the open doorway and the white linen curtains that stirred in the breeze from the courtyard brushed her bare shoulder.

"We'll move out tomorrow. Cobb says Arnaud has a place for us across Pontchartrain, little shotgun shack."

"Sounds gritty."

"But then we should split up, keep moving, motels, hotels, maybe even fly out of here for a week or two, go, I don't know, to LA or somewhere, just to set some false trails." He handed her a utilitarian phone he'd gotten at a drugstore. "Here's a phone to use to call me or any of us."

"You said I could stay with you," she said, play-pouting, lower lip out.

"You can. I just have to be movable for a couple days while I get some of the heavy lifting done."

"What does that mean? Is it like holy commotion, Batman?"

"At least."

CHAPTER 19

At West Jefferson Med Center, Brandi Binaggio, Antonio's second trophy wife, sat curled in a plush chair by the large picture window overlooking Tenth Street traffic, playing a game on her iPad. It was a private room.

"So you met this bugfucker?" Binaggio said into the phone, chewing on an unlit cigar. He lit them rarely, mainly due to spousal concerns and objections. In this case, because he was talking from a hospital bed. Brandi didn't like "them stinking dog rockets." Sometimes he acquiesced, sometimes not.

"Sho did, Anthony. Had a little red dot on me at the most unusual times."

"Rookie bullshit."

"Nope. Tell you what, Antonio. I got the feeling this boy wants to die in the saddle. He don't give a shit for nothin'. 'Cept maybe the money."

"Big deal. I'm gonna give him his wish." His words sounded muffled to him through the bandages.

"No. No, you're not. Not until we get every scrap of what he's got to sell."

"How we gonna do that?"

"We got options here, Tony bony baloney fo-foney."

Binaggio bit down on his cigar, causing his cheek to ache more. He hated this name game bullshit Rafferty pulled. Had to be fucking Alzheimer's.

"Option one: we pay, and that's it. Two, we find him or a loved one, and we question the living shit outa them. I have a feeling a boy like this don't collect too many loved ones, though."

"That's the option I want. Lemme at him, the fuck."

Brandi looked up from her game, attuned to action brewing, or unpleasantness in the air.

"Now Tony, that's emotion speaking. You know better than that," Rafferty said.

Binaggio was suddenly tired, having upped his morphine feed. He said goodbye, set the phone down on the side table, and slept.

⋐⋑⋐⋑

Brandi picked up her husband's phone and walked out into the hall while pressing redial.

"Tony bo-bony?" Rafferty said.

"Brandi bo-bandy," she said.

She stood by the chauffeur, Julio, who sat in a chair outside the door and slid his hand up her skirt. She allowed this to happen.

"What's up, purty lady?" said Rafferty.

"What was all that about? Eek!"

The chauffeur had pulled her twat ring, as he called her intimate jewelry, and hard. She slapped his arm and scurried away. He smirked.

"Come over and we'll talk about it," Rafferty said.

"I might just do that."

"Tell you what. Meet me at the bad office."

"Twenty minutes." She hung up, scowled at the chauffeur, and walked well around him when she went in to replace the phone. The bad office was where drug and money drops took place. It was also a staging area for "long rides" that had dubious endings for passengers. More recently it had been the scene of Binaggio's unscheduled pistol-whipping.

၉၁၉

Julio, the chauffeur, was not only boning the boss's wife, he was living dangerously in another way he had no inkling of. The bull-necked haunter of gyms and strip joints was slated to die for being in Dallas the night of Melissa Bradley's death and for the possibility he had something to do with Vinita's death.

He felt full of life, full of himself, and the juices of quickies and whatever gratifications the next few minutes would bring.

He was well paid as a chauffeur and bodyguard, even though he'd lost a notch or two in the boss's regard, due to the recent pistol-whipping incident. He wore Armani and Versace, ate at the best New Orleans restaurants, drove a tinted-windowed Escalade of his own when off duty, and had the run of the boss's garage as well. A pissyellow Lamborghini was his favorite, but a Tesla interested him too—it just didn't make enough noise for his tastes.

Fucking Brandi Binaggio was a sometime thing, depending on her libido or boredom factor, but it supplied him with an adrenaline rush that other dangers just didn't match. He leaned the aluminum chair back against the wall of the hospital corridor and opened *Ripped*, a bodybuilding magazine.

The chicks in there were too small-titted for him, though he'd like to fuck a female bodyworker just to see what it was like, all those rips and cuts and standout veins. Sorta like a guy. He felt a pelvic sensation and thought back to prison.

Cobb, his executioner, was drawing near in a stolen Mercedes, checking on Julio's whereabouts. The tracking device on the Binaggio limo brought him into the hospital parking lot.

೧൧೧

At the bad office, Brandi Binaggio was working to bring Rafferty off but it was an uphill struggle.

"I tole you to wear that schoolgirl outfit and pigtails," he said, breathing hard.

"No time, sweet pea. *Vouz poude?* Don' pout. I make it right for you."

೧൧೧

Back with beignets and coffee, Travis keyed the door and, hearing something odd, hesitated. He opened the door a crack then walked in on Emilie, holding the electric toothbrush as a microphone, as she danced naked through the room and out into the courtyard, singing a song by The Crystals.

> "I knew what he was doing when he caught my eye,
>   Da do ron ron, da do ron ron
>   He looked so quiet but my oh my
>   Da do ron ron, da do ron ron"

She didn't hear him, earbuds in her ears, iPod strapped to her arm. It was all she wore. He stopped, entranced. She did a duck walk, a hop, some west coast dancing, whirled and turned, skidding to a stop on the worn tiles, blushing red, then recovering, bowing, curtsying, and dipping into a bow. "Thank you, thank you very much," she said into the toothbrush mic and bowed again.

Travis set down the bags, and clapped. "More! I thought you just had The Chemical Brothers and Mississippi Shakes on that thing. Wow, 'Do Ron Ron,' that's from way back."

"Well, so's Chopin, but we don't just drop it because it's not on the charts."

"Glad you recognize that." He held up a bag. "Coffee, tea or me?"

"It's Alabama Shakes, by the way," she said, standing with her hands clasped behind her back.

How did he ever, *ever* luck into this gorgeous naked lady? Indescribable. Even in his best college days he'd never laid eyes on anything like her. "Love your outfit," he said, walking toward her. They made love standing up by the catawba tree while the coffee cooled and the jasmine filled the air around them.

e/oe/o

The courtyard danced with Monarch butterflies as Travis and Emilie sat on the stone bench.

"They are migrating south. Did you know they travel across Pontchartrain with the cars? On the long bridge?" When tired or spent, her pronunciation relaxed back into Creole and she said "wis zee cars" and "zee long brishge."

"On the cars?"

"Non. Alongside. Avec," she said.

They coupled again in the sunshine.

e/oe/o

After showering, while dressing, she said, "Do you believe a hurricane begins with a butterfly movement or a bird wing somewhere over the ocean?"

"I believe in a lot of things now I never thought I would before."

∽∾∽

Travis met Cobb at Bumstead Burgers, a greasy spoon in Algiers where the coffee was either very good, or he'd been lulled by the tourist taste of the French Quarter.

"Chicory," said Cobb. "You had it all the time back home."

"That's what it is. Man, that hits the spot."

A gum-chewing Creole girl, with nose studs and a couple of rings in her lower lip, splashed more into their cups. She waggled her mini-skirted butt as she walked back behind the counter to get their order of biscuits, gravy, and eggs with burned sausage bits.

"Okay, Cobb, here's the deal. I'm of two minds. One is, drop this and head back to KC, LaCygne, pick up where I left off. But with Emilie."

"Travis, you're welcome at the place. So's she. But her daddy's probably younger than you are. How long do you think that'll last?"

"Shit, I don't know. I don't care. She's it for me, Cobb. I mean, you knew, remember?"

"Hell, yes, I remember. But they wasn't the big age difference. She's still forming her opinions. This right now is exciting to her. She don't know how dangerous it is."

"I think she does know. Anyway, the other way, is finish this off, get the money, then you and me and her are fixed for life."

"Shoot, Travis. I don't want the money. I *am* fixed for life. Always was. Now I just want to get back on the Marais Des Cygne, live a while longer. I miss the hell out of Vinita, Travis. Something's gone outa my life. There's a hole in it I ain't never gonna fill, never repair. The only thing that comes close to helping is being on the river. I don't understand it, but there it is. I'm close to her out there."

The girl brought their food. "Anything else I can get ya?" she said to Travis with a smile. Her blouse had one more button undone since the last visit, he noticed.

"They know," Cobb said, nodding at the girl as she flounced off. "They know when you're tight with a woman, and they just want to jack with you. Wonder how they know."

"Pheromones," Travis said.

"Fairy moans. Is that anything like awmby awnce?"

Travis laughed. "Something like it, yeah."

"Useless shit you learn in college. Anyway, there's no way you can stop now. You done dropped the bait can. The worms is all over the boat."

"I just don't want to get her involved."

"That bus done left. She's involved, I am. There's a circle around us, Travis. All involved. Smart as you are, I can't believe the way you're thinking."

Travis sighed, looked at his untouched breakfast.

"Reno Pete wanted it all," Cobb said. "He realized it wasn't possible, but he was crazy about Rose. He only knew his way of life, though. You've run up against that now. You're more like him than you think."

"I'm not like him," Travis said with little conviction.

"Have it your way," Cobb said, forking some gravy-soaked biscuit into his mouth, "but I'll tell you, I feel like I'm settin' across from him. And that ain't a bad thing, Travis. Especially now. We need us a little Reno Pete, right now."

A Black homeless type shuffled up to their booth.

"You gen-a-mans got a dollah to spare?" The apparition wore a long overcoat, despite the weather, and shoes that were duct-taped. The hand he proffered was filthy and grained. Travis gave him a buck. The person looked at Cobb, and said, "I said gen-a-mens, mofuckah, dat means you too."

Cobb's eyes narrowed and his face went hard. "You best get to truckin' while you still in one piece, mofuckah." He drew out the last word.

"Cobb, it's Elsie," Travis said quietly.

Cobb untensed, shook his head.

"I meet you mofuckahs outside by the dumpsters behind this place," Elsie said. "It's private. Ten minutes. Enjoy yo eats." He waved the dollar bill at Travis, said "Bless you. Mofuckah."

Elsie sidled up to another booth, and the fry cook yelled at him. He did a step-n-fetchit move out the door. "I's leavin' boss, 'dis me leavin.'"

Cobb rolled his eyes and Travis began eating.

ↄↄↄ

Back of Bumstead Burgers near the dumpsters in an alley with no visible sightlines to nosy people in windows, Elsie flopped his overcoat open to reveal a shotgun.

"Carry all the time now, boys. That's an order from Gallery Ghost. Just don't shoot a cop."

"What's he know?" Travis asked.

"Just about every damn thing," Elsie said, with a high-pitched laugh, bumping fists with Travis, "but the carry order is, shall we say, informed."

"They onto us?" asked Cobb.

"They beginning to zero in. Big Julio was found dead in a hospital parking lot. Scairt the living shit outa Binaggio. Scairt equals pissed in his world. He don't know what to do, so he got all his troops out there looking. And some a his troops are feds and cops."

"Okay, so we carry."

"Cobb, I don't want to know too much," Elsie said, "but we kind of know who done in Big Julio, right?"

Cobb nodded.

"That .22, it gone, right?"

Another nod.

"Nice clean job, though. Look like a gang hit, base of skull, in his trunk, all that."

No comment, no expression.

"I need the tracker back."

Travis looked sideways at Cobb, who handed a paper bag to Elsie.

"Well, I got to run, boys. You, Travis, get out of Maisson de Vries. Today. Cobb, you move somewhere other than Broussards. They don't need the heat. And you—" He looked at Travis. "—get your dick used to being lonely. Get that girl out of town."

He whipped the coat off and around the shotgun in one movement, walked to a rusted white van with a Murphy HVAC magnetic sign on each door.

He removed the signs, tossed them in the dumpster, and drove off.

"I'da told you about that piece a shit Julio," Cobb said. "We did agree it had to happen."

"Yes, we did. It just seems like you went off on your own on that one."

"You were busy. Need to know, all that. Just doin' my part."

"Revenge have anything to do with it?"

"Little bit."

"Feel better?"

"Nope."

ℰↃℰↃ

After they checked out of Maisson De Vries, Travis packed their things in the Land Cruiser. The car now had legal Louisiana plates on it, thanks to Arnaud. Emilie had gone back inside to check the room for anything left behind and to say goodbye to the catawba tree. She picked up one of the blossoms from the ground and put it behind one ear. They headed to Lake Pontchartrain.

On the causeway, the water reflecting blue sky and speckled with diamonds, Emilie moved close to Travis. "Any idea where we goin', lover?"

"Waterfront property, so I hear."

She kissed his cheek and curled up against him to sleep.

ℰↃℰↃ

As he drove, his mind reeled along with the straight-line concrete bridge railings.

You're thirty years older than this girl. It's not even close to realistic. Without her the money wouldn't mean shit. It didn't before, but I thought it did. Now it only means something with her. A couple of good years, then cut her loose, let her live her life without some old fart cluttering it up, give her a bundle, pay off her student loan, have a trust fund to go forward with, good memories. Then what's left for me? Money. Fuck that. Who knows if I'll even get out of this alive? And I've drug her along. What do I do? I get the money, engineer the trust, the loan repayment, give her a chunk, and let her know she's not obligated.

Jesus, that's even hard to think about. Is that what love is? I thought it was like a good movie, happy ending. Not the case, no way, I should know that by now. Okay,

I'll do this deal as best I can, try to get out of it clean with the money. Do something good for a change, for someone.

He knew better than to pray.

☙☙☙

When they reached the other side, he turned left to Ponchatoula and checked the directions Arnaud had given Cobb. Through the little town and past a tattered billboard that said *Are You Saved?* with the D and the question mark almost illegible. At his side, Emilie made a sound and nestled deeper into sleep. The road they turned down reminded him of Cobb's place, remote, untended. A recent rain had made the dirt road slippery and he slowed to engage the Land Cruiser's four wheel drive. At least it wasn't a long road. The shack came into view. Brick pattern tarpaper sides. No Maisson De Vries.

He pulled up in front and stopped.

Emilie awoke, said "Hmm?"

She wiped her eyes with balled fists, yawned, stretched. Planted a kiss on Travis's cheek, smiled. She woke up well. He usually watched her wake up. It was a pleasure. This time, the foreboding dimmed it. He almost ducked as a large shadow floated over them. It was a turkey buzzard, circling low over the grounds and trees behind them. It didn't mean anything, shouldn't anyway, just something dead in the bayou. The swamp was full of dead things. He'd put some of them there.

But the shape was wrong. The still air was too mute. There should be something more filtering into his consciousness. Tire tracks, fresh footprints in the mud—might mean nothing.

"Charming," she said. "Did you pick it out?"

"Your kin did. Maybe they don't like you."

"God, do you suppose there's running water?"

"If we hate it, we'll get a motel. No big deal."

"I hate it."

"Come on. I'll carry you over the threshold."

"Not here, you won't." She got out the passenger side door, leaving her purse and bags.

In the yard, she slumped her shoulders exaggeratedly stood limp.

"We'll find a place, don't worry," Travis said. "Arnaud was thinking of any port in a storm. And I was thinking maybe I'd send you to Kansas City, anyway."

She spun around, fists on her hips. "Oh, ho, ho, no, you won't. I'm all in. You said so yourself. I'm not going anywhere. Even if we stay in this hovel."

"We're not staying here."

"What's the matter?"

"I don't know. Something. Let's see what else is available on the highway."

His cell rang. Nobody knew the number but Cobb and Elsie. He answered.

"Yeah?"

"Oh, man, where are you?" Cobb said.

"At this picturesque shack in the swamp."

"Don't go in there. Do not go in the cabin."

"Okay."

"It's wired. Semtex. One of Arnaud's boys got bent. Money, we think. They were gonna take care of it in one blast."

"No shit? We were ten feet from going in. How much do they know?"

"We're finding out now. They questioning the dude back in the shop. We think they don't know much, just that the guy they were looking for was gonna hole up in the cabin. They don't know about anything other than that. They think Arnaud is out of the loop, that his guys were doing some freelance for money. This need to know stuff works pretty good."

"So what happens to the shithead who talked?"

"Need to know?"

"No."

⟨∽∾⟩

They left in a hurry. Escaping the cabin could have been the last of his luck, he thought, as the Land Cruiser fishtailed onto the highway from the greasy road and he disengaged the four-wheel-drive. As they proceeded the way they'd come, he noticed, in the rearview mirror, a big dually Silverado turning onto the road they'd just left.

"Call Cobb," he said. "Ask him about a black Chevy dually that just turned down that road."

After a short conversation, she said, "He thinks it's the people who wired it. Going back to check it. And we are to take the Land Cruiser to a place in Ponchatoula called Ace's Tinting & Detailing. Now. It's on US 51 and Pine. Get the vehicle off the road and out of sight."

They were on US 51. "Left or right?"

"I don't know," she said, looking dazed, detached. She shook her head, and looked out the window.

The highway was a long, calamitous strip of signs, thrift shops, bait shops, used car lots, and auto repair garages. If his luck was running low, he wouldn't find any more in this shit heap of meanness. He passed Pine, pulled into a Quick-Loan lot, and turned around. He saw Ace's from there and crossed the busy highway. He heard a distant "whump" in the direction of the cabin. He looked at Emilie as he pulled into Ace's. She showed no sign of having heard it.

Another Arnaud-looking place with high chain link and razor wire atop that. A garage door opened in the six-door block structure and a short, muscular-looking older man with shades atop his shaved head motioned them in.

The door closed after them. The man said to Travis, "Anything you want outa this vehicle, get it out now. Hope you got no sentimental attachment to it."

"I don't, but the owner might."

"They can look for it in New York tomorrow." He moved a toothpick back and forth in his mouth.

Travis and Emilie went through it pulling bags, papers, and searching the glovebox. As she bent over the man appraised her legs and the short shorts at the top of them. Travis was getting used to this.

"Call me Ace," the man said and offered a grimy paw, after wiping it with a pink shop cloth.

"Junior," Travis said, shaking his hand.

Ace's eyes slid toward Emilie, back to Travis, and he smiled, showing a gold tooth in front. It may have had a skull in it but the smile was quick. "You folks are now the proud owners of a 1998 Honda Civic stealth-mobile." He led them to the car parked in the corner of the shop next to a raised platform Dodge truck with black windows and fancy striping. "Give me your ID," he said, adding after a pause, "Junior."

Travis handed it over. Elsie had provided him with an Arkansas driver's license that would stand up to a police computer check with the name Herbert Ellsworth McCain, Jr., address in Eldorado, Arkansas.

A bespectacled older woman did some paperwork in a back office and handed it to Ace. Registration, plates, and insurance certificate, all in state envelopes.

"Car gets hot, call this number and tell us where you left it. If you can," Ace added, handing him a Post-it. He spit the toothpick out. "Beats standin' in line at the fuckin' DMV don't it?"

"It does, yes," Travis said. "Thanks."

"Don't thank me. I just do what I'm told. Tank's full. Runs like a striped-ass ape. Stroker package. Bored out. Dog leg gearbox." Ace winked. "Don't let it get away from you. She's a hot little bitch." He took another look at Emilie and flashed a gold-skull-toothed smile.

❧

Travis was getting used to feeling buffeted. Cars, identification, directions, compliments of Gallery Ghost, no doubt, but he had no real feel of control. Loss of control was as bad as loss of luck. Luck was finite. It ran out, it filled up, you had it, or you didn't. He felt the last of his luck may have flown with the shadow of the turkey buzzard. You made your own control. For Emilie's sake, he'd project it.

They pulled out of Ace's into traffic.

"Where to now?" she said.

"Well, we can go pretty much anywhere, now," Travis said. "For a while anyway. They won't be looking for this car. So any motel that looks good."

Sirens sounded behind them. Travis pulled over. A fire engine and two state troopers passed, heading in the direction of the cabin they'd left. He pulled back onto the road and headed for the causeway. He turned on the radio, caught the tail end of a weather bulletin about Hurricane Oswald. The water on Pontchartrain was black and white capped, and he could feel the wind around the little car. It would have been more pronounced had they been in the taller-profile Land Cruiser he thought. He hit the accelerator and the Honda growled as it surged forward.

❧

"I know, Cobb. But it was hot as a nuclear waste pile,"

Travis told him, when he explained the car switch. "We'll get something else when we get back to Kansas, something Vinita would like. She'd understand."

"Tell Elsie I want that car back in Kansas. Not New York."

Travis rubbed his temples. "Okay, okay."

After Cobb stomped off, Emilie massaged his neck and back. "It's all he's got of her," she said.

"I know. I just never thought." He punched the phone for Elsie.

"Yeah we can do that," Elsie said.

"What are we talking about?"

"Well, let's just say your new little boat didn't cost as much as the plates did. And for them to ship the Toyota back to Resume Speed, Kansas, you could have a trip to Maui, you and your squeeze. Up to you. Just chips."

"Send it back."

"Yassuh, Mist' Travis. I's be do that."

"Listen, Elsie? Can they just hang onto it? We'll drive it back. Or Cobb will."

"Not a good idea man. It's too hot right now. Just let us handle it."

"Right. Thanks, man." Travis hung up.

Back at the bayou shack they'd decided against, a spiral of smoke blended with the darkening sky. Red and blue flashing lights from various official vehicles strobed the overhead canopy of cypress trees, and police radio exchanges battered the relative quiet of the surrounding swamp.

The mangled remains of the black dually lay on its side, smoking, and the cabin was history, a blackened patch of ground. The swamp sounds had settled in again, undeterred by the intermittent squawking of the radios.

☙❧☙

At Arnaud's, Travis held a cold bottle of beer against his forehead, rolled it back and forth. Sitting beside him, Emilie leaned against him.

"We told the dumbass it was a phone set charge," Arnaud said. "Sent him back there with a cell phone and told him to key it from a distance when you all drove in. But first, he was to go inside and get a small cashbox out of there, put it in his truck. Something we forgot." He lit a Cuban cigar. "Boom." He blew a smoke ring, then another within it, held the cigar out at arm's length, looked at it as though it might do something surprising.

"So, what are they thinking, Binaggio and Cornpone?" asked Travis.

"Who knows? It was our guy that got fried. Maybe they think it's over, but I doubt it, if they knew his truck."

"Thanks. They must be close. We'll get out of your way and quit associating."

"Well, we're not without resources. The mob doesn't fuck with us. Usually. But that other thing you've…awakened. That's something we all left behind in the sixties. New Orleans is the epicenter of that. We have people involved. They have people involved. Seems like half the town was in on it. So, yes, might be good to have some distance." He looked like a fish with the cigar in the center of his mouth and his lips luxuriously around it.

"Sorry about your guy, Arnaud," Cobb said.

"Oh no, no, don't waste any sympathy there. That was a favor to us, finding out an employee is freelancing."

"But the cabin, that's a loss."

"Oh yes. Travis, if you and Emilie had gotten inside, you'd have stayed. All new stainless steel appliances. Reclaimed timber flooring. Entertainment center. Central air. *Une belle maison.* I slipped over there now and again, just for the quiet." Arnaud stood, as they prepared to leave. "Yesterday is history, tomorrow a mystery, *n'est-ce pas?*"

"Hang on just a sec," Emilie said. "I need a gun. Got a LadySmith?"

Travis was taken aback. Was that a good idea? Did she know how to use one?

She conferred with Arnaud for a minute. Then the two disappeared into the rec-room area downstairs. When they emerged, she looked the same, physically—shorts and a top. She reached behind her, pulled a pink-gripped .38, opened the cylinder, spun it, snapped it shut, smiled at Travis.

"I now have a moll," he said to no one in particular.

"She knows what to do with it," Arnaud said, seated again. "More important, she knows what not to do with it. Right, Emilie?" He looked at her pointedly. His head was lower than hers and he only moved his eyes up to meet hers.

"Yes, sir." She pulled the clip holster out of her shorts, inserted the pistol, and put it into her purse.

"No paper on that piece. You got it at a gun show in Bossier City, Civic Center, anybody asks." He addressed this to Travis. "And when all is shot and done, store it in the Pontch, off the causeway." Another smoke ring.

"Thanks, man. Thanks for all the help." Somehow he felt like he had when he'd shipped out for Afghanistan, leaving the familiar behind.

Arnaud waved away the thanks with his cigar. "You need anything, you know where to come. You're blood, all three of you. Here's a number with a scrambler. No one can trace it either."

He repeated it to Emilie in a whisper until he was sure she had it.

CSCS

Cobb sat in a dusty Jeep with Mississippi plates and a rusty exterior, but a strong, beefed up motor. "I'll find a place near you outside of New Orleans," he said out the driver window. "Sorry I got bent outa shape on Vinita's car, bud. I know it's a shit for brains move, but I just want that Land Cruiser."

"I shoulda asked. I get it. It's on the way to LaCygne as we speak. Breeze is picking it up on Highway 69." He patted the top of the Jeep. Cobb chirped the tires as he drove away, waved out the window.

Travis eyed the threatening sky. Weather coming. Soon as they found a place to stay, he'd check the local weather on TV.

"What's that on the windshield?" Emilie pointed. Written in the grime and moisture, Travis read, backward, *GG 3P*. Obviously from Elsie, Gallery Ghost, three pm.

"Sonofabitch, that guy is everywhere."

"Gallery Ghost or Elsie?"

"Both. Like shape-shifters, you know? I meet The Ghost at three, looks like."

"Glad they're on our side." She paused, then, "They are, aren't they?"

"Either they are or they've got an extended sense of cat and mouse."

"Shudder," she said. "But I love Elsie."

Travis looked at his watch. A couple of hours before they had to meet. Time to find a good place to stay, preferably with more than one entry/exit. A low floor balcony would be good. Ghost was paying the Amex bills.

There was a quickening in the air, he could feel it. The weather, the score, something was happening, many things coming together. He needed to be rested, up for it all. And he hadn't had his workouts in days. He needed to sweat. A lot. Get rid of toxins. A health club, a sauna. A good grade motel, Residence Inn type of place might have that.

"Em, get on the laptop…"

She moved quickly, squeezed his crotch. "Yours?"

"I wish. The MacBook. Find a motel with a spa, sauna, you know, health club, I've gotta work out until I drop."

"Can I come too? A sauna? Wow. I'm on it, boss."

"You're a moll. I mean a doll."

"I'm Bonnie, Clyde. We will kick some ass. I mean it, man. I'm ready for a life of crime if it's with you, Daddy."

ℰℐℰℐ

The Montmartre Arms Motel had a ground-floor unit with both a front door and a sliding glass patio door, plus the car could be parked within feet of the front door. It wasn't in the French Quarter but close enough for access to the Effigy Gallery.

"I miss our courtyard," Emilie said, lower lip out just a bit.

"You wouldn't miss it if Binaggio's goons treed you in it."

Hurricane Oswald was a few minutes from announcement and the sun shone brightly through the front window. Emilie pulled the shades, picked up the TV remote, and fell on her back on the big bed, bouncing. She aimed the remote and the TV came on in the middle of a Dr. Phil soliloquy in which he wondered why a guest couple got married in the first place. He kept using the word, "deflecting."

"What a dick," she said, changing channels.

"…and Binaggio isn't talking," said a sleek woman reporter standing in the street in front of the hospital.

"Not about his injuries. Not about his heretofore missing bodyguard, who was found today in the parking lot of this hospital, stuffed in the trunk of Binaggio's limo, executed gangland style. Conjecture on the street is that drug territory has been transgressed and rival factions are vying for turf."

"Travis?"

He turned from his laptop, looked at her.

"Are you killing people without me?"

"God, you're a bloodthirsty little thing."

"Yeah. Ain't it cool? What happened to Julio, seriously?"

"Seriously? Something serious. He got connected to a crime that happened in Dallas a couple months ago. Unfinished business that just got finished. Except for the fact that he killed someone innocent, looking for information about me. And that will never be made right."

"Two wrongs don't make a right."

"But three do, thank goodness." He folded the screen lid down on the laptop and an email from Detective Holt.

She arched her back on the bed and slid out of her shorts. "Come here, Mr. Right. Wrong me, right now."

They made love as the attractive weather girl made swooping motions with her hands showing how Hurricane Oswald might flow all the way to the Gulf and New Orleans. The sound function muted as they rolled onto the remote.

"Ouch!" She took it from under her and dropped it on the floor.

***

To:Wildlife@gmail
Subject: How's job search?
Travis, good hearing from you. Got a job yet? Know

anyone named Binaggio? Seems like wherever you go, shit happens. Binaggio got beat up and his "chauffeur" stuffed in the trunk of his limo.

Funny, but the vic was someone we liked for the Melissa deal. In fact, I was coming down there for a look. Still might. Know of any coon hunts? Probably not, as you're busy looking for a score. I mean a job, of course. More soon. Bet on it. Holt.

☙❧☙

"Okay Em. I have a distasteful task for you. Call Binaggio's granddaughter's school and try to arrange a pickup for the girl today. Tell 'em it's an emergency."

"Oh, Travis. I can't. We can do godawful things to godawful people and I just don't care, but—"

"Don't worry, hon, they won't let you do it. She's got bodyguards closer than three coats of paint. I just want them to know we're out there and circling."

"Hmm. Well, yeah, sure. It won't frighten her?"

"Shoot, they won't say anything to her, except don't go anywhere with strangers, the usual stuff. I have no intention of ever even seeing her."

He showed her a typed script on the computer screen and she called the number from a disposable cell. As assumed, the teacher came back with, "Who is this?" and a muffled exchange as they tried to trace the call.

Emilie hung up. She made a face and hunched her shoulders. "Now that did make me feel dirty. Ew."

"It's just theater for Binaggio and that crowd. He's the dirty one. It brought us a little closer to our endgame."

"Which is?"

"Take the money and run. Have us a time from now on out." He did a Cobb dance shuffle on the deep carpeting and howled softly.

Em tried not to laugh, biting her lower lip and breathing hard through her nose.

The room phone rang. They both looked at it.

"Nobody knows we're here," said Travis. "Let it ring."

"Might be the front office."

"Let them get ahold of us some other way if it is."

The phone went silent and a red message light flashed on. Travis picked it up. Elsie's voice said, "Yo, Junior. Don't ask how I know your room number. De Shadow knows. Hoooowahahaha. Anyways, guess who wants a meet. Three p.m. Today."

Travis hung up, looked at his watch. 2:10 p.m. "The gallery at three. How about we head over to Napoleon's? I can walk from there. You can move the car if you don't mind."

"Can I go like this?"

She had put on a crop top so short the bottoms of her smallish but perfect breasts showed if she moved a certain way. Her shorts were short and her long legs ended in the white Nikes. His mouth line compressed.

"Yeah. And we'll both wear signs that say 'I'm with stupid.'"

"I'll throw on a sweatshirt," she said sweetly. "But I can't help it if I've got a great ass, I just can't."

"We can get you some butt pads and a caftan."

She drove and the little car growled as she shifted. Travis watched her appreciatively as she geared down at corners and stomped it through the straights. Somewhere, she had learned to drive a dogleg stick, and quite well. He wasn't surprised. She smiled as she felt him looking at her, dimples deepening.

"What?"

"Just watching you drive. Where did you learn to double-clutch anyway?"

"I was a hot-rod chick in high school. Flagged the

street racers and stuff. My boyfriend was a drag racer and now he's a top fuel, nitro freak—poor, good-looking dumbass."

"Should I be jealous?"

"Hell yeah. Taught me everything I know."

"Everything?"

"Well, you helped me with some stuff." She down-shifted and pulled expertly up in front of Napoleon's, backed into a snug space with only a couple of twists of the wheel. She turned to face him. "In my never-ending quest for education."

"I've got your education."

"I believe you do. And I hunger for knowledge."

"Right here on the street?"

"No, not this time. I'm going to get something to eat."

He handed her some twenties. "Move the car so we don't get a French boot."

"I will. See you in an hour?"

✧✧✧

The tropical disturbance, that spun the small boats off Sierra Leone, meandered inland following the monarchs' playful trail, kicking up winds in Bobo Dioulasso, scattering old books and paper items in the market area, pulling at the merchants' rugs, and snapping laundry on lines. One book that survived the sudden sand-filled gusts was found by an Englishman, an archaeologist, in Bamako as the storm took a sudden left, heading west. It was a 1960 first edition of *Alpaca* by H. L. Hunt. Paperback. Covers sunned, heavily rubbed, darkened, creased.

Other than sand between the pages, the book was in remarkable shape. It had found its way to the marketplace through Libya, having been read by an amused Mohammar Quadaffi a few years after nationalizing Hunt Oil. It was thrown away then surfaced again in a book stall in Brazzaville, where it was bought by a French motorcyclist who was killed for his backpack outside of Lome. The killers scattered the contents, finding nothing they could use, and the book was picked up by a villager who traded it for a coffee in Accra. From there its trip to Bobo Dioulasso was an unremarkable series of trades and barters, usually along with other household goods. Nobody could read the strange language. The book espoused, among other things, more votes for those with more money in a utopian civilization.

The storm, gaining in strength, confidence, and shriekability, crossed the Sahara, driving nomads into buffeted tents, or at least into the confines of their robes, coughing but not cursing. It was Allah's will to send the sands awhirl and screaming. Camels sighed and closed their eyes. It was a photo in National Geographic in 1911 or 2011.

NOAA satellite viewers saw it as faces and fingers forming over the Atlantic. "Look at this, Josh. No shit, looks like a face!"

Josh ate his Subway chicken bacon ranch and nodded. "Now it looks like a splatter painting, you know those things like you get at a fair for your kid." He wiped his mouth with a paper napkin, typed a message into his computer after checking the hurricane names list. Looked like this one was Oswald. The Black community was pissed, someone said, because there weren't any Black names, like Shoricia or Towanda. Josh was Black and, personally, he didn't give a shit what they called them. They could call them Shitaree Number Three for all he cared. He just knew, from the satellite shots, what they looked like forming. Evil motherfuckers.

෴

The afternoon seemed unnaturally still and the light was off a little. Blue sky to the north but a darkish cast to the east. He stood in the quiet street, quiet for the French Quarter on a weekday afternoon, turned to watch Emilie's fine backside disappear into a yogurt shop.

He wanted this thing over with. It was all so unscripted, so labyrinthine. Too much waiting, then rushing. He hadn't yet decided how the money transfer would happen and that needed to be in the next day or so, fresh after the demise of Julio, before the opposition had time to strategize, to protect their flanks, and take the offensive. But then, maybe they already had. He watched street reflections in the storefronts. *Quit thinking. Soak up the surroundings.*

He stopped at the window of a smart women's shop, with a crow for a logo and no name, using the dark glass as a mirror. Behind him, across the street, foot traffic, tourists, locals reading newspapers at a sidewalk café, no one looking at him, or even in his direction. He looked to either side. No one stood out. They wouldn't, of course, if they were any good at what they did. And his adversaries could afford the best. He stepped inside the shop. He had a good fifteen minutes before he had to meet the Ghost.

A couple of young women scraped the hangers back on racks, searching. He wandered deeper into the store, descended to a lower level, the stairs a rusted safety tread, like Cobb's old flatbed, the railings stainless steel and airplane cable. There were mirrors everywhere and arty mannequins in extreme poses wearing short dresses and thigh-high boots or threadbare jeans, carrying backpacks and large studded purses. Jeans his aunt threw out went for big bucks here. Distressed.

An exotic looking Asian girl about Emilie's age and build approached him. "Hi. Looking for something special for someone special?"

"Well, I'm just looking, but yes, it would be nice if I could find something for a girl, young lady, just about your size and age. But I haven't got much time." *And she's hotter than a two-dollar pistol and movie star gorgeous. And you ain't too damn bad yourself, Asian chick. Shame on me.*

He wondered, at just that moment, how Emilie always looked so fresh and stylish even though she had brought so little with her. A young woman needed clothes, shoes, cosmetics. She had precious few of those things, being on the move with him. Not that he wanted to weigh them down, not now, but he'd like to get her something, take her somewhere nice again. He'd lost her a little bit over that cabin blowup.

She'd showed fear. Good, in a way. "I'm thinking something she could wear to dinner, you know, at a nice place. Dressy but young."

"If I'm not right in this selection I'm going to insist you buy her, she can bring it all back, no questions asked. Is she daring?"

"To a fault."

"Is she kinda sexy?"

"Very."

"So, not to get nosy, but we're not talkin' your daughter here, right?"

"Right."

"Okay, I was going to wear this very outfit, but in the interest of a sale…follow me."

She smiled a rather wicked smile, whirled around, bustled into a row of dresses, plucked a multicolored one off, then headed straight for a display of stockings and tights, pulled a package from the shelf, picked up some ethereal undergarments from another, checked their sizes, turned, and said, "Shoe size?"

He remembered a conversation in which she'd complained about her "big long seven-ass feet" and said, "Seven, I believe?"

In Shoes, she picked up one that was on display, a red pump that matched a red in the dress, held it to the dress, then held the dress to her own body. She took the pile of clothing to a register, looked at her watch. "Six minutes. Bet you never shopped with a woman in such a short time."

"No. Wow. Looks great, too." *I've never shopped with a woman, period, but it's kind of fun.*

"Tell you what. If you have another couple minutes, I'll put 'em on for you. I'm *craaazy* about this outfit. Come on." She took his hand and led him into a dressing room.

Before he could do or say anything, she slipped out of her one piece shirt-dress, and turned to put on the selected one. No bra, brief flowered panties, her bare, olive-skinned back to him, she put the colorful dress on, said, brightly, "Zip me."

He did. She stood, one hand on his shoulder to steady herself, and stepped into the shoes, backed away and did a "voila" move and smiled, cocking her head.

"Beautiful! You look...beautiful." He squinted his eyes to blur her and see Emilie instead. The dress was short, very short, and showed one bare shoulder with a slash of material across the top of one breast. The colors were all dashed upon a white clingy background, and a ruffle decorated the hem.

"Unzip me."

This time when she slipped out of the dress, she did so semi-frontally and he saw her breasts were about Emilie's size. He looked away, feeling color in his cheeks. At the register, he wondered if the intimacy was in preparation for the bill. Just chips, he thought, as he handed her his latest credit card.

He wasn't used to signing a name other than his own on a credit card slip.

When he walked out of the shop, the large bag with only a crow on it in hand, she waved through the window, and he waved back. He wondered if all young women were so uninhibited. He had been born way too soon, he thought. His watch told him he was about three minutes late and the walk to the gallery would take another three to four minutes if he hurried.

CHAPTER 20

The gallery was empty as usual. His footsteps echoed across the hardwood floors. The large painting of the nude with mask had been replaced with a nude lying on a couch with a remote in her hand, half asleep, the light from an unseen TV illuminating her. A menacing figure, half seen in the dark background as there had been in the mask painting. Obviously the same artist had done both. Realistic, but bordering on the surreal. A brooding unease radiating from both paintings.

"Sir?"

The attractive older woman was standing across the room, hands laced in front of her. She was attired, as last time, in an expensive matching top and skirt. Glittering but not showy jewelry. She looked like she was used to expensive homes, elite social gatherings.

"Yes?" He walked a couple of steps toward her.

"Shopping I see. I like that shop." She smiled, nodded toward the bag. "I take my granddaughter there." Then she resumed her official capacity as gatekeeper, saying "They'll see you now."

She led him to the office, opened the door after a discreet knock, stood aside. The door closed behind him.

This time, the statuette was a girl standing a bit

spread-legged, hands behind her back, holding a riding crop. She wore stockings and a corset that bared her breasts. Ivory and some kind of metal. It looked Art Deco to Travis, and he remembered having seen something like it in art history at KU.

"A Bruno Zach, this time. Often confused with Demetre Chiparus. The original. Not that rubbish you see on eBay or in the gyp markets. There are so many copies of this, some very good, that it hardly makes sense to have an original, but someone badly wants it. I'd say their interest was prurient, but no matter. Do you know what the name of it is?"

"No, but I've seen it somewhere."

"In yo dreams, funky White boy," Elsie said, as he walked in, offered his fist to Travis, who bumped it.

"Whipping Girl," said the voice behind the revolving piece.

"They all the same," said Elsie "When the whip comes down. Out to hurt yo ass."

"Apt, Elsie. That time has come. Any plans, Travis?"

"Contact Rafferty. Arrange for a pickup."

"How simple."

He felt rebuked. "I know it's not."

The Whipping Girl revolved between them. Her 'twenties-era bobbed hair was intricately carved in yellowing ivory, as were her features, her eyes, her lips. There was humor in her face, but no kindness. Her eyebrows were ever so slightly arched and her look was one of undisputed domination. It was a masterful piece of work, if only for that expression.

"Is there some way you can have him contacted?" Travis asked.

"Many ways. But it can't come back to me. I'll attend to it, however. How can he reach you?"

"I have a disposable cell, but even that's too risky. The

guy is powerful enough to manipulate a TV station to drop a hint on the news or weather, say. He can't do a drop and expect me to pick it up like the old days. I don't know, there has to be a way he can get word to me that the money is ready. Then there has to be a way to get him the materials. But not me, not Cobb, not Em."

"Not Elsie," Elsie said with a laugh.

"Travis, you have the hole card. The materials. Once they have those, you have no edge. Not fear. They don't fear you. You killed Julio, you whipped Anthony, you upstaged Jerry. So far, so good. But they will simply set in motion their machine to exact—call it revenge, call it punishment, tit for tat, whatever—and their method is to escalate far beyond the inciting incident. And what's frightening is their lack of emotion."

"My main concern is getting the money and then getting the hell away."

"One amusing facet of this, Travis, is that all concerned are still looking for a South Boston motorcycle tattoo. I wouldn't repeat that little bit of disguise ever again, if I were you."

Travis could even hear the smile in Gallery Ghost's voice. He wondered what the Ghost really did. In the sixties. Now. He might be an art lover, but galleries weren't his thing. Up against bad asses, Travis felt this guy was badder ass. And he, Travis, was slipping back into a place akin to when he was young and a bully-hunter, full of fear and anger, an all too explosive combination. "Advice taken."

"Something that Elsie has uncovered. Anthony's wife is having affairs and one of them is with Rafferty. The reason this is valuable to us is because she can be the delivery of time, date, method. Knowingly or not, makes no difference."

"She dresses up like a schoolgirl for ol' Cornpone.

S'only way he gets off these days. Man, she is some hot mama, though. I got the movies to prove it. Ol' Julio was even dippin' into that."

"One plan is to sacrifice her," said the Ghost. "War between Rafferty's group and Binaggio's would be interesting. But that could be distracting. And, by the bye, young man. The six hundred eleven dollars you just spent on your attractive lady friend, that's on your tab, not ours."

Travis flushed a bit. "Of course."

Elsie took a call on his cellphone. "Mm-hmm. Got it. Hang out there. Be witcha *vivement*. Sorry," he said to Ghost, "my hotline. Couple goons watching Emilie. Maybe just the physicality of her, umm, physicality, but these two are known freelance badasses. We done here?"

No answer came.

"We done here," Elsie said. "Coming?"

They walked fast, Elsie on the phone. When they reached the street across from the bar, they could see Emilie through the big windows. Elsie said to Travis, "Cool it, man, no rough stuff. We do not want to draw attention. You go on, call her. We take it from there."

Travis called her on the throwaway. She answered in the bar, while stirring a drink with a straw.

"Em, walk out of there, turn right, and I'll be about thirty feet behind you. Keep walking until I call you again."

"Sure thing, sailor." She gathered her purse, left a dollar on the bar, and headed for the door.

"Got a date, sugar-tits?" said one of the men watching her. They were seated in a booth and this one was leering.

She decided to play the part. If they thought she was a whore, she could defuse this. "Yeah, I'll be back, though. 'Bout an hour?"

"We'll be right here."

He got up and watched her walk away. He whistled loudly and yelled, "One hour."

She never looked back, just waved over her shoulder. Travis walked past the door with his shopping bag, acting as though he might enter, then looked at his watch, continued on. She turned the corner, then Travis did. She looked both ways then flashed him a breast with a quick raise of her sweatshirt, said "I only have an hour, sailor, but I bet we can get it done."

"Where's the car?"

"About two blocks on Rampart Street. What's your problem?"

"Those two guys ogling you are bad guys, Elsie didn't say whose."

"Oh. I'm pretty sure they thought I was a ho. What's in the bag?"

"Surprise. Let's get the car and get outa here."

ᴄ⁄ᴑᴄ⁄ᴑ

The whirl of weather that was rapidly becoming Hurricane Oswald carried Sahara sand in the inner rim of its eyewall, and would bring it across the ocean with various flotsam, including pages of books from the bazaar in Bobo Dioulasso and a lost military mail envelope from 1943 with rare Mauritanian stamps. The envelope was addressed to General Omar Bradley and was from General George Patton. Buried in the sands of the Sahara Desert, it was in fair condition until it met a struggling Cape Cormorant and exploded into small pieces.

ᴄ⁄ᴑᴄ⁄ᴑ

At the motel, Travis handed the bag to Emilie and felt an embarrassment he couldn't explain.

She took the bag. "Awww, Travis, you shouldn't have."

"Why do people say that? I do a lot of things I shouldn't, but why is this one of them?"

"I don't know. It's just something people say when they're a little overwhelmed and pleased at the same time." She unwrapped the tissue on the boxed dress, held it up to her, then unwrapped the other items. She smiled at the undergarments. "Wow." Then, "So, did you have help selecting any of this?"

"Yeah. A girl you'd probably like."

"She has kick ass taste. Kick. Ass." She slid out of her shorts and top, wrestled her tennis shoes off. He thought of the girl in the dressing room and compared their lithe bodies. Emilie won. She laid the underwear on the bed and slipped the dress on over her naked body.

"Zip me."

Déjà vu. He zipped her up in back, kissing her neck. She steadied herself, one hand on his shoulder, and put the shoes on. "Wow, how did you get the right size? Amazing."

She looked even more stunning than the salesgirl in the colorful dress. With her wild hair and green eyes picking up greens in the dress competing with the red splashes, she was a picture of jet-set nightlife in New Orleans café society, something out of a magazine, or a red carpet scene on TV.

"Damn, I'll have to buy a suit."

"I'd love to go on that shopping trip. Hugo Boss would look great on you. But I want to wear this tonight. You'll be fine in jeans and that blazer. In fact, you look so cool. Club night, okay? Dinner and boogie? Come ooonnn."

"Might as well. We're blowing this pop-stand pretty soon."

"How can I thank you?"
"You'll find a way."
"Unzip me."

❧❧❧

Ross Holt shifted in his seat and thumbed through the airline magazine while he waited for the plane to land at Louis Armstrong International. The weather was getting to him. He was sensitive to barometric changes and something was going on weather wise. They said something about a hurricane on the weather but, for some reason, he thought it was heading up the east coast. It made him jumpy. Irritable.

There'd been no sign of Travis since the last email. His phone went directly to voicemail. He seemed to have disappeared. Holt's sources thought he was still in New Orleans but they'd lost him. He knew now that Travis had been AdvanceGroup in Afghanistan then in New Orleans during Katrina. This guy was way more than he'd let on. But aren't we all? he thought.

Holt needed to question him thoroughly about this Binaggio chauffeur thing. He was pretty sure the garbage bag, Julio, was responsible for the stew's death in Dallas, but now there were some odd connections to Binaggio himself, and some other old New Orleans money that were intriguing. Then again, according to New Orleans street sources, Julio might have been done in by gang activity. Word on the street wasn't particularly trustworthy, in Holt's experience.

Someone was rattling cages down there and it had something to do with the death of Binaggio's bodyguard. Travis had been all over that JFK thing in Dallas, but then a lot of people were fascinated by all the loose ends in that deal. It was like the Lost Dutchman goldmine. If anyone ever did find it, there'd be a lot of disappointed armchair prospectors.

But Binaggio, the old Marcello group, and that Rafferty guy were, peripherally at least, involved in the JFK conspiracy. And someone was raising hell with them. It was like the old days when Garrison started digging around in New Orleans. The ripples had affected some Dallas people.

Since Holt had gotten permission to pursue the Melissa Bradley killing, he'd followed it here. What connected everything seemed to be Travis Meachem. Seemed to. Albeit not very substantially. It was a hunch, he had to admit. However, his subconscious had set him off in the right direction more than once. Thing was, he liked Travis. Not a bad guy at all. He knew he didn't do the Melissa thing. Could he have offed Julio? That garbage bag needed offing, in Holt's opinion. But it was still murder one. And in his book, it still came with penalties.

Once down, he collected his single piece of luggage, and took a shuttle to Budget car rental.

e/ɔe/ɔ

"Junior?" Cobb's voice said on the phone. "Johnny here."

"Hey, John."

"Knock, knock."

Sigh. "Who's there?"

"Juneau."

"Juneau who?"

"Juneau there's a hurricane coming?"

"What are you talking about?"

"Hurricane. You know about them, right? Can you say Katrina?"

"No shit?"

"Oswald this one's named. They say it might be heading for the gulf, and New Orleans."

"How soon?" *Oswald. Jesus.* The goose walked on his grave again.

Cobb's information was spotty but various weather reports had it reaching Louisiana or Mississippi within two days. Something caught Travis's eye. His regular cellphone was flashing a message since he'd put it on a charger and plugged it in between the two motel beds. One bed, unused, held papers, clothes, his laptop. The other was used. He was lying on the used one, inhaling Emilie's perfume from the pillow, and thinking. He told Cobb he'd call him back and picked up his other cell.

"Ross Holt, Travis. You get this, call me back. I'm heading to your neck of the woods Wednesday about noon. Flying. I'll pick up a car at Louis Armstrong. Sure would like to meet up with you. Call me."

Fucking hurricane. Holt, too. Travis would have to get the pickup arranged and get the hell outa Dodge by day after tomorrow. Friday. Gone. He wondered if Emilie was coming with him. They'd never really discussed it. Would she want to stay near her roots or would she even consider Kansas and a remote, rural existence. If they got the money, they could go anywhere, travel, but Kansas was home.

And how would she take to the Marais Des Cygne and the refuge? Because that was where he aimed to build. Spend time. Spend his life.

Who was he kidding? She'd get tired of fishing in about a week. An hour. And the winters were a bitch. He liked nothing better than to be snowed in, especially in a self-sufficient atmosphere like Cobb's. Would she get cabin fever? They'd have to talk. He'd simply disregarded a future, living from hour to hour. And, before Emilie, he just didn't care. Now he did. A lot.

"Travis? I'm taking the car to go pick up some eyeliner and a couple of things. Want to go with?"

"Yeah, I could get out of here for a bit."

❦

Holt drove into New Orleans parish, then the French Quarter, using the rental car's GPS. He'd honeymooned in New Orleans with his first wife, but didn't remember how he got there. He recognized a street or two then found the Maisson De Vries where they'd stayed. A big comfortable suite with a featherbed and a courtyard. Expensive as hell. They'd fucked their brains out in that place. And after a couple of years of marriage, she'd gone on and honeymooned with half a dozen guys before he caught on. A drug bust at a Dallas motel put him face to face with her and a small time dealer. He'd sprung her, divorced her, sent the dealer away for a stretch. He didn't much like New Orleans.

He tried calling Travis again. Voicemail. He drove on to the small hotel he was booked at. He'd found it online. They had overstated their charm. The elevator was out of order, so he walked up three flights with his bag. Luckily, he traveled light. He'd arranged an interview with Anthony Binaggio on the pretext of investigating Julio's death, though he wanted to seal the deal on Julio's Dallas visit. He also wanted to find out what had happened to Binaggio, though it was out of jurisdiction.

He turned the TV on out of habit. Whichever channel he flipped to, they were talking about a hurricane. Just his luck to be stuck down here in a frigging hurricane. Why hadn't someone told him? Why hadn't he paid attention to what the weather hottie in Dallas had said, instead of just trying to figure out how she was put together under that nubby silk old-lady outfit. She had been talking about something in the ocean that looked like a weedeater diagram. Must have been this Oswald storm. Jeez, he hoped it went up the coast but they kept saying it was going to the gulf. *Hit Mississippi, you fuck. Oswald. Isn't that a kick? Wonder if Travis got the irony. Or is he back in Dogpatch, Kansas?*

Holt splashed some water on his face, ran a Speedstick under his arms quickly, pulled his polo shirt back down, and threw on his seersucker jacket. Needed a shave but that was supposedly a good look nowadays. He stuck his snub-nose in a clip holster inside his jeans, put his badge in the watch pocket. Another look in the full-length door mirror. Man, he was getting old.

He strolled down the street to his car. Weather was weird but not especially bad. He stopped, lit a cigarette, and watched an unusually large bunch of monarch butterflies bouncing all over the place.

The meter still had some time on it. He pumped some more quarters into it and walked to a likely looking watering hole. He surveyed the place quickly in a cop's glance, saw two troublemakers in a booth by the door, drunk and loud. Otherwise the place seemed okay. He sat at the bar, ordered a tap beer and a shot. This was partially vacation, partially work, didn't matter if one slopped over on the other. The bartender kept an eye on the two by the door, didn't making any moves to quiet them. They looked like hard guys.

One of them bumped Holt aside as he took over a spot at the bar and said to the bartender, "You hard a hearing, jagoff?"

"No more for you, or your pardner," the bartender said, looking him in the eye.

"I'm gonna bet you could do time if someone caught you drinking, *and* making a public disturbance, am I right?" Holt said.

"Who the fuck are you?" The man swung around to face Holt.

The barkeep reached under the counter. Holt shook his head at the bartender, pulled his badge, one hand on the holstered .38 in back of him, coat swept away conspicuously.

"I the fuck am the po-lice, pencil-dick. And if you got brain-cell-fucking-one, you and that weasel you're with are going to haul ass."

The man backed away. "Hey, I got no beef with you."

"You got a good start on one, asshole."

The barkeep exhaled in relief as the man conferred with his friend, indicated Holt with his thumb. The two left.

"Whaddya got back there?" Holt asked the barkeep, resuming his elbows on the bar position.

"Just a sap, but thought I'd need a whole lot more. I think them two are on crank. You NOPD?"

"No, Dallas. I'm in town on a possible extradition," Holt lied. "Off duty right now, though."

"You guys carry all the time, right?"

"Supposed to. What do you know about this hurricane?"

The bartender shook his head. "Not much. Just that it's coming this way. I hope it veers off or something."

"Me, too." Holt circled his finger at the beer and shot. He looked over his right shoulder as the bartender waved to someone on the street.

"Whoa. Now *that* is nice," Holt said as he eyed the wild-haired, green-eyed beauty on the street.

"Yeah, comes in here sometimes. With her old man. Older guy."

"Like her father?"

"Nooo. Not unless there's some incest goin' on in the family."

"Ah. Sugar daddy."

"Not really. Can't figure it out. Sure stuck on each other, though. Nice guy. Quiet. Funny sense of humor. There he is. Coming the other way."

Holt almost didn't turn to look. "Oh shit!" He jumped up, started out, remembered his order, threw a five on the bar. "Be right back."

"Travis! Yo, Travis!" he yelled, hurrying to catch up with them.

Travis turned to face Holt after looking in all directions to see if anyone had noticed. He made a quieting motion to Holt, and Emilie just looked mystified.

"I'm...I'm kind of incognito, Ross. Or, at least, I was."

"Oh sorry, man. When I blow cover in Dallas, we just get off the street, quick."

He half pushed Travis into a doorway, which turned out to be a voodoo shop. They entered, and Travis quietly introduced Emilie to Holt. Holt looked Emilie up and down, smiling. She excused herself to go ask the proprietress if she could use the john.

"Nothing about how you and I met, okay?" Travis said.

"Oh, we're old coon hunting buddies. Dog fanciers. Man, oh man, oh man, I have a whole new respect for you, dude."

Travis grimaced, looked out the window to see if anyone had noticed the reunion.

"Been trying to get ahold of you. You don't answer your phone much," Holt said.

"I just got your message today. I'm kind of using disposable phones right now. And maintaining a low profile."

"What the hell are you up to, boy?"

"Nothing you'd care about. Why are you here?"

"Melissa Bradley case. We thought we had the dude, then someone snuffed his bad self."

"Case closed then, I'd say."

"Not that easy, sport. Some funny shit going down here in The Big Easy, and some of it has to do with that bad boy and his boss."

"Yeah, it's been on the TV."

"What's been on TV?"

"That Mafia killing. I assumed that's what you're talking about."

"I didn't say," Holt said, looking appraisingly at Travis.

Emilie and the voodoo lady were involved in animated conversation and laughing. The proprietress had a curiously deep voice and was exotically dressed in flowing silks, showing what looked to be an augmented breast job. Her long fingers were topped by talon nails.

"So you can really do *le voudou*?" Em was saying.

"Honey, I could conjure yo man into a cat if I wanted to."

"Oh, please don't. I love him the way he is."

"Oh, you'd still love him. He'd just be easier to keep, is all. No smoking in here, mistah!" She addressed Holt who'd pulled his pack of Pall Malls. "Is he a cop or what?" she stage whispered to Emilie. "At night, I sing at *La Fleur de L'acier*. Come on in tonight after eight p.m. These'll get you in the door." She handed Emilie two passes. "Believe me, it's crowded. You'll need 'em, honey." Her accent was a Brooklynese Creole with smatterings of French.

She put the tickets into her purse. "Cool! Thanks, Yvonne. Matter of fact, we're going out tonight. We will come by *La Fleur de L'acier*."

Yvonne gestured to her to come close and hugged her. "You special, Emilie. You got de way of *loa*. Did you know dat, girl? Take dis too, it be *veve*, protect you. Although anybody fuck wit you, need it woise." She laughed, a deep enveloping sound that turned the men toward them.

After making some curlicue marks on a paper, she handed Emilie a diagrammatic drawing—small, cross-like.

"You draw dis where you go, want to influence events. It bring you spirits, *loa*. Draw *veve* in de dirt, on a wall, scratch it in wood, tattoo it. It be one of a kind. It be yours, pretty girl."

Emilie looked closely at the drawing. "Tattoo," she mused. "Where?"

"Close to de wahmest paht of you body, girl." She winked and patted her own crotch.

Emilie smiled. "See you tonight. Thanks."

Outside, Travis said, "Yvonne, your new buddy, is a female impersonator, I believe."

"She's almost there for real," Emilie said. "Just needs the operation. She gets that in a month or so. Meanwhile, she's on female hormones."

"Did you exchange life histories?"

"Nice boob job he's got," Holt said, lighting a Pall Mall.

"Don't be *bete*, you guys."

"Means foolish, stupid," Travis said to Holt. "Pardon her French."

"We're going to see her sing tonight. She has such a cool voice, bet she's good."

"In a couple months, she'll hit those high notes," Holt said.

Travis looked away, tried to turn a laugh into a cough.

"*Bete,*" Emilie murmured, walking ahead of them.

☙☙☙

As she walked to the car the two louts who'd been kicked out of the bar staggered around the corner, almost bumping into her.

The loudest one said "Yo, beeyotch!" and looked at his friend.

Both were suddenly animated by the chance meeting. Their day was looking up.

Emilie walked faster, but they ran to catch up with her. One grabbed her arm and the other blocked her path on the sidewalk.

"Better let go," she said.

"You're late, but that's okay. You can give us a discount. Go get the van," the loud one said to the other, a compact thug with big arms, greased short black hair and a feral look. His whole face seemed to follow his nose.

Holt and Travis were almost upon them before they noticed what was going on.

Holt drew his .38 and smacked the one grabbing at Emilie across the face, then drop-kicked him in the ribs as he went down.

Travis tackled the feral one, rolling him to where he could get a good aim and started beating his face with short piston-like blows, scattering blood on the sidewalk. A small group began to gather.

Holt pulled his badge. "Unless you want to be arrested for interfering in a police matter, start walking. Now!"

The gawkers dispersed and Holt and Travis dragged the two thugs into an alleyway. One started to get up and Holt kicked him in the head.

The other was spitting teeth. Travis hit him once more then held his fist. "Hard-headed motherfucker."

Emilie was busy scrawling her veve on the forehead of the loud one with a sharpie, referring to the paper Yvonne had given her.

"I think it worked," Travis said.

"We'd better get scarce, people," Holt said. "Come on."

"I'll pick you up at Charbonneau and Jackson," Emilie said. "Go, go!"

They all took off in different directions to confuse any witnesses, hiding their faces. Holt and Travis met at the appointed corner.

"Man, I am never bored when you're around," Holt said, "but I know damn well I'm alive."

"I can't be all bad, then, right?" Travis said.

"You might be. Could be what I like about you. Your girl is a pistol. Like to buy you guys a drink."

"Far from here. Here she comes." The Honda purred to the curb.

ぐうぐう

Police who attended the scene sent the two thugs off in an ambulance under guard, having recognized them as warrant-evaders.

A policewoman mused, "You see the *veve* on the one dude's forehead? They must've run afoul of some voodoo practitioners."

Her partner, taking notes in a small black book, said, "Must have hit them with a lead chicken."

ぐうぐう

The little Honda growled when Emilie opened it up outside the French Quarter. She wound it out, shifting smoothly into fourth.

"Take the 610 to Metairie," Travis said. "There's some roadhouses out that way."

"I haven't been here an hour and I feel like a fugitive," Holt said.

"Well, that incident wasn't part of what we're doing here," Travis said. "Did you know those guys, Em?"

"Nah. They bothered me at Napoleon's. Thought I was a streetwalker and got pretty insistent about it. It wasn't like I could call the cops."

"Well, I ran into them at the same place," Holt said. "I could tell they were cons. I chased 'em out of there. They were drunk and hassling the barkeep."

"Em's a bad-guy magnet," Travis said.

"I got you, didn't I?" She signaled, downshifted, pulled into the gravel lot of a place called Charlie's M's.

Travis was awed that she knew a dog-leg shifter was opposite of a regular manual shift. The uninitiated jammed it into reverse for second. "You did, indeed."

When the two large men extricated themselves from the small car and joined Emilie, a sudden gust of wind swept the lot and dust scudded off it to the west. They looked east to the darkening sky.

"One drink, then we've got to run," Emilie said. "Would you like to join us tonight, Detective Holt? We owe you a night on the town, at least."

"Call me Ross, and no, I couldn't—"

"Sure you could. You're dressed fine for it right now," Travis said. "She's the show pony. Nobody'll be looking at you and me, anyway."

"Well, you're right, there. Maybe I will. If you promise to stay out of trouble."

"Can't promise that," Emilie said. "Can you dance, Ross?"

"Does a bear wear a funny hat in the woods?"

❧❧❧

They stepped into the '60s when they entered Charlie's M's. Three pool tables at one end of the cavernous structure anchored the dance floor, and a deserted go-go pedestal mushroomed out of the dance floor on the other side. A small stage with vintage amps and sound equipment caught some sun from a window facing the lot. The incoming clouds from coastal weather allowed light and dark to play on the dance floor in schizophrenic bursts.

After they ordered from an older gent in a worn plaid shirt, showing long john sleeves underneath, and suspenders, Holt dropped some quarters into the juke box, punching *Wabash Cannonball* by Hank Snow.

"Rest of the plays are up to you," he said to Emilie. "Anyone for eight ball?"

"I'll take the winner for five bucks," Emilie said as she searched for anything she could recognize on the juke box. She finally settled for some Doug Kershaw Cajun music for the rest of the selections.

The decisive crack of the racked balls, music, and banter of the three newcomers lifted the spirits of the owner and he bought the second round, to which Holt had added a shot of bourbon.

Holt beat Travis so Emilie racked the balls and chalked a stick. Holt broke and left a table full of targets, sinking none. Emilie walked around the table, then splayed her long fingers on the faded green baize, sighted down the stick, and decisively smacked a stripe into a side pocket. She proceeded to run the table of striped balls in unhurried fashion. Then the eight ball.

"Corner pocket," she said.

She leaned far over the table, one leg out, tendons prominent behind the knee—attracting Holt's appreciative eye—tapped the cue ball off the cushion barely kissing the eight ball, which sat on the edge of the pocket for an instant then dropped. She bowed to the applause. Travis was reminded of her naked curtsy in the sun-flooded courtyard at Maisson de Vries and *Da Do Ron*

Ron ran through his head, as did her lithe form. He smiled, seeing how Holt was eyeing her. Most men did. Kershaw came on with a slow one, and she held her arms out to Travis in a dance pose. He would only dance the slow ones. He held her close as they danced to a ballad called "When Will I Learn?" and she hummed along in his ear. Holt bought a round and included the bartender. Time slowed down, "Orange Blossom Special" played, and the four people inside Charlie's M's didn't give a damn about the outside world.

CHAPTER 21

They dropped Holt off at his hotel, promising to pick him up in an hour. Back at the Montmartre, Emilie took a luxurious bubble bath with her hair up, and Travis rummaged for a clean shirt, found a new one still packaged and full of pins from Brooks Brothers, a shirt that Emilie had bought him when they'd strolled Canal Street. He whistled at the price tag. But it was a damn nice shirt, yellow with window pane lines crossing. He found a fresh pair of jeans and laid out his ostrich skin boots and blue blazer. She came out of a steamed up bathroom in a towel, hair still tied up on top of her head.

"You look like a bird," he said, patting the top of her head.

She opened the towel and let it drop. "Bird, huh? Bird this."

He grabbed for her but she spun away. "Get dressed, horndog. Look at the time! And don't shave—that stubble looks groooovy."

While he showered, she checked her arms for bruises from the encounter with the goons—just one thumbprint on the inside of her arm, not bad. And it was on the side of the new dress that had fabric over that arm up high. She stood naked in front of the full length mirror, turned and looked over her shoulder at her back, her butt, her legs. She sprayed some perfume in the air and walked beneath it. Sprayed a little on her hands and rubbed it here and there. Near her warmest spot as Yvonne put it. Where the *veve* would go.

Emilie found some bright red bead earrings in her bag, cheap but sexy. *Like me.* She smiled in the mirror, applying the earrings. She slipped the dress on, straightened the slash of openness so it sat on the curve of one breast, zipped it as far as she could. Kick. Ass. She put the shoes on. "Emilie's in da *house*," she growled.

"Wow," said Travis. "Double freaking wow."

"You're a good little shopper, Travis. Zip me."

She turned all the way around for him. Then she pulled her hair back in a severe ponytail and tucked the tail up with a red barrette. She found the bright red gloss she'd bought that day, applied it. Brushed on some sort of darkness that accented her cheekbones even more, checked her red nails. They'd do. She grabbed a small red clutch purse and stood at the door.

Travis opened the door, flicked off the light. When he opened the passenger side door for her, he said "You just Paris Hiltonned me," as she climbed in.

"A little preview of what's to come, big boy."

"Those undies were a waste of good money."

∽∾∽

Holt was waiting at the curb, smoking.

"I'll get in back," Em said.

"No Paris Hiltonage for Holt, hear?"

"I'll watch it, sir."

"I heard my name," Holt said, "Should my ears be red?"

Emilie smiled at him as she transferred to the small

back seat. He flipped his cigarette in the gutter and climbed in. "Man, somebody smells good and I know it ain't me. Great duds, Emilie. You look gorgeous!"

"Thanks. You guys both look very with it and handsome tonight, yourselves."

They agreed on a restaurant on Jackson Square so they could walk to the club, left the car with a valet. Travis tipped him a ten, stressing quick access to the car, and warned him about the dog-leg shift that had reverse on the wrong side.

The restless, starless night would have appeared threatening to those less ebullient than the trio approaching The General's House Restaurant, the gusts of wind snatching at Emilie's ruffles and raising wings of hair on the men's heads. Their wordplay and laughter rustled and danced, like the newspapers in the street, and ricocheted off the wind-blown, wobbling stop sign at the corner.

A TV van had set up down the block, revelers parting and walking around it like a rock eddying a stream. An interviewer talked to a group of college boys, boisterous and giddy with beer and the approaching storm. One wore a T-shirt that said *I got crabs in Maryland*, and he referred to it often. A joke about FEMA meaning "Fuck 'em all" got bleeped. Shop owners were busily applying plywood to store windows and the harsh sounds of power drills, hitting the ratchet-stop when screws had been driven home, punctuated the interview.

Emilie got some wolf-whistles and a comment or two and the cameraman swung around to record her passing by. Travis and Holt averted their faces from the camera lens for different reasons.

の中の

Binaggio, at home now, watched the TV, a drink in his

hand. As Emilie passed by, she and the two men with her meant nothing to him, other than a hot girl accompanied by two men who looked a little like cops or gangsters or manufacturer's reps from Cleveland. He thought, if the girl was a hoor, she was out of their league. If she wasn't, what the hell was she doing with them? These kids babbling at the camera about how little they cared about the storm. They needed their smart asses kicked. Maybe they'd get washed out to sea if this Oswald amounted to anything. If it came inland like that fucking banshee bitch-ass Katrina, he'd have to head north himself. The irony of an Oswald returning to New Orleans to wreak havoc did not escape him.

"Need anything, hon?" Brandi was dressed in a micro nightie that showed off her long legs and gym-toned arms. She was buffing her nails. "I'm thinking of going to bed, Tony bony."

He raised his head and looked at her, his expression the same as when he gazed at the aquarium tank of fish in his office, or watched a red light waiting for it to change to green. But a rogue neuron was firing off somewhere in his subconscious, triggered by the name-game rhyming.

❧❧

Travis, Holt, and Emilie, having dined well at The General's House, re-entered the night—a night no less festive and full of drink-toting tourists than it had been earlier—and inhaling the suddenly still, humidity-sodden air, salt and fish-laden from the sea, were silent as they strolled toward the Fleur at crowd pace. Holt rolled a toothpick back and forth in his mouth and eyed the crowd like a cop, while Travis took note of anyone who seemed a bit more interested in them than was normal.

Emilie checked her makeup in a compact mirror, briefly watched two college-aged boys behind her whose eyes were glued to her butt, and smiled. Travis looked around at them and they stumbled, fell against one another laughing, sloshing their drinks.

The thing that made this night different from any other in the French Quarter was the plywood window coverings popping up on storefronts. The filligreed balconies were still full of partyers, some of whom, when asked to do so from the street, raised or lowered t-shirts or bandeaus to reveal breasts to great applause and shouting. One or two showed more. Few seemed concerned about the approaching storm.

"Willya look at that line?" Holt said, removing the toothpick and patting his pocket for a cigarette. The line to La Fleur de L'acier, The Steel Flower, snaked back on itself, then disappeared around the block. At the door a burly tattooed young man in a black muscle-tee was allowing a few in at a time.

"She's that good, huh?" Travis said to Emilie.

She fished in her purse for the two passes, held them out to him. "What about Ross?" she said. Travis took the tickets, folded one back, held them so they looked like three. "Follow me, guys."

As they walked past the line in the street crowd, Travis edged over to the bouncer, held the tickets up. The man unhooked a velvet rope on a brass standard, motioned them in, to some consternation from the next few in line. The bouncer smiled appreciatively at Emilie, said, "Now that's what *I'm* talkin' about. Go in there and class up the joint."

She bumped his outstretched fist and exploded it with him. "*Merci*," she said.

Holt slipped him a twenty as they went in.

The Steel Flower was all stainless steel and gleaming mirrors, accented with rusted steel cutout floral panels, softly lit. Black chrome tables caught the lights and re-flected the upper halves of those seated at them.

A dangerous-looking man shot his cuff to look at his watch and two young men next to him ducked. He grinned crookedly and said something to a sleepy-eyed, anorexic girl-woman who smiled and licked her already glistening lips.

Elsie, moving through the crowd with a drink, ignored the three. He was dressed in tight jeans, hi-top Varvatos sneakers, a turquoise silk shirt hanging out and open, and a black tux jacket with the sleeves pushed up. A Rolex glittered on one wrist, and ropes of gold jewelry showed beneath his open shirt. His chest and stomach muscles were pronounced.

Emilie poked Travis's stomach. "You could use a little of that, big boy."

He instinctively tightened his gut, grimaced.

Emilie whispered in his ear, "Aww, I was kidding. You're fucking *parfait,* perfecto. And I want some right now." She kissed him, and squeezed his thigh.

Elsie had disappeared upstairs somewhere among the dancers and watchers. They were seated by a hostess at a small table where they ordered coffee and liqueur drinks. The loud DJ music stopped abruptly and a circular re-volving stage lit up, then the lights lowered, and mist rose from the floor as Yvonne stepped out of an alcove and onto the stage.

A voice said, "We give you the reason vocal chords were invented. Yvonne!"

The applause was enthusiastic. "Damn," Holt said. "She's sure enough fancied around these parts."

The crowd grew quiet. A ghostly violin solo contrast-ed with the synth and house jam that had pulverized the silence before. Yvonne looked down at her hands on the microphone stand. She wore a magenta, sequined, tight-fitting dress and the spotlight blossomed and played on it as she composed herself for her opening notes. The song was "At Last," and when those words came out of her, Emilie gasped. There were quiet runs when one had to almost lean forward to hear, and there were voluminous, powerful passages that threatened to blow the speakers.

Yvonne made the song something different than the pop ballad by running a scat riff or two when least expected but always appropriate. Her Creole and New Orleans Brooklynese disappeared in her delivery.

Emilie's hand sought Travis's.

"World-class," he murmured. He breathed deeply during her strong ending. "Wow. I see why the line's so long." He looked at Emilie and squeezed her hand. "I bet those passes are hard to come by. She must like you."

"Simpatico," she said, tears glistening in her green eyes.

After a few Sinatra-like ballads and a Black Eyed Peas cover, she bowed her head and the lights went up, then down, and she disappeared. The synthesized dance tracks of the DJ came on and suddenly Yvonne was sitting at their table.

A waiter materialized, almost as mysteriously as Yvonne, with a champagne bucket, stand, and flutes. He popped the cork on a good Krug, pouring for all of them. Yvonne waved aside their compliments, skewered Holt and Travis with a look, and said "Freak's not supposed to sing good, right, *mahn*?" Then she laughed to show it was not malicious, patted both their hands. "I don't know where it comes from, dat voice, it just comes out. As long as it does, I will use it." She put her hand over Emilie's on the table and smiled. "Meanwhile, champagne! Do de tings dat passion tell you. *Hahve* fun, *mahn*!" She got up, smoothed her shimmering sheath dress, and made her way to the back of The Steel Flower table by table of admirers, grasping their hands on the way. Before she was out of sight, she turned and smiled at Emilie, placing her hand over her heart.

"I think you've got a friend, Em," Travis said.

"Feeling's mutual, for sure," she said, tracing the *veve* symbol on the onyx chrome tabletop in champagne.

CHAPTER 22

The sun was a white ball in a gray sky, clouds moving across it and obscuring it.

"Here's what we know, Tony bony," Rafferty said.

They were sitting alone in Binaggio's limo in their industrial park. Binaggio flashed on Brandi just then and his face darkened as he turned to look at Rafferty.

"What?" said Rafferty.

"Nothing. Go on. What do we know?"

"Okay. Your boy Julio was in Kansas and we know why. You went off the rez, Tony moroni. Linked up with MK13 on some fucking marijuana property in *Kansas*. MK13? Kansas? What were you thinking?"

Binaggio, started to protest, but Rafferty shushed him. "Julio had some lowlife kill a person or persons and set a fire, but none of it worked and the lowlife got caught. Well, they sent MK13 his ears and scalp. Sound familiar? This ringing any bells?" He paused. "Now a little before that," Rafferty continued, "Reno Pete cashed in his chips over in Daytona. Right? Just blink your eyes if you understand."

Binaggio looked at Rafferty. He could waste this fucker pretty cheerfully.

"Well, Tony fofoney macaroni, what your rocket scientist thug had done was kill someone in that same family. They broke with tradition by just stuffing him in your trunk, no ears, no scalp. They were throwing us all off the trail, and the cops too. Looked like a mob hit. Still with me?"

Binaggio's eyes had narrowed. He looked straight ahead and nodded slowly, as the wind buffeted the limo.

"You listening? We searched Reno's place thoroughly, no sign of anything linking him to Dallas. Nada. The girlfriend took off with his ashes to Tulsa. We left her alone, and after checking her out pretty well, figured she doesn't know dick. We don't kill people just for the hell of it. It draws attention. Your Einstein Julio killed a Dallas stewardess just because Reno's boy was laying her. Probably figured he was telling all in the throes of love. After they determined she didn't know anything, he offed her. Brilliant."

Binaggio nodded again.

"Thank god someone finally shut that idiot down," Rafferty said, shaking his head.

Binaggio made an impatient gesture for Rafferty to go on. "So where we at?"

"My feeling is we're dealing with Pete's boy. And some others."

"So let's find 'em and kill 'em."

"You any relation to this Julio employee? Marcello must be spinning in his grave right now. And, by the way, Kansas pot? What were you *thinking*?"

"It's better than what we're running, and it's cutting into ours. We weren't going off the reservation. We were just taking our own business back. Fuck Arnaud and those assholes."

"So you want to start a war with the Frenchmen over some pot out of Kansas and you don't even know how much there is or if the source is limited?"

"Our intel says supply is unlimited. It's grown on some wildlife refuge and it's better than anything we got."

"Refuge means government land. Which means there's more crazy people in this than just you and me, Tony cojone. Unless the gov is involved and I'd know about that."

"So we don't need it. We'll coexist with the frenchies. We got good sources all over."

"My point exactly." Rafferty shook his head, decided not to lecture Binaggio on greed. The heavy black car moved, wallowing a bit in the wind. Binaggio's new chauffeur stood in the lee of a concrete block storage building, collar up, holding onto his cap, and trying to smoke a cigarette. The wind was fierce on the outer wall of the weather coming in. Papers and detritus blew by. A seagull struggled in the wind, trying to fly against it and, gaining no distance, allowed itself to be flung in the opposite direction, veering low past the black car as it found its flying balance again.

"I'm pretty sure I was talking to Reno's kid. Right age," Rafferty said. "He was all halloweened up in long hair and a porkpie hat, padding maybe, but those eyes—"

"The guy who fucked me over had a tattoo. Harley. South Boston."

"So did the person I talked to. I'm going to hazard a guess it was a red herring."

"Naw it was Harley, Southie…"

Rafferty looked at the ceiling of the limo. Carlos Marcello had been a smart man. Those were the days. Gone forever. Only the liabilities remained.

"Anthony, here's what we're going to do. We're going to fly five million dollars' worth of gold Kruggerands to Las Vegas. Leave them at the old test site. And go away.

Simple. Then we're done with this. It's not as though we can't afford it. Business expense."

"I want that fuck dead."

"And that kind of revenge thinking is what gets you future heartbreak. For instance, when your dear little granddaughter grows up, if she grows up, and gets married, say. The wedding, say it's in New Orleans, or even Switzerland…"

Binaggio turned swiftly, looked at Rafferty with fear in his eyes.

"Oh, we have our ways of knowing where Debbi is, just like they do. At any rate, say it's ten years from now, and the wedding ceremony is the culmination of all your dreams for her, marrying a young man with pedigree, listed in the social register, graduated from Harvard, and a drone flies overhead, unseen by anyone, and missiles shriek. I would say, Tony baloney fo-foney, you'd best pay up now."

"Are you workin' with these fucks?"

"Surely you know better than that."

"You talk like you're with them."

"My business is built on speculation, informed speculation, I—"

The explanation was interrupted by both doors flying open. They were both thrown to the floor and Binaggio swiftly unarmed and frisked further until the ankle pistol he was clawing at was taken. Rafferty looked up and out the opened door for the chauffeur but he was nowhere to be seen. A large man in overalls with some kind of a feed sack over his head was busy handcuffing him with plastic pull-ties. He heard duct tape being ripped. Then he couldn't see any more.

He heard Binaggio say "No, please, I'll do it, I'll pay—"

Then more duct tape ripped, and he was silent.

Then he heard the large man say, "Listen to me. I just as soon kill you as spit on you, both of you. I git joy out of things that most folks don't even wont to think of. That grand dotter of yours? Whooee. Do you not think anybody else can git to Switzerland? I and my friend here, we can. First thing we buy over there is a chainsaw. Do you not think they sell such a thing over there?" He pronounced thing as thang. Think as thank. He wheezed inside the feed sack and made other unearthly sounds.

The other large man was silent, until he said, "Looka this little drop gun he had. I might just keep this purty little fucker."

Rafferty didn't recognize their voices. Neither belonged to the one he'd talked to in his study.

"Whyn't we just kill 'em?" the latter voice said, in almost a whine.

"Becuz they gone pay the money, yuh dumbass," the other voice said in a school teacherish, patient way. "They don't, *then* they get theirs. And we mop up all of 'em. Family. Friends. Fish in the Eyetalian boy's aquarium. Ever thang."

"I kindly hope they don't pay," said the other voice. And then he laughed in a sort of huh, huh, hunh snorting way that bubbled in his nose.

"I know. I know," said the first one, the one who seemed to be the leader.

Big Ray and Dammit Ray were trying hard not to laugh for real. They carried Rafferty under his arms and by his feet into the office where Binaggio had received his beating, set him in a chair, ripped the duct tape from his eyes, but not his mouth.

In the stormy day's dim light, Rafferty shuddered involuntarily as his eyes adjusted to the room, to the two men in overalls and feed sacks with eye holes. Mutants. They were truly terrifying, like something out of the distant past. Hillbilly train robbers. Night riding psycho-paths.

"Show him the lady. I want to see it agin," the young-er one said, repeating his odd laugh.

"I'm fixin' to. Got to work this thing right." He set an iPad in front of Rafferty, keyed a video of Rafferty with Binaggio's wife dressed in a schoolgirl outfit, pleasuring him. Out of the corner of his eye, Rafferty saw the one overalled moron rubbing himself and making snuffing noises. *Good Lord,* he thought, *next I'll hear the banjos from* Deliverance. *This may be a nightmare.*

"Want us to show the Eyetalian feller?" Big Ray said. Then to Dammit Ray he said, "Stop that, Earl!"

"Mm-unhh," Rafferty said, shaking his head violently. "Mm-nnnh."

Big Ray laughed. "Don't think he wants us to show the Eyetalian how he's porkin' his ol' lady."

Dammit Ray did his awful hunh, huh, glottal snog. They went back to the limo where Binaggio had gained his feet and was running headlong into buildings, bounc-ing off corrugated metal garage doors of the storage units.

They caught him and let him go, caught him again, walked him into the office, taped his ankles. Dammit Ray pretended to unbuckle Binaggio's belt, jerking on it.

"What the hail you doin, boy?" Big Ray said.

"Kin I git him in the bung like them college kids we caught under the bridge, huh, Earl?"

"Naw, we ain't got time for that. Leave him be."

"Won't take long, can I?"

"I said no. We'll pick us up a hitchhiker."

They slammed the warehouse door shut, leaving Binaggio and Rafferty in the dark. Then they ran to the limo, clambered into the front seat, and shut the doors before they burst out laughing, pounding on each other, pulling off their feed sacks.

"You see the eyes on that one dude?" Dammit Ray said. "Big as silver dollars."

"That fucking Binaggio, never go out of his house again. Where in hell did you get that godawful laugh?"

They drove the limo to Cobb's Jeep, wiped it down good with a shop rag and a small bottle of alcohol, wiped the keys, and tossed them under the floor mat. Big Ray got in the front seat with Cobb, Dammit Ray climbed in back, and they drove off down the stormy deserted street, boxes and newspapers blowing around in circles.

"What did you do with his driver?" Cobb asked.

"Taped him up and left him in a storage unit with the door up a little He was a pussycat. Man they are getting some weather around here."

"Appreciate you boys coming down here," Cobb said as he drove, craning his head so he could see the sky. "We'll take care of you if we live through it. So far, so good."

"What you got goin' on here, Cobb? Does it have to do with Vinita?" Big Ray asked.

"Not any more. That score'll never be even but we done what we could back at the refuge and down here too. This here is Travis's operation now, and it's a shita-ree, I tell you. Have to ask you to be quiet about it. Tell you more some night out on the Marais Des Cygne."

"Good enough," Dammit Ray said. "Been fun so far." He laughed his hunhh, huh theater laugh and got Big Ray to giggling.

"Well, you boys'll have to get the hell outa Dodge. They are gonna be turning over the rocks and the wood-work now, and you two are too easy to spot. Besides the hurricane is coming and it looks like it's gonna be a billy blue hell sumbitch."

Cobb pulled up to their motel where the big red Dodge dually with Kansas plates was parked. "Hate to not party with you boys a little bit, but you really have to make yourselves scarce."

Outside the Jeep they hugged all around. The Rays took off while Cobb paid their bill.

ᏋᏬᏋᏬ

"I think that was a come-to-Jesus for Rafferty and Binaggio," Cobb said, in Travis and Emilie's motel room. "Should get some action. Far as they know, Ray and Ray were mouth-breathers from the swamp."

Travis shook his head and chuckled again at the Rays' part in the game. He knew they'd terrified the smug bastards. They'd scare anyone, and with gunny sacks and that hillbilly act, they'd have to have been unforgettable.

"I made 'em take four hundred dollars for the road, so I'm running low on cash," Cobb said. "You got any handy?"

Travis searched in the greasy Burger King bag, pulled out a stack of twenties and fifties, counted out five hundred for Cobb. "Hopefully, we're on the back end of this thing now. We can always get some money from the Ghost, but we're into him for about two hundred K as it is."

"Where's Em?" Cobb asked.

"Out getting a tattoo, can you believe that shit? She found a guy who'll open up his shop. She should be back anytime." He looked at his watch, the outside by parting the blinds. The wind buffeted the outside walls and Cobb's Jeep rocked slightly in the lot. A beer can rolled across the asphalt, picked up speed, and was flung against the car.

Travis noted Cobb's incredulous expression. "Hey she's a woman, you know? That means she's part crazy. She was bound and determined."

"A fucking tattoo? As a hurricane's coming down? Did you know they're evacuating the coast areas? If this thing is Katrina-sized, we have to get the hell out and postpone this whole deal. Man, just as I was thinking she was a smart cookie. Well, where's Holt?"

"Probably nursing a hangover. Haven't heard from him today."

"Is he gonna be a problem?"

"I don't think so, but he's a stone cop all right."

Cobb looked off toward the parking lot. "Then he's a problem."

ひとつ

Travis wasn't so sure. The previous night, the "Night of Yvonne," as Emilie referred to it, the three had gone to an after-hours jazz spot where they'd talked and drunk into the morning hours. By the time they'd said their goodnights, Holt had picked up a reasonably attractive session singer and he'd walked back to his hotel with her. In the interim hours between The Steel Flower and leaving the after-hours place, they'd relaxed into a friendly bonhomie which included plans for the future.

"Ever wanted to go into business for yourself?" Travis had asked Holt.

"Sure. I think of it all the time. But the details keep screwing it up. Bookkeeping, health insurance, staff changes, all the damn headaches." He stirred his drink, leaned back on two chair legs, and seemed to soak up the quiet late night jazz riffs of the piano, sax, bass, and cocktail drum brushes. Then the singer, who had been humming and swaying at the microphone, began some Norah Jones-like version of "Moonlight in Vermont."

They were all quiet for a while. Emilie excused herself to go to the Ladies'.

Travis said, "What would you think of a private security service with offices in Dallas, New Orleans, and KC?

"Cool. But the startup for something like that is crazy. I've looked into it on a smaller scale."

"What if all that was taken care of?"

"Let me ask you a semi-personal question, Travis. Are you sort of bending the law some here and there?"

"I'm shattering it. Taking a pickaxe and a eight-pound hammer and a machete to it."

"Well, just so it's quasi legal." He took a drink, leaned toward him, elbows on the table, tie loosened. "Tell me more."

And so, that night, an alliance was not so much decided as strengthened.

"I just want to know. This won't come back and bite me in the ass, will it?"

"Not if we—me, Em, Cobb get out of New Orleans all right. Then it'll be behind us. We're dealing with some bad people and right now we have to be worse than they are."

"Anybody dead yet?"

"You asking as a cop on a case or just interested."

Holt swirled the ice in his glass. "The latter."

"Yes. But no one who didn't desperately need it."

"You know, we'd have to be clean to start such an operation as you describe. What do I bring to it? Not money."

"You bring expertise, determination, commitment, a good sense of how it all works, contacts. Invaluable. It wouldn't work without a Holt."

"And you?"

"I bring the wherewithal, the startup, and a willingness to learn, not be a boss type boss. I've run a small business successfully. And I ain't lazy."

"Could be exactly what I'm looking for. Let's talk when we're both sober, bud."

When Em returned, the singer was into "Where or When" and sounding very much like June Christy. Outside the jazz joint, the wind whistled through the alleys and toppled loose garbage cans.

⁊⁊⁊

The City of New Orleans had gone to some lengths not to be caught unawares again. The mayor was in close contact with the governor of Louisiana, and the National Guard was at the ready. FEMA management was on twenty-four-hour standby as was the entire police department of New Orleans and adjoining parishes. The President of the United States was awake and advised by Homeland Security, The Corps of Engineers, and a war room full of weather watchers.

In the pump rooms of New Orleans, equipment was checked time and again, and emergency generators were run and shut down. The levees had been fully vetted by the Army Corps of Engineers and deemed strong enough to withstand a category-five hurricane, the level of which Oswald showed signs of attaining off the Mississippi shore.

Travis wondered if his old AdvanceGuard unit was hanging around the ritziest part of town, guarding the property of the ruling class, wrists resting on slung M-16s and street-sweeper shotguns.

The businesses in the French Quarter and all over New Orleans were battened down with plywood and the revelers replaced with police patrols and concerned citizens' auxiliaries. A few Escalades and Navigators roamed the streets. Looting, murders, rapes, and other lawless behavior had run wild during and after Katrina, and the eyes of the nation, perhaps the world, watched now. Red and blue lights of prowl cars cast eerie shadows through waving trees. Here and there a sheet of corrugated metal would pry loose and plane through the air, clattering and banging along the street when it landed, careening off a plywood covered storefront. Nervous police officers slowly patrolled the deserted streets, side arms ready, radios up to catch the latest briefings, and calls snapping through the static.

Big and Dammit Ray watched it on TV in a diner in Shreveport, the big dually sitting outside in a driving rain.

Big Ray ate his last shrimp, and wiped his hands on his napkin, drained his coffee. "You 'bout done there, Earl?" he said to Little Ray, who gave him his glottal snog, one more time.

It was wearing thin, though, and reminded them of dangers beyond the storm for Cobb and Travis and that knockout girl they'd picked up along the way.

The TV reporter stood near the Maisson De Vries, in a slicker that crackled and blew in the fierce wind, and he ducked as a corrugated piece of tin hit the street behind him. Gripping his flapping hood in one hand and the microphone in the other, he said, "It's getting wild here on Dauphine Street. Few, if any, people remain in the buildings. Certainly, they aren't on the streets."

At that instant, Ross Holt and the jazz singer hurried past behind the reporter, Holt holding an ineffectual jacket over them both against the driving rain.

"Well, exceptions do exist. At their peril. Back to you, Mary," the reporter shouted into the microphone after seeing the apparition on the monitor.

The crew hurriedly collected their equipment and the TV van left. Holt and the singer were on their way to his rental car to take her home, then back to his hotel, double park, pack his stuff, and wait for a flight to open up. A police car prowled slowly down Dauphine, lights flashing, rain sheeting off the sides.

∽∾∾

Cobb, Elsie, Travis, and Emilie conferred at the Montmartre, sitting around the table, the wind and rain battering the south side of the building. Elsie drank from a bottle of water, which he capped and uncapped often, the only outward sign that he was possibly a bit nervous. Otherwise his face was impassive, and he was relaxed in the chair.

"Did they put up plywood at The Effigy, Elsie?" Emilie asked.

"Oh yeah," Elsie said, "Moved the best art yesterday, just in case." He turned to Travis, said in a lower tone of voice, "Some a them Blackwater types, the movers. Maybe ol' buddies, Travis?"

The lights and the TV flickered, dimmed, then went out.

"Never been in a hurricane before, Elsie," Cobb said. "We in trouble here or what?"

"Well, speaking as a Katrina survivor, this one is only scary because it's almost a direct hit. The pumps are working. The new levees will hold. It's a bitch, but we'll make it. Seen 'em before."

Travis's attention was on a map spread on the table. He took a pull from a Red Bull, set it down on the corner of the map.

"Here's the Mail & More where Rafferty himself will drop off the box. He'll use a prepaid label and bar code we send him to a G. Melchior in Nashville, leave it on the counter, drive away. Inside the Mail & More, Elsie will take the box, strip it, leave any GPS trackers inside, remove the bonds, put them in a padded bag to be delivered to Cobb. We'll be able to detect a tracker in the bonds, remove it, drop that bag on the outgoing counter. The truck picks up the box and the bag, both are delivered. The box goes to Nashville, the bag goes to Cobb. Questions?"

"What happened to the Kruggerands?" Cobb asked.

"The Ghost switched it to bonds. About eight hundred pounds lighter," Elsie said.

"How much do we owe you and the Ghost?" Travis asked.

Elsie took a small book from his pocket. "As of now and this bottle of water—" He held it in the air. "—it be one million, one hundred thirty eight thousand, seven hundred twenty two dollars and forty cents, plus or minus a nickel—itemized bill to come."

A noise outside the door prompted Emilie to get up and part the blinds, looking outside. They all turned to see what she was doing. Cobb pulled a .38 from his Carhartt jacket.

"It's a little dog," she said. "A puppy, I think. Awww, poor little guy." And she opened the door enough to admit it.

Cobb breathed, put the gun away. The pup was soaked, half drowned, crying as she scooped it up and took it to the bathroom where she rolled it in a towel.

"He's shivering. Cold or scared or both," she said.

"What is he?" asked Elsie.

"I do believe he's a hound," Cobb said, "Look at them feet and ears. Black and Tan."

He picked him up by the loose scruff of his neck and dangled him over the table. The dog whimpered, looking at Em. She took him back.

Travis said nothing. Just shook his head and smiled.

"What'll we call him?" Emilie asked.

"Jack," Cobb said.

"No such thing. He's Oswald. Ozzie for short. The storm brought him to us."

Elsie stood. "It's a sign," He waggled his hands and made a whoooeee mystery noise.

"Well, it might be," Em said. She looked at Travis with a question in her eyes.

"Hey," he said, "I know when we've got a dog and when it's a drop off at the shelter mutt. Damn. Just what we need."

"Shoot, I'll take him back to join the Jack pack," Cobb said, "He gets to be a handful."

Red and blue lights flashed in the parking lot and the short whoop of a siren cut through the storm sound. "Well, I gots to leave this doggie-love session, people." Elsie put on a blue rain jacket that said POLICE in big yellow letters on the back. He opened the door to the storm, slammed it, and was gone.

"Man he's got contacts everywhere," Cobb said.

Travis said nothing, just looked at the door Elsie had departed through.

"Okay, here's the deal," Travis said. "Two real UPS drivers will be gagged, tied up, and left in two different places. They'll be paid. They won't know jack about the operation, and they won't see anybody, so they can't say much to cops or the other side, should that come about. They just won't be of any help.

"Then, Cobb and I and the electronics guy will be in the one truck that picks up the package. We'll check it for explosives, just in case. They won't be that stupid, most probably, but you never know. Then we repackage the bonds in a much smaller box. The electronics guy will remove the tracker or trackers that will almost certainly be in the package, and put them in a dummy package filled with newspapers."

"Wait up. Bonds?" Cobb asked.

"Government bonds. Negotiable. As I understand it, these will go to the Federal Reserve, a Gallery Ghost contact, be converted to dollars. Checked thoroughly. Shipped or wired or whatever to Switzerland. Transferred to the Caymans where our accounts will receive them. By that time the trail is erased. Anything bigger than ten grand is followed by the banking authorities here in the US and reported, but that won't be a factor."

"So that's why Reno had all those accounts for nine thousand dollars," Cobb said. "They must've done that back then, too."

"They did. He just had to go to more trouble back then to hide it. I imagine some of those accounts still exist. As legal heir I might check 'em out."

"I'd let them sleeping dogs lie."

"You might be right, Cobb."

"Usually am. Anyway, why don't they just ship the bonds to the Fed in the first place?"

"A bunch of reasons, but the main one is, the Ghost's contact would be outed and it would all unravel. They don't have the slightest idea what we're going to do with 1960s government bonds. They can't even cash them in anymore without some scrutiny in their direction. We can. When they discover them, it will appear they've been there since the '60s and simply accrued interest, which, by the way, Ghost's contact will keep."

"You know, in the movies this stuff is all slick as a gut. Like *Ocean's Eleven* or something," Cobb said. This is…I don't know…seems like we make it up as we go."

"I guess we could go back to the Marais Des Cygne, start over," Travis said.

"If we could, bring back Vinita, leave that shit buried in the yard," Cobb mused. "Well, is there any trail on these bonds? Paper trail? Like a bank check?"

"None. Except back to the JFK thing, and nobody

wants to open that up. That's why they're still paying authors to write 'lone nut' books." He did air quotes with both hands.

"Wow," Emilie said, stroking the pup. "Intricate. By the way, you know what they call those air quotes?" She waggled her ring and index fingers in imitation of Travis. "Dick fingers."

Cobb swallowed his coffee wrong and coughed.

"It's exceedingly uncool is all," she said, recapturing the puppy, which was exploring. "We have to find a vet and some dogfood."

"Good luck with that. Maybe he'll eat pretzels for now." Travis held up the bag.

"He needs shots, and maybe wormed, Travis. And a collar and tags, and good food and love and care."

"Don't we all? But, you know, hurricanes and stuff?"

The TV and lights came on, and they cheered, causing the puppy to pee in Emilie's lap. She held it out from her, the stream dissipating.

The now-functioning TV said that Oswald had taken a northern path, doubling back into Mississippi and was rapidly losing strength as it traveled inland. Evacuees were told to wait a day before streaming back to the coastal areas. Levees had held, pumps were in good order and not needed, even though the storm surge had pushed water inland but not as far as the French Quarter. Lake Pontchartrain was already receding.

≈≈≈

Holt moved his car into the covered parking area and walked back to the hotel, soaked to the skin. The rain pelted down but the wind had let up and debris was no longer a flying danger. Branches lay everywhere on the streets, as did plywood scraps and Styrofoam coolers, drink containers and boxes. Some business owners were already removing the plywood window protectors and stacking them on trailers. This place never slept, he thought. He was actually beginning to like it here. That damned Travis was beginning to influence him.

He was conflicted about Travis. His instincts told him Travis was all right, not a career criminal type, though certainly he had committed crimes. Holt was of two minds about revenge and justice. He'd sworn to uphold law, and that had meant something to him over the years. But he'd seen too much. Seen too many bad people go free on legal technicalities. Seen too many unpunished hardasses thumb their noses at the law, to the point where he was thumbing his as well. He knew Travis was ex-AdvanceGroup, just a step above Hell's Angels in his opinion, but Travis—he was different.

Private investigation could be a breeze. Divorce cases. Missing people. Insider theft. Providing protection. And with his contacts Holt could skirt a lot of legal crap. He'd made some good friends over the years and his reputation had few blemishes. It was time he took off on his own, or with someone he felt was trustworthy and solid. Travis had a good resource pool, with his past repo, bounty, merc experience. Privateers, but manageable in a business like they were talking about. And Travis, well, he had morals, only slightly soiled in the past. And now.

He'd done some homework on Travis. Brought up in Kansas by rednecks, his old man was a shadowy entity, probably a merc. His mother had spent a year at Oklahoma University, been a stewardess, married Travis's dad. She'd been killed in a truck explosion, not meant for her, most likely—never solved. There were some scalps taken, literally, over the last couple months, MK13's, and that was fine with Holt, dandy in fact. They might have been associated with Travis somehow. And the disappearances of two thoroughly skanky meth-heads. They had brushed up against Travis somehow. Holt knew that. But even the New Orleans police shrugged that off.

The Melissa Bradley case was not a Travis deal. It had been "taken care of," however, most probably by Travis and his people. Maybe Holt would go back to Dallas and close that out, say he couldn't find trails. He couldn't bring Melissa back, but at least he could let her only relatives—a sister and an ailing father—know she was clean, had bumped into a gang operation, and the killer had been killed. No justice really, other than the old fashioned kind, but some closure for them. And for Holt, himself. He no longer felt a cop's need to pursue it.

The power was on when he reached the hotel. He tested the shower for heat. There was plenty. Soon the bathroom was steaming and he was singing one of the songs that Trish, the jazz singer, had been singing the night before at the club. "I got the world on a string…"

❦❦❦

The next day dawned gray and raining but Oswald had lost force. Television coverage of the damaged areas was coming in through phone videos and helicopter cameras. Parts of New Orleans parish and the Gulf had been declared disaster areas once again, and Federal Aid was promised. The death toll was far below usual hurricane level. Through some freakish happpenstances of weather fronts, Oswald had skittered off as a tropical storm and had spared most of Louisiana and Mississippi. Traffic was up again on the city streets and plywood was coming down.

Cobb located a vet for the pup, who he called Jack when not in earshot of Emilie, and was waiting patiently in the vet's office off Canal Street. Two women behind the counter were conversing. The younger woman in tight jeans and a T-shirt had earned top honors in Cobb's mind, firing off the "I'd like to git her agin" synapse. She smiled at him, said, "What's his name?"

"Jack," he said. "He come with the storm."

"Why don't you call him Oswald then," she said.

"'Cuz the storm didn't do jack, not like they said it would."

They both laughed.

When he left, the puppy had a new collar, tags, and a fairly clean bill of health. Cobb had packs of heartworm pills, flea treatments, and tightly jeaned Doreen's phone number.

"Aw, he's a harmless old guy," she said to her counter-mate. "Must be seventy."

"With a gleam in his eye. And probably Viagra in his pocket."

"Oh you think that's what was in his pocket? I thought he was just glad to see me."

And they both laughed hard enough to turn heads.

☙☙☙

Rafferty's people explained the box to him. Double boxed with a layer of Styrofoam peanuts in between. Each box had a small chip inserted in the corrugations, so small as to slide down the tube-like corridor. The outer box had plain red circles, one on each side, in order to be noticeable from a distance. He was to leave the box at the Mail & More on Robert E. Lee Street, and drive away. If he didn't drive away, the deal wouldn't happen. If the store was watched in any way, the deal wouldn't happen.

Rafferty would receive the materials promised by the same method. They would be delivered to his office by UPS the next day. He had no guarantee that this would happen, other than a clean delivery of the government bonds. If the delivery didn't come off clean, death was certain, but not instant. He, for one, believed it. And he was pretty sure Binaggio got it by now, as well. But Binaggio didn't think they would keep their end of the bargain.

"Why wouldn't they?" Rafferty asked. "It's in their best interests. The stuff does them no good, other than to hold us up. And if you think for a microsecond they won't kill your granddaughter now or ten years from now, you don't get it, Tony. They know it would be all-out war if they didn't keep up their end. They don't want that, I wouldn't think."

"I dunno, Jerry, they seem crazy. Like the fucking Russians. You just have to kill 'em. Can't reason with them." Binaggio sighed. He thought back to those hooded country mutants. Jesus Christ, they were awful. He had thought his leg-breakers were scary. Shit, they didn't hold a candle to those freaks. One was actually going to have sex with him. He shut his eyes tight and tried to get that out of his mind, that and what could happen to his grand-daughter. Jesus.

It was like those overall Big Smith horrors had disap-peared. His guys couldn't find a trace. Neither could the cops he had freelancing for him. They were like a true nightmare.

Even the guy who kept cracking him with that gun didn't bother him as much as they did. Fucking retard psychos. Earl. His guys had picked up dozens of Earls in overalls. None were the one, not even close. Eeeesh. Fucking weird.

"Okay, I'm going to deliver the package myself," Raf-ferty said. "Then go away, far away. Nobody, hear me? Nobody is to watch that store. We got it covered. The trackers will tell us everything we need to know. We'll follow the truck when it leaves after we pick it up from the GPS. Trust me."

"How do we catch them?"

"We don't. We find out who they are." He said this like a teacher talking to a very slow student.

"What good does that do us, if we don't have them?"

"Well Tony bo-bony, if they don't come through with the goods, we hunt them down and suck every last bit of information out of them. And you can pistol-whip them if you want."

"I want."

"The Company is helping us on this."

"Good damn deal. What's the address on the box?"

"Nashville. We already got people in place."

"So if they're stupid enough to pick it up there, which I really doubt, we should've had 'em by now."

"You're catching on. We may have to just live with it. Chalk the five mil up to expenses. Enjoy life again.

"We got trackers in each box and in the bonds too, right?"

"Right. But don't count on them not figuring that out."

"Well, if it's the fucking Snopes boys in their Big Smiths, we got 'em."

"They snookered *us*, Tony, don't forget that."

"I just can't stand the fact of these fucks walking with five million bucks."

"It's not like it's out of our pockets. We never would have seen these bonds. It's covert money. Converted from jap gold after World War Two. We've already spent too much time and energy resisting, so suck it up, man. Unless you want to risk your granddaughter."

Binaggio chewed his cigar.

"If anybody is going to find these guys, it'll be a little division of...well, you don't need to know. The same guys, essentially, that took care of King and Bobby."

"Are they after them?"

"Let's say they are engaged. I have met with them. They are extremely interested in keeping the materials offered out of circulation."

"Yeah, fuck it. I'm out of it, then. But you tell me when, where, how, these sonsabitches get theirs."

∽∾∽

"Jerry?" Travis spoke through a voice-changer, for its psychological effect.

"Yeah?" Rafferty was driving his cream-colored Mercedes SLK to a Mail & More he was familiar with, having passed it dozens of times on the way to his office on Poydras Street in the financial district.

"Anyone watching the Mail & More?"

"Nope."

"Which one you going to?"

"The one near my office."

"Great. Just so you get it to one that's open and send that package. Insure it for a hundred bucks, okay?"

"Sure."

"If no one is watching, Tony bony won't see you porking his old lady."

"Ever?"

"Ever. Like it won't go, you know, viral."

"Times have changed," Rafferty said with a sigh.

"Yeah, done got more complicated. That's for sure."

The phone went dead. Rafferty pulled into the Mail & More lot, carried the box inside, and handed it to a smiling Black man with dreadlocks and rimless specs. He handed the man the address, said to insure it for $100, and waited as he typed it into a computer, slapped a label on it. Then he paid cash, $14.25, took his change for a twenty and walked back out. He stood in the lot for a minute looking up at the clearing sky, punched his fob to unlock the door of the cream colored Mercedes SLK, got in, and drove to his office.

e/ɔe/ɔ

He could have gone to any Mail & More so no use watching this one, Rafferty thought. But then these people were smart, they might have known he would most probably stop at this one. It made no difference. The deal was done. They'd pick it up at the other end.

Elsie watched Rafferty leave. He snapped on thin latex rubber gloves. Pushing the blade on a box cutter, he opened the outer box, pulled the large packet from the inner box, weighed it, replaced it with magazines, checked the bond packet for a tracker chip. When he found it taped to the inside of the padded envelope, he re-taped it to a magazine, resealed the inner and outer boxes, left it on the outgoing counter with the pile of boxes and envelopes.

He then released the proprietor of the Mail & More, told him to lay low for another five minutes before he took the blindfold off. "Better to do that than risk some bad shit, my man. Plus there's a little bonus for you under the scale. Five minutes."

"You got it," the young man said.

A cab waited at the curb near the lot. As it sped off, Elsie held up one of the bonds to the light. *Something too easy about all this*, he thought. *Way too easy*. And these bonds didn't feel right. He directed the cabbie to the address of a philatelist on Royal Street.

e/ɔe/ɔ

"I'm afraid this series of bonds was never printed in

the 1960s, Elsie," the old man said. He then perused the paper with a loupe. "Plus these have been printed on a laser printer, to boot. Where'd you get them?"

"You know, eBay, doc. Got to be more careful."

"Sorry, Elsie. I'd like to have better news for you. You still interested in the Mauritania Dakar cover?

"Sure am. Might as well get that while I'm here." Elsie had collected rare stamps for years; it was his 401K.

He paid the old man and took the vellum stamp envelope and the phony bonds with him to the waiting cab.

❧❧❧

"I think Tony suspects something, Jerry," Brandi said as she changed.

"I did Viagra, Brandi. Don't ruin it by bringing up that clown," he said from the king sized bed. He lay there in his boxers and black socks in their usual suite at the Monteleone on Royal Street, curtains drawn. This time he'd had it swept by a security team. No cameras. No microphones.

She came out of the bathroom, acting like a simpering young schoolgirl in short plaid skirt, hair in doggie-tails, a tight white blouse, knee socks, and saddle shoes. She dropped her backpack on the plush carpet, said, "Oopsie," and bent to pick it up, revealing to Rafferty that she wore no underwear.

"You've been a bad girl," he breathed more than said to her. "Come to the principal."

"Oh please don't tell on me," she begged, "I'll do anything."

"Anything?" he wheezed. He unbuttoned her blouse as she straddled him.

❧❧❧

Travis gave Emilie a good chunk of cash and told her to go shopping. She'd protested, but he said it was something she needed to do. She took the car and headed for some shops she knew and liked.

Travis realized that she might need a little time away from him. In trying not to be his father, he was fast becoming his father. It was easier than fighting it, especially living this kind of life, day to day. Soon he would have all the money he'd ever need, a sort of lottery winnings. But the odds carried more consequences.

Em kidded about being a moll, but she was in a stage of her life where she was impressionable and, if she liked, or thought she loved someone, she would do what it took to stick with it. He had to be careful not to allow her to lose a pretty good sense of morality.

She wasn't really all that impressionable, he told himself. She had seen a good deal of life, being a stripper in a seedy locale. Contemplated being a prostitute with a good business sense. Left that behind as not being feasible or agreeable to her sense of herself. She was kind, tough, vulnerable, beautiful, feisty, sensitive, creative, probably high IQ. What was he doing with a girl like this? Was it just a huge mismatch? A weird thing that would end some morning when she woke up and said, "What the hell was I thinking?" She carried a gun because of him. That right there was a felony, good for hard time. She didn't deserve that. Could he, himself, do time? His old man could. And did, more than once. He sure as shit didn't want to, but he felt he could do it if he had to. He knew what was involved.

Shoot, his one honest job, flooring, was a form of doing time. Fuck that.

A solid rap on the door brought him out of his reverie. He checked the peephole. It was Elsie. He let him in quickly, looking around the lot.

Elsie was not his usual hiphop casual self. He tossed the envelope of bonds on the table. "Take a look at a phony payoff, my man."

Travis opened the envelope, looked at Elsie. "Phony?"

"We been wastin' our time. We didn't scare 'em enough or something. My guess is that they thought they'd get to us by now, so they didn't even try very hard to make this shit look real."

"Rafferty and Binaggio? I can't believe that."

"Here's another thought. Someone bigger than they are engineered this. They may not even know. But we can find out pretty quick."

"How?"

"Voice analyzer. I have a really good contact."

Elsie made a call and they cabbed to a recording studio on Dauphine Street. The studio was austere on the outside, angled gray wood, stainless steel letters with the address only. Inside a pretty girl at a reception desk welcomed them, seemed to know Elsie. "Andre is in room one, Elsie. Go right in."

The room was dimly lit, built with two stages of wood floor, couches on the upper level, a cocktail table with a large bowl of candy bars and granola bars, and some music industry magazines. Comfortable plush chairs on the lower level. Black soundproof walls. Andre sat at the large console, a mass of dials and buttons, about five feet long. A large curved screen monitor hung above him, and glass walls showed two session rooms, one of which contained a full set of drums and some guitars on stands. Matte black Bang and Olufsen speakers mounted on either side of the curved screen looked like something Effigy Gallery would display as art.

Andre rose and greeted Elsie, hugged him, shook hands with Travis. "Make yourselves comfortable, gentlemen." He set up the phone line and gestured to Travis to make the first call, while he flipped some switches and slid some bars on the console. "It's a patch and untraceable," he said, "But make it short, a minute or two."

"Tell him Reno needs to talk to him," Travis said to Rafferty's secretary.

"Reno," Rafferty said.

"The bonds are fake," Travis said, with no preliminary talk.

"I'm sorry?"

"You will be. Fucking fake. Not smart."

"I have no idea what you're talking about. Did you get them already?"

"Yes. Why did you think you'd get away with this?"

"I—I—don't know what to say. Are you sure?"

Andre pushed some more bars, and the flat screen showed the sound pattern as Rafferty talked. A series of green perpendicular lines raised or lowered to the volume and pitch of Rafferty's voice.

"Oh I'm sure."

"But—but the source. Impeccable. I was assured. From the—I can't conceive of them being phony, believe me I wouldn't *dream* of fucking this up. Shit house mouse. It's too important—"

Andre nodded. Travis said, "We'll talk again today. Answer your cell at three p.m." He hung up.

Andre played the voice back several times, examining the vertical stripes of the speech pattern. He pointed out several areas with the cursor from the console computer.

"He's for real, guys. It was a total surprise to him. He could act it, of course, but in examining the pattern it would show and I would see it. He's not acting. I do this for the FBI here in New Orleans, and for spook central."

"Thanks, man. Want to try the Dago?" he said to Travis.

"No. He's just a secondary in this."

"Bad news, guys?" Andre asked.

"Well, we got screwed royally on a deal. But you know me, Andre. It gone be made right."

"I heard that, brother." They slapped and tugged hands. To Travis, he said, "Elsie is someone you do *not* mess with."

ⰎⰎⰎ

In the cab, Elsie exhaled a long breath. "Aaight, we not at square one, but we in the shit. They wouldn't pull this unless they close to findin' us out. That's bad. We know it though, and that's good. We still in the game, you know?"

Travis was silent. He nodded, thinking back over the arrangements. Then he said, "Elsie, we got to pull some monumental shit here. It's upstairs from Binaggio and Rafferty."

"The Ghostman. He's next. He will not be happy. That's good for you, bad for the marks."

Elsie leaned forward, gave the driver an address two blocks down from Effigy. Then he got on his cellphone, made a call, said nothing after allowing it to ring a certain number of times. He called once more and hung up immediately.

Elsie had Travis get out first. Travis walked to the Effigy Gallery, taking care to absorb his surroundings, and watching reflections in storefronts. He took an up escalator at a glass building and took the back stairs to the street. He approached The Crow and peered in. Business as usual. No Asian cutie. He walked to Effigy, taking his time, a tourist. All the stores were open. No sign of Oswald's presence anywhere, other than scraps of trash still in the wet streets.

Inside, a couple, man and wife, marveled at some

Plexiglas sculptures that turned on motorized bases and threw off light flashes. He stopped at the vulture piece in the standing coffin and the gallery hostess appeared beside him. She was dressed in a khaki suit with shoulder epaulets and brass rings at the pockets. The jacket was cut in a deep V in front and showed off a tanned chest and the sides of breasts.

She smiled. "You like Alfonso? He's sort of a pet. We have a few things by the same artist in here." She guided him by the elbow to the office door, shutting it softly behind him when he entered. Elsie was already seated. The sculpture was a Modigliani, a tall bronze figure, turning as if on a turntable, lit from above, the various facets collecting light or disappearing in shadow.

"It's a shame when chicanery tarnishes simple business transactions," said the Ghost. "But, in certain areas of government, it's a way of life." He cleared his throat behind the hologram. "Binaggio's a fool, but not behind this deception. Rafferty is, I'm sure, deeply embarrassed, and there will be repercussions down the road that don't concern us. The good thing is, we can now easily double the payoff. We'll go for ten million now, in gold. Krugerrands. Two million and expenses to us."

"Mm-hmmm," Elsie said. "And some attention-getters, pretty quick, I'd say."

"Sad, but true. Everything doubles. There will have to be some very quick, very dramatic collateral extremes."

"I have some in mind," said Travis. "No real extremes needed yet. These'll be out of Psych 101. We work on Rafferty and Binaggio again, and unravel these guys. That will get to their...what?...handlers? Bosses? They won't want these two going nuts. And to try to get to the bigger bigwigs, that could take a long time and a lot of money."

"Good thinking, Reno. Implement them, with Elsie's…ahh…oversight." said the Ghost. "And now the plan is this. They will helicopter the gold to exact coordinates at the old nuclear test site in Nevada outside Las Vegas as originally planned. We will take it from there. Wheeled carts. Seems dangerous, but it isn't, really. There are tunnels there, and only a few of us around who still know them. Did you know we used to sit on Liberace's pink Cadillac hood and watch the atomic bomb tests? What magic times those were."

"Magic. Mm-hmm," Elsie said. "Like to have been back in the day."

"Oh, yes. Oh, my, yes. The colors of the sunrises on the desert. Spectacular. We drank gin fizzes on that awful florid Cadillac and we saw God in those times. We did. Boom. There He was. Liberace was quite a patriot, you know. So were the Rat Pack, bless them all. Las Vegas rising up out of nothing…well, I seem to be reminiscing like an old fool. Next thing you know, I'll get all weepy. Another time, you can indulge me my stories."

"I'd like to hear them," Travis said.

"Thank you for that, young man. Reno. That's a compliment, by the way, not brain slippage. I feel like I'm back there, alive again. For that, I thank you."

Travis knew he and Elsie were alone then. The Ghost was gone.

"He's got some doozies," Elsie said. "Well, we gotta get busy. Lay out some of this Psych 101, my man."

Travis had him laughing as he described what could happen and how it would affect the oilman and the mob boss.

"You somethin' else, Travis, You truly somethin' other than else. But it won't be cheap."

"Just chips, Elsie."

CHAPTER 23

It started with Binaggio's fish tanks. The ones in his home and in his office. All the exotics, indeed, all the fish were floaters. No explanation. The aquarium people were called in, and they cleaned the tanks, tested for substances and allergens. None were readily found.

When Rafferty awoke the following morning, he saw a plaid short skirt like a schoolgirl would wear sitting folded on his slippers on the floor on his side of the bed. He grabbed it and hid it from his wife, wondering how and who, in the night. In his house! His bedroom!

When Binaggio called his chauffeur who had a stupid *The Good, the Bad, and the Ugly* theme ringtone on his cellphone, he was standing impatiently by his limo, drumming his fingers on the hood. There was no answer but Binaggio thought he heard the ringtone. He called again and walked around the car. No doubt about it, the eerie theme ringtone was in the trunk. His jaw dropped. He hung up. His phone rang.

"Yeah?"

"Yo, Tony. How come they moved your granddaughter from the Alps to LA? That's much closer and easier." Awful laugh. Hang up.

A package arrived that same day, Federal Express from Los Angeles to Binaggio. The return address was where his granddaughter was sequestered. The package contained a filthy pair of overalls with the seat cut out and a scrawled note that said "Ware thes wen we com get U. XXX"

Both the address and the note raised the hair on Binaggio's neck and arms. Then a sniper's bullet left a clean hole in the window he stood by and pierced the overalls and the FedEx box, leaving a furrow in the carpet.

Binaggio pulled his ankle pistol as he hit the floor and fired five wild shots through the window. The neighbors called the police and Brandi shrieked from the bedroom.

He ran to the bedroom to see Brandi, hands to her head, standing over what looked like human feces.

৩৩৩

"Jerry, I can't take it no more. The fucking cops were here. Someone got in and shit on the floor in the bedroom. The fish are all dead. Al was tied up in the trunk. What the fuck is going on, man? None of the guards were here…" He trailed off.

"I'll take care of it, Tony. My fault. I trusted those psychos in…well, in the gray area. The spooks. They fucked us over. Right now our adversaries are just playing games with us, but if we don't get right with them, people will die. I know. They told me and I believe them."

"Pay the fuckers!" a red-faced Binaggio screamed, veins standing out at his temples.

"The price went up."

"I don't give a shit. Pay! I'll help! I can't stand this anymore."

"Yeah, well, it's double now. Ten mill. And you know what? I don't blame them. They're pissed. No more paper. It's back to solid gold now. Dropped in Vegas."

"I got people in Vegas," Tony said.

"Back. Off. If this doesn't go smooth, I hate to think, Tony…"

"You're right. But—"

"But nothing. I'm working on getting Krugerrands. Do you know how much that weighs?"

"A hundred pounds?"

"Try eight hundred."

Binaggio hung up. The carpet people were moving furniture upstairs and replacing carpet. The aquarium company had installed new tanks. His own people were watching closely and supervising. It was a madhouse.

୧୬୧୨

Emilie had picked up some items for Travis on her shopping spree. A tweed burglar cap. Another Brooks Brothers shirt. Colorful ribbed condoms.

"Okay, I modeled my stuff. Now you."

Travis put the cap on. Frontward. Sideways. Backward.

"Oh, nice! I love it!" she said. "*Chapeau a la modeou,* have to wear it, please, what a disguise." Then, "The shirt brings out the blue in your eyes! Love it!" She opened the box of condoms. "Here, let me help you with these, see if they fit right. That one does. And it brings out the purple on your—Cool! Let's see if it works!"

They put Oswald in the bathroom, where he slept— after unrolling the toilet paper.

୧୬୧୨

"It's time to move again," Elsie said. "I took care of y'all's bill here. Ghost wants Em to go to Vegas, get settled in. Then we go, one at a time, a day apart."

"What do we do? Where do we stay?"

"You do some moderate gambling, stay at the Mandalay, run into Em at the casino, then you hook up again. We have a persona for her, looking for a job. That way, it looks like what happens in Vegas stays in Vegas, natural. You don't recognize me or Cobb, vice versa. I have some friends there. We get stuff done."

"Bet you do. What did Ghost say about all this to you, Elsie?"

"He fall back on that old passive construction, 'mistakes were made.' He don't get all bent outa shape, know I'm sayin'?"

"I can imagine. The calmer the badass, the badasser, the...something like that. What's next?"

"Ghost wants to move fast before gold loses value, or the bubble pops on that madness. His bonds guy in DC is pissed. Some spook heads will roll on that deal. And we have to pitch in some gold to the DC contact, but it's only six figures. Plus our two mill, plus that old bugaboo, expenses. Vegas will rack up a tab."

"Of course."

"But the bad guys actually did you a favor. You're coming out of this—if you come out of this—with double the purse."

"Is it a big if?"

"Bigger than it was. But Ghost's intel points to some very dumb and dumber adversaries. It's just a problem to be solved. Most people, by now, would have pulled out, said whew, I survived. Now's when the rubber meets the road. They dumb. We less dumb." Elsie smiled.

❧❧❧

Brandi was pouting as she changed back into her street clothes. "I know you had Veronika Roxoff at your party, Jerry."

"Never heard of her." Rafferty tied his Ferragamo cordovan shoes with some effort, breathing hard. "Is that a real name?"

"It's her stage name. I danced with her at TNA."

"Tits and ass?"

"Omigosh, no! TNA. It's the name of a club on Bourbon Street. Is that what it means? Tits and ass?"

"Well, duh. Tony owns it."

" OMG! I did not know that. The name I mean. Anyway, Veronika said she was body painted at your party. She was bragging about doing it with a billionaire."

"Oh, her. She was just eye candy. It was a beach theme. You and Tony were invited, as I recall." He thought back to the relief he'd felt when she'd said they'd be out of town. Vegas.

"You didn't plunk her, did you?"

Rafferty laughed. "She's a porn star, Brandi. I'm not crazy."

"Oh, Jerry, please don't go with anyone but me. And your wife."

He squeezed her breast. "It's just you, hon. Exclusive."

"Oh, almost forgot. There was another TNA dancer there. Emily something. I think her dance name was Vicki Volvere."

He adjusted the Windsor knot in his tie. "Is there a point to this?"

"I'm getting to it. Anyways, she was there as a caterer. Veronika thought it was odd because she didn't really do anything but sort of snoop around."

"What's she look like?"

"She's kind of mixed race, Creole maybe, but drop-dead gorgeous, a college girl, you know, making extra money dancing. But she wouldn't put out so Tony's manager fired her. Veronika sent me a phone picture."

She thumbed her iPhone until the picture came up, enlarged it, and handed the phone to Rafferty. He studied the photo. Hot girl. There was an arm reaching for her butt and it had an interesting tattoo on it.

"Can you get more background in this shot?" he asked.

She manipulated the picture. There he was. The badass in the porkpie hat and Harley tattoo. Just enough of him to be sure. Could be he just pinched a pretty girl's ass, but maybe the guy knew her. He had people at the party.

ᐒᐁᐒ

The crewcut young man Travis had handed the ketchup to in the restaurant in Kansas City was standing at a third floor window in a federal building overlooking Camp Street in New Orleans—544 Camp Street, to be exact—where it all had begun before he was born, and Bryan Sample could see it from where he stood, waiting to be called into his superior's office. Guy Banister, the ex-FBI nut and his proteges David Ferry and Lee Harvey Oswald had worked out of the Camp Street office, building a legend for Oswald while also training for a Cuba invasion in 1962.

Bryan knew he was going to be chewed out at the very least. Possibly demoted in grade and pay. He had let Travis—the son of Reno Pete Meachem, aka Pete Wood, aka Pete St. Cyr—slip away in Kansas City after breaking into his car to see what he'd brought back from Daytona. But Meachem had taken his suitcase into the hotel. Then he'd disappeared off the face of the earth. Go figure. Guy comes home, goes to a hotel? Didn't make sense. And he wasn't registered besides. Then when they finally copped to the overnighter, the stewardess had gone back to Dallas and Travis had gone to his apartment, then poof. Gone again. He should have followed him, but Travis was acting hinky. Bryan figured he'd just give him some rope, catch him on his flooring job in some rehab house where they could cover the noise with power tools. But he was gone. And Binaggio had gone off the reservation with his questionable contacts, causing severe repercussions, to say the least.

Bryan scowled and glared at the traffic on the street when he thought of savages in Kansas sending ears and scalps around the country.

Travis Meachem, or St. Cyr, had to be behind this circus going on in New Orleans now. Crazy shit. The remnants of the JFK old guard were being run ragged. It didn't help that The Company passed off some fake bonds to buy some time and save a few bucks. A move that had enraged the perps and now they'd doubled down. What they had to sell was worth a lot more than they were asking, but it would only be safe when they were all dead.

Who knew what their safeguards were, though? If they caught and terminated a couple of them, how many more were out there to up the demands, yet again? Or blow the top off the JFK thing, and possibly RFK, MLK and Malcolm X. And he, Bryan, could have headed it off. Possibly. It was a volatile situation. He knew one thing. He wanted to hang onto his scalp and ears for a long, long time.

"He'll see you now," said a sweet voice behind him. She was an intern loaned from DOJ, cute and trying hard to be businesslike.

He managed a smile, eye contact with his steely gray-green eyes. That usually left an imprint. He'd have to invite her for drinks after work sometime. She flashed a glance at his rumpled suit. *Maybe not*, he thought.

"Sit," said Colonel Varnum.

I'm not a fucking dog, Bryan thought. But he sat.

"This problem is not yours, Bryan. It belongs squarely in the laps of a bunch of bizarre individuals who came very close to instigating World War Three, back in '63. Half are dead. The other half are fucking wackos and rest-home droolers. Trouble is, they spawned a cloud of winged monkeys to follow. You familiar with winged monkeys?"

"Wizard of Oz?" Bryan said.

"It's an apt metaphor. Scary little fuckers of which we are two. I didn't say that, by the way. None of what I say will be attributable. Let's take a walk." Varnum motioned to the door, looking at his watch.

സ🙵സ

Rafferty gave the enlarged printouts of the photo to his fixer. The fixer, a sometimes PI and bondsman, whistled softly. "She's a looker," he said.

"Spread that photo around," Rafferty said. "Fifty grand to whoever leads us to one or both of these people. The guy is most probably in disguise. He may or may not have that tattoo. He may be the son of Reno Pete Meachem, I'm not sure. I don't know who she is other than an ex-dancer at a Binaggio club, and an LSU coed. They were both at my beach party a couple weeks ago."

"I'm on it. Send me a link for the photo, please."

"They are not to be harmed. Much. If possible. And if they aren't found soon, say the next couple of days, we may have to widen the search to include Vegas."

സ🙵സ

Travis kissed Emilie at the airport. "I'll take a plane in the morning, and set up at The Mandalay as a sports agent. Same name as the Honda registration. Call me any time on the disposable cell. You check into Bellagio and I'll join you there. Be careful. Watch your surroundings. I feel them getting closer. In a couple days, we should be gone. And rich."

"Gone where, Travis?"

"First we go to Costa Rica. San Jose. I know people there. Then anywhere we want for a while. Then back home to the Marais Des Cygne maybe. I don't know yet, but it will be up to us, actually. We have to be careful for a time, not too long."

"Are we going to get out of this? Alive?"

"I wouldn't be doing it if I didn't think so. Know so. Especially with you involved. I won't lie to you. It might get rough, starting about now. We've been lucky. And a little careless."

"Yeah. Some of it has been…I don't know…a lark. Sort of pretend dangerous. When those meth freaks got me, I did think I was in for a horrible end. That woke me up to how real this is."

"Me too, believe it or not. That's when I got more careful, myself. Want me to go in with you?"

She gave him a worried smile. "No. I'll be fine."

As she walked away with her wheeled luggage, through Sky Caps and limo-borne business people and tourists, he was reminded of Melissa Bradley leaving the KC Marriott, and his life. He knew better, but he prayed anyway.

∽∾∽

"Yeah, I know she's a knockout, but shit, man, you throw a stick out here and you hit ten of them. That's the best disguise you could have in Vegas or Hollywood," the Las Vegas PI said to Rafferty's fixer.

"Well, her hair is crazy. Like springs. And she's got a face like, well, it's just beautiful. She stands out."

"Not here, she don't. But we're looking."

At Bellagio, Emilie went to the spa and made an appointment to get her hair straightened. Elsie had suggested it and it made sense. The girl at the desk said, "Really? Oh, hon, it looks so cool the way it is. I'd give anything to have your hair."

"It always looks like I stuck my finger in a socket, you know? I'm tired of it. And if I'm going to get a job here, it's got to go."

She left wearing it over one eye, like Lauren Bacall in *The Big Sleep*.

When she opened the door for Travis the following night, he stepped backward, startled. "Jeez, Em. When did you do that?"

"Don't you like it?" She let her robe fall open. "I'm the same everywhere else."

"It's just so different. It's a good look. Wow."

"Get in here."

CHAPTER 24

He's here, Mr. Binaggio" said the floor man at Bellagio. "Gambling, playing blackjack, small hands, and he's with some babe looks like an old movie star, only young. Veronica Lake, maybe."

"Veronika?" Binaggio said, thinking back to Veronika Roxoff from TNA. No, no, Veronica Lake played opposite Alan Ladd back in the day. He remembered her. Way back when he was coming up in the Marcello organization, she was hitting the skids in her acting career. Or was that Hedy Lamarr?

"Well, taller. Tall as him in heels. Gorgeous. He's got good taste in women, I'll say that."

"Yeah, yeah. Well, he was running around with some afro-haired creole down here. She wasn't bad either. Looked like a dancer used to be at my place. Where's he staying?"

"Working on that right now."

"Do not lose him, hear me? Do not lose him."

"Yes, sir."

❧❧❧

The dealer watched as a solid looking man with a bro-

ken nose sat at the blackjack table, a beautiful girl with a
'40s 'do, standing at his side.

"Want to play?" the solid-looking dude asked the girl
beside him.

"Only with you, hon." The hot girl slid a hand over his
shoulder, and nuzzled him.

The dealer, a woman with a line of studs in one ear,
glanced at Emilie. Hot girl, older guy, must be the sugar
daddy. *She's playing it right if he is.* When he said "Hit
me," and smiled at her, she smiled back. *He's not too
hard to take, actually. Got some miles, but not bad. Street
nose job, but a good-looking dude, I can dig it.* She
slapped a king down. Then an eight. He picked up his
hand, turned it over. He'd had a three of spades. Cards all
around.

The girl looked like a '40s movie starlet. Really beautiful. Not some hooker or pole dancer.

A man passed close behind the girl and, seconds later,
she collapsed. Just fell where she was standing. *Something's happening*, the dealer thought. *Watch the chips,
the cards.* The guy slid off his chair, knelt by the girl, and
took her in his arms. He looked wildly around. The dealer
watched the cards, the chips, signaled to the dome camera
above her for a floor man. This wasn't a diversion for a
robbery but it wasn't a normal drunk patron collapsing
either.

"I'm a doctor," a man said, from another table, rushed
over. Travis was off the chair, cradling her head and
shoulders, listening to her chest, checking her pulse. He
looked up as the doctor checked her vital signs. Management informed Travis an ambulance was on the way.
We're in the shit, he thought. *This is it.* But he had no
plan, no balance.

The floor man seemed solicitous. "Can you tell me
what happened?"

"She fucking fell. Where's the ambulance?"

"Here they come, the paramedics. Out of the way folks, let the paramedics through," the floor man said solicitously. He cleared an aisle way. The paramedics put an oxygen mask on her face, listened to her heartbeat through a stethoscope. She looked so vulnerable to Travis. This was unthinkable. Yet it wasn't, not at all. She was alive.

"Any allergies?" the attendant asked.

"None," Travis said, sizing up everything in the commotion around him.

Once on the gurney, they covered her with a sheet, wheeled her quickly out to the waiting ambulance. Travis walked alongside, noting her breathing, saw her eyelids flutter.

"Are you a relative?" asked the paramedic closest to Travis when they'd secured the gurney inside the vehicle.

"Husband," said Travis. He wasn't about to be refused admittance with her.

The medic hesitated as though he hadn't expected this. The other one, the driver, nodded to him.

Travis climbed into the ambulance with the medics and sat on a bench parallel to the gurney. They slammed the doors from inside.

"Hang on," one of the medics said. He was readying a hypodermic needle.

"What's that for?" asked Travis.

"It's for you, sedative. Did you realize you're hyperventilating? She's gonna be fine. It's you we're concerned about, now." He raised Travis's shirtsleeve, swabbed a spot with alcohol.

Travis caught sight of the man's fingernails. They looked dirty. Weird for a medic. Travis slammed him against the ambulance wall and grabbed the wrist with the syringe. The other one hit him with a sap, hard, and the interior of the van circled in his head, his last memory before unconsciousness, the smell of the alcohol and Emilie's perfume mixed together, the sight of her eyes fluttering open, the fear in them. He heard voices echoing from the bottom of a well, then nothing.

⠀⠀⠀

"We got their ass," Binaggio said to Rafferty.

"I told you to stay the fuck out of this, Tony."

"Who you think you're talking to? One a your flunkies? You fucking maggot, I'm tired of your superior shit."

"Sorry, Tony. Calm down. It's good that you got him, but we have to be extremely careful now."

"Why? I'm gonna fly out there and kill this maggot myself. And his fucking family if he has one—"

"Can't let you do that, Tony-boney."

"How you gonna stop me? And cut that name-game shit."

Binaggio, unaccustomed as he was to taking orders, was not stupid. He did realize in some small pocket of his mind that Rafferty was a dangerous man, ex-CIA, and well up in the hierarchy when he was active. He'd been told that Rafferty was to be tapped for the highest office, or second-highest in that organization. The man was personal friends with an ex-president or two and rumored to have "disappeared" more people than a certain South American dictator, also a close friend. So he eased off his adversarial stance.

"Aww, Jerry, you know how I feel about this psycho. I want to pistol-whip him like he did me. I want to stomp his ass into a mudhole. I want to have ten chimpanzees fuck his girl while he has his eyes forced open to watch. I want—"

"I know, Tony. And, we'll make sure he gets his. But

first, and far more important, *far* more important, we must have those materials. And we must know that all safeguards they have in place are as carefully dismantled as an IED. You understand?"

"Oh, I get it. Yeah. But we have him now, see? I got that done."

"You did good. You did what all the flying monkeys out there couldn't do. Don't harm him. Or the girl. I understand the girl is with him?"

"Yeah."

"Where are they?"

℀℀℀

Travis began to come around. They weren't moving. No traffic sounds, no voices. He barely opened his eyes. He was on a hard floor, face on cool dusty concrete. His hands were tied, but not his feet. He had a headache, that arced and stung with each heartbeat, and double vision or at least trouble focusing but he didn't want to open his eyes fully in case he was being watched. He felt he had probably suffered a concussion when he was struck. It was going to be difficult to do anything about his predicament. Emilie! Where was she? He did smell her perfume in this cell-like place, musty as it was. His body was stiff. He had to at least roll over to get some feeling into his legs. He decided to take the chance.

"Travis?" She spoke quietly, seeing him move.

He groaned. "Mmm. Yeah." And rolled in her direction. God, he ached. His legs, his head, his shoulders.

"I don't know how long they'll be gone," she said.

"Are you all right, Emilie?"

"I think so, not sure what put me out, a shot of some kind. We're in a bomb shelter. Out by the old test site. I heard that much on the way. They had to use a GPS, and

I gathered there were a whole lot of shelters out here."

He craned his neck painfully and the walls doubled up on him. Two Emilies merged, moved apart. "They were used to test soldiers for radioactivity back in the fifties." It hurt even to talk. "Who's behind this, you know?"

"I thought I heard Binaggio, but they could've been saying Bellagio. One of them sapped you hard. He was worried it might have been too hard, so they must want us alive. Are you all right?"

"Yeah." The only thing they had going was the release of materials upon their death, and torture could probably make him tell how the stuff could be accessed. Except for the fact that Cobb had removed the tubes and had them reburied.

And YouTube was sitting on the film with only a touch of a button from Breeze, if he didn't call in every other Thursday and let him know they were still all right. Same with the KC lawyer and the release of statements and DVDs. If they hurt them too badly, he'd just go with death, but he couldn't stand the thought of Emilie in pain and danger.

This was his fault, all his fault, and now they were in for it. She didn't know the details of the whereabouts and subsequent release of materials, but that could be worse than knowing if these people were not sophisticated inter-rogators. If they were, they were not about to let her go, anyway.

His mind raced, getting nowhere. Concrete walls, floors, steel door, and crappy ventilation system. He deserved what he'd get.

He knew that. But she didn't. He'd been vigilant. Had his peripheral paranoia relaxed? Had he been too arro-gant? Pissed off God? Was this part of the big plan, added pain from her part in this now, to pay for all he'd done in his life, and paying for Reno, too? He began to get angry. *Why her? Come on. Let me take it from here. Just let her go*. Then he passed out again.

Ͽ/Ͽͼ/Ͻ

When he came to, he felt a little bit stronger, more rested, less confused. One more hand and they had planned to go to lunch. Walk down the strip, look for a nice place. Or maybe at the casino. Things changed in a fucking heartbeat.

He looked around. Emilie was gone. Jesus, he hadn't even registered that. He had to figure out how to get out of here and find her. He had to take a whiz. Would they let him? Would he have let them?

He craned around to see what was holding his wrists—it had felt like a plastic tie, the kind one pulled through a slot and the teeth on the tie lock, impossible to get out of unless you could start a tear in the plastic. That's what it was. Time to see if he could get up. His legs felt wobbly, but he stood against the wall, easing himself up from the knees, allowing the blood to circulate. Then he walked from one corner to the other and back.

The dim light in the cell was provided by a one-foot diameter tube up to ground level, he assumed, a thick coke bottle-like lens at the top. Impossible to climb that—too small. There was a hatch in the ceiling, obviously an entry and exit door. But any access to it had been removed.

The cell was about eight by ten, eight foot ceiling. One side was all metal shelving. For canned goods and water, no doubt, for whatever length of time they'd designated back then.

There shouldn't be a lock on the outside. These were built for survival and eventual emergence into the post nuclear world, so all locks and closers should be on the inside.

The deal he made with himself or any power that might be listening was that if he got out of this, with Emilie, he would never take her for granted, he would let her go when the time came, as it probably would, with no strings, with dignity, and good feeling between them, no guilt, a healthy trust fund for her. He'd killed people but not with blood lust or any joy. He would try always to live with some moral integrity as a compass. End of bargaining. He'd try, that's all.

He checked the metal shelving for any sharp edges and found it was attached to braces with sheet metal screws, the pointed ends of which protruded from the braces. He rolled under the bottom shelf, located a brace, and found a screw end to engage with the plastic, awkwardly began to saw the plastic tie against the point. He counted each saw-like gesture and stopped at ten to rest. Ten more. In the midst of the third ten the tie popped off.

Thank God. He felt and rubbed his wrists. The circulation began to flow back into his shoulders now that they were no longer drawn behind him. His watch showed 3:15. This whole misadventure had taken only two, two and a half hours, so far.

Standing shakily in the middle of the room, he got his balance and windmilled his arms, breathed in and out hard enough to start coughing, bent over forward to stretch his back, try to touch his toes.

Whoa shit. He almost fell over. His head ached but he could stand that. The double vision was beginning to soften. He was up to it. He circled his head, hunched and unhunched his shoulders several times, threw punches, danced from one end of the small cell to the other until he was breathing heavily.

He looked at the shelves, gauged their length to be six

feet each. If he dismantled two of them, he could reach the exit porthole, using the screws to reattach the two as sort of a ladder/ramp that would lay against the porthole opening and the floor. Would it hold him? Would he have time to do it before they returned? Impossible to know, of course. They could return in thirty seconds or thirty minutes.

The other option would be to wait, arms behind him, possibly overpower one and grab a weapon to overpower the other if there were two. It would be like an unfair cage fight with two armed opponents, the short-fused element of surprise his only advantage.

The decision was made for him. He scrambled back into his previous position as he heard the porthole door clanking open, creaking, some sand falling down as they lowered the metal staircase into place. He watched through barely opened eyelids and saw a pair of booted legs in jeans descending.

The figure stopped about midway, peered down at him. Travis's eyes were closed enough to seem fully shut. The figure straightened up and he heard a voice say, "Fucker's still out like a light." Another voice answered, "Shit. I don't want to carry his bulky ass outa there. Is he alive?"

The figure descended into the bomb shelter. Footsteps approached. *Calm down*, Travis told himself. *Easy now, he's going to test for a pulse. Easy, want it to be low*. The man grunted as he knelt, felt for pulse on his neck, straightened back up. He climbed up the metal ladder, shouted outside, "Yeah, he's just still out. Plenty of pulse."

The other voice answered, "Okay, give him an hour. If he's still out we'll bring a rope and haul his ass outta there with the Caddy. He might be in a coma. Let's check on the girl."

They left the ladder. Emilie must be nearby, he thought.

The porthole door was open.

He could hear their voices receding as they walked away. He jumped up, his head throbbing painfully, climbed the ladder carefully, and looked out the porthole. Nothing to the right. And the open porthole door was hiding the view to the left. He looked under the circular hinged metal door. They were at a neighboring bomb shelter. They hadn't taken her far at all, merely separated them. Smart.

"Come on outta there, Lundy. You can get all the pussy you want later!" The man was hunkered down by the porthole door of the next shelter over, wrists on his knees, looking down. "Come on, dammit! They want her in tiptop shape. You want paid, doncha?"

He started to rise as Travis approached his back. Had to be perfect. No noise. His arms snaked around the man's throat, both front and back, grabbing his own bicep and elbow, vise-like quick pressure. The man made a gakking sound while clawing at Travis's arms, then he was out. The effort reignited Travis's head pain, but he wasn't seeing double now. He kept applying pressure and rolled his forearms quickly, hearing the snap. He wanted no doubt.

He dragged the man halfway back to the shelter he'd just climbed out of, patted him down, took a nickel-plated Beretta 9 mm semi-auto from him, and a tiny, five-shot .22, the size of a starter's pistol, from an ankle holster. The land was flat, nowhere to hide the body, no time to get him down into the shelter. He'd have one shot only.

He slid the action back on the Beretta slowly, saw the tail end of a brass cartridge in the chamber already, slid it back quietly, pulling against the spring loaded action. He lay flat on the ground, both hands out, safety off.

"Yo, Mick! The cunt bit me! Take a look at this!" The voice sounded hollow, resounding as it did inside the shelter, as Lundy climbed the metal stairway, preoccupied with his wound.

His head popped out of the doorway and, in the instant Travis saw it and squeezed off the round, he thought of the prairie dogs he and Cobb used to take potshots at with the Ruger long-barrel target pistol.

Before the shot, the man swiveled toward him, said "Oh shit!" The shot hit square on, right above the nose. He dropped back into the shelter. There was a scream from Emilie, then silence.

Travis sprinted to the opening and looked down. The man named Lundy lay in a heap at the bottom of the ladder. Travis shouted down the hole. "It's me, Em. It's me."

He climbed down.

"Oh God. Oh God. Travis!" Emilie said. "I thought you were dead."

The rest of what she had to say was unintelligible through the sobbing and hysterics. The straps of her sun dress were over her shoulders and her breasts were bare. He hitched the straps up quickly, covering her chest, turned her around to check the plastic tie. "Hang on, Em. It's okay, it's okay. I gotta check this guy for a knife, keys, anything to cut the cuffs off you."

He found one gun, a snub-nose .38 S&W revolver, laid it on the concrete floor. No other guns. Small, worn Case pocketknife, probably one the goon had carried since he was a boy. Travis opened it, cut her wrist ties in swift sawing motions, blade toward him. Hands freed, she immediately rubbed her wrists, moved her shoulders as he had done. He helped her to her feet.

"Em? We have to get up out of this place. Can you? Can you walk, climb up the ladder?"

He was shaking, not from fear, from the GI jitters. He'd had them in Afghanistan after a firefight, adrenaline coursing through him, tripping wires, firing off synapses of survival, taking a year off his life but saving the rest of it—the tradeoff of Reno's profession, the efficient soldier.

"I lost a shoe. Damn useless high heels." She searched around but couldn't find it, so kicked the other one off. They climbed out of the shelter, Travis helping her up rung by rung. He looked around, checking in a wide circle. Empty desert. One black Cadillac. He waited, watched. He couldn't wait any longer.

"There's a car out there about fifty feet away. I can carry you that far. Or move the car back here. You can't go barefoot out here." He looked around again. One hawk riding a thermal breeze way up high. Nothing moving, except a tall tuft of grass here and there. He ran to the car, head throbbing, adrenaline level in the redline area. His deal with himself was intact, he felt. There was no other way to handle these captors. It was down to that, now—survival.

He opened the door of the Caddy, felt immense relief when he heard the annoying repeat bell announce keys in the ignition.

It started smoothly and he wheeled it around in a cloud of dust to where Emilie stood waiting, her light sundress wrinkled and stained, her hair unkempt, blowing in the slight desert breeze, arms around herself as though cold in the ninety-degree heat. If they ever got through this, he'd never let her out of his sight until she wanted to be.

She hobbled to the passenger side where Travis helped her inside. He shut the door, looking up at the pale sun to get his bearings before getting back behind the wheel. The gas tank registered three quarters full. Mountains sat off to the west, about thirty miles. Must be the same ones they'd seen from Las Vegas, walking westward on the strip. He drove over desert ground slowly in a wide arc, looking for a road, found it, and headed southeast, somewhat parallel to the mountains. He knew the distance to the test site was about sixty miles from Vegas. Less than an hour's drive.

Their phones had been taken. He didn't want to use the captors' phones which lay on the back floor with a small pile of guns and keys.

"Em, for now, take this." He handed the small .22 across the console to her. The other man's .38 snub-nose lay on the console next to him. She took the gun, silently, then started sobbing.

He reached across, took her shoulder, and squeezed it. "Hey, hang in there. Those guys are—"

She interrupted. "I have to clean up, Travis. I feel so awful." Then, as if to reassure him, she said, "Nothing they did to me, other than keep me locked up. I fucking peed my pants. Twice." She laughed through her tears.

"I thought you didn't wear any," he said.

"Figure of speech. Are we going to the hotel?"

"Better not. Those guys had some cash in their billfolds. First we'll stop at a motel on the outskirts, get a room. Regroup. Clean up. Figure out our next move. I've got an emergency number for Elsie. We'll figure it out."

"Maybe we should just run for it."

"Nope. This car is already hot, or will be in an hour, maybe two. We're smarter than half these guys. The other half? We're meeting them. We'll just have to play it out. We, for sure, can't get caught again."

He was talking nonstop, like he did after a firefight in the provinces. He quit talking. *Think*, he told himself. *Think it out. You have some time.*

She looked at the .22 in the palm of her hand. "I hear that. Loud and clear."

She was shaking, he noticed. Natural, but it couldn't continue. She'd fall off into helplessness.

"The pendulum is swinging the other way now, Em. Get it together. Payphone up ahead at that rest stop, I imagine. Got a quick call to make." He pulled over in the waning afternoon sun, Mojave dust blowing back over the car as he stopped. There was a working payphone in an actual phone booth, or what was left of one, its glass shattered, the interior oddly full of candles and dolls. The receiver hung by its metal wrapped cord. He pumped some change into it.

"Talk, mofo," said a lackadaisical voice on the other end.

Travis looked around at the deserted road, the Cadillac. "It's me."

"Call you right back," Elsie said.

Waiting, Travis read scrawls and messages inside the shelf-like enclosure. One said, *The Holy Sprit Command you to wait for call from Sgt. Xeno, Pentagon.* It almost made sense. Nothing was too odd to believe right now.

The phone rang in its battered shelf. "Where you been?" Elsie asked.

"In an eight-by-eight concrete cell. Emilie, too. In your boss's old stomping grounds. No sign of Liberace."

"Anybody on your ass?"

"Will be soon." He explained their circumstances in short clipped sentences.

"Okay. Arnaud has a detail shop contact in Henderson. Get the car over there. He'll take care of it. Name is Hongo." He gave Travis directions and a phone number. "There's a no-star motel over there called Cezar's Other Palace. You'll be fine there for a couple days. The Company was behind that snatch by the way. It was way too weird for Binaggio and them. But Binaggio knows and is trying to muscle in. You do anyone in?"

"Two guys. One name Lundy and one with first name Mick. I got their IDs in their billfolds. Need them?"

"No. Give their shit to my man. He'll shred the plates, take care of the car. I will handle Rafferty and Binaggio. They won't jump ship again, gar-own-teed. The payment was being assembled, but the spooks stopped it, saying it wasn't needed. They may reconsider now. Where are the bodies?"

Travis gave him directions, telling him that only two of the underground shelters would have their hatches open. One body was inside. One was on the ground.

"I see them," Elsie said. He gave a specific latitude/longitude to someone. "Here's the deal. You have a dandy signature sort of calling card by now, if you follow."

"I think I do."

"Reno did too. I have two morticians on the way right now. They will take ears, scalps. I be sendin' them FedEx to the right peeps. Get it?"

"I'd have done it myself, but I had to run. Know what I'm saying?"

"Uh huh. This should spook even the spooks. They knew they had you. Knew it. We knew it too, just didn't know where and no way to find out. This is good, mofo. May not seem like it, but this is *real* good. How's Em?"

"She was shook up. Thought it was end of the line. Funny but I never did. But I'm like the little boy who got manure for Christmas and says there must be a pony somewhere."

"Mus' be a pony, huh, White boy? This one be solid gold. Get over to Henderson. By the way, you know what you're calling from? The last working phone booth in the whole Mojave Desert. Over." He hung up.

Travis knew they were far from out of the woods, despite Elsie's optimistic words. He opened the trunk on a hunch. "Well, lookie here," he said softly. Inside lay their billfolds, Em's purse, their IDs, guns, cellphones, even their shades.

The man called Hongo drove them to their motel in a freshly painted BMW sedan. A big man with a long braided ponytail and a pockmarked face, he said little and asked no questions. Emilie sat in back and appeared to watch whatever was outside as they drove, but Travis knew her eyes were unseeing, glassy from shock They passed a western tack and clothing store within walking distance of the motel. Hongo dropped them off at Cezar's Other Palace, a seedy-appearing casino/bar/motel with a neon slot machine sign lit against the darkening sky. The S was burnt out and it flashed *$1 LOTS*, and beneath it an added-on sign proclaimed *Loosest in Nev.*

In the room, Travis approached Emilie, intending to hold and reassure her, but she turned away from him, averting her eyes. "I feel really awful, Travis. Filthy and…" She held her arms across her breasts as though cold, shivered once. She didn't finish her sentence, turned, and went into the bathroom. The door shut softly.

He heard the shower hissing and spitting, then catching hold. The metal rings of an old fashioned shower curtain slid and shrieked on the overhead bar and the water blasted against the plastic.

Something was ending here. He had the buzzard shadow feeling again, but it could be just residual bad-assitude from getting his head busted up. He'd had similar moments after getting wrecked in the ring. They were hardly out of danger, but he felt they were safe enough for the moment. He checked the small ankle pistol he'd taken from one of the men at the test site, stuck it in his waistband, and pulled his shirt out to cover it. He knocked on the bathroom door, opened it. The little bathroom was clouded with steam and it felt good.

"Emilie? Can you hear me?"

"Yes?"

"I'm going out for maybe twenty minutes. Don't answer the phone or the door."

"All right."

Nothing else. No question, no admonition. She was someone else now.

He picked up the motel key, looked in the mirror of the outer bathroom. He looked like hell. His head didn't ache so badly now but the skin around his eyes was dark and he had a scrape on his right cheekbone. He splashed cold water on his face, dried it with a thinning stiff terry-cloth towel.

He checked for signs of the gun in the mirror. Satisfied it wasn't showing, he dropped the key in his shirt pocket and let himself out, quietly closing the door, checking to see that it was locked.

He looked toward the motel bar. Some pickup trucks, a multicolored car made up of junkyard fenders and doors, a couple of choppers with extended front forks. Typical hard luck outfit with the patrons to match. They'd be shooting eight-ball and talking about how the slots were ready for payoff, he thought. This was the outskirts of Henderson, some storefronts in a strip mall to his right, tax prep and CPA, consignment and damaged freight store, a nail salon. Beyond that, a filling station/food plaza, brightly lit, a few people inside and cars pulling up. In the other direction, the tack and western clothing store, about two blocks away. He started walking, and picked up his pace when he noticed some of the store's window lights being turned off.

He felt relief when he pulled the glass door and it opened. A girl, maybe twenty-five with a shadow of annoyance crossing her freckled face, smiled gamely. "It's about closing time…"

"Won't take long," Travis said, "and I'll try to make it worth your while." He smiled.

She relaxed. "Take your time. I *will* put the closed sign up though." She paused, looking outside. "Where's your vehicle?"

"Wife dropped me off, back in a few minutes. I'd like to surprise her so if we can hurry, I'd appreciate it."

"Fine by me. What do you need?" The girl was country, probably a barrel rider, cute in a rodeo-following way. She was dressed in snug jeans tucked into stovepipe boots, buckaroo style, tight western shirt, horsehair belt with a huge ornate buckle that proclaimed championship at some horse-related event.

"Just about what you've got on. Big buckle included. All about one size smaller than you."

The girl did some bustling, found an ornate trophy buckle that wasn't inscribed, laid it all out for him to see. "What size boots?" she asked.

"Seven shoe size. Seven B I think."

"Okay, size seven and a half boot, and some boot socks. Should be a little loose in the heel, tighter up front. If she don't like 'em bring 'em back and we'll exchange. If they ain't worn, you know."

"Great. Wrap it up." *I'm just a women's clothes-buying fool. I could be a fucking buyer for Macy's, something to fall back on.* He pulled a pair of jeans from a shelf in his size, a blue work shirt, a packet of undershorts and some socks. He picked out a Bailey U-Rollit straw hat, put it on his head, tried on a western cut sport coat, added it to the stack. He was already wearing the ostrich skin boots. *Yippy-tie-yi-yayy.* As an afterthought, he grabbed some T-shirts and shorts for Emilie.

The girl punched the items into an old fashioned cash register while also code reading them with a corded device. She put everything in boxes, tied them with string, and after he counted out the cash, said, "Hope she didn't stand you up. I've really got to close."

"I'll be fine. I'll just walk down the road and she'll be along. Thanks." He looked back toward the store when he was half a block away.

The girl locked the door to the now-darkened store and hurried to her truck. Travis knew he looked scary, wrinkled and stove-up as he was. Feeling his age, sore and limping. She glanced back and waved once as she drove off. Had to be the best sale she'd had in a while. *Probably thankful she hadn't been robbed.*

He walked back to the motel as the horizon in the west showed crimson over a mountain range then gave up the night to a three-quarter moon in the desert sky. He let himself in, balancing boxes against the door and his knee.

The room was steamy from the long hot shower. Emilie was wrapped in one of the skimpy motel towels, drying her hair with another. Travis saw the spring was back in her hair, if not her step, and hoped it was a good sign.

"I need clothing," she said.

But the way she said it implied she'd gotten some of her mischief quotient back, Travis noted. She was perking up. A hot shower might just be the ticket for him, too. Wash off the desert grit and miseries of the past couple of days. It seemed like weeks.

"Wait'll you see this getup, cowgirl," he said, as his disposable phone sounded, the one for which only Ross and Cobb had the number.

᯽

"Travis! Where the hell are you?" Holt practically shouted.

"Can't say, Ross. I only answered to touch base. Can we make it short?"

"I guess I'm not the detective I thought I was. Everywhere I went to look for you, it was like the place never existed. Yvonne's not at The Steel Flower, The Effigy Gallery is no longer there—"

"How'd you know about Effigy?" Travis interrupted.

"Tailed you there. Anyway that voodoo place Em met Yvonne in? Gone. Empty. Want to let me in on what's goin' on?"

"Where are you, Ross?"

"Back in Big D, pardner. I'm not independently wealthy as it appears you are. We still talking about that deal, by the way?"

"Yes, we are. If I get out of this without doing some serious time."

"Well, just don't do anything illegal."

"Got to run, Ross. I'll be in touch, promise."

ⓔⓢⓔⓢ

"What was that about doing time?" Emilie asked as she worked at pulling on the boots.

"Nothing. Just a Ross question. He's a cop. I have few leanings in that direction."

She stood and walked around the room. No full length mirror, she discovered, but the one over the sink showed her what she wanted to see.

"Man, you are a bull rider's dream," he said, admiringly.

"Think so?" She hooked her thumbs in her pockets and affected an exaggerated stance. "I don't look like someone in the cast of Oklahoma?"

"Hey, I'm a better women's clothes buyer than that. You look authentic. And authentically hot."

"How do we get mobile?"

We have a car coming from Mr. Hongo, compliments of Elsie and company."

"God. That Hongo guy creeps me out. How much do we owe by now?"

"No idea. But we're scoring double, don't forget. Or triple by now. The Ghost is pissed."

She popped the pearl buttons on her denim western shirt, opening it to the waist. "Speaking of scoring."

CHAPTER 25

Hongo brought the car, a dusty nondescript Dodge Charger, at noon the next day. Elsie was in it. They drove Hongo back to his shop and Elsie to a field about ten miles east of Henderson.

"Whuddup, boys and girls? Tell you whuddup wid us. FedEx delivered various auditory and dermatological remnants. The legend grows. And a doubling of the last amount. Twenty now. You in for sixteen large, and we in for four of that. Stakes are higher. But it's still pocket change for those Fannie Mae and Federal Reserve types. Occupy Wall Street." He thrust a fist out and laughed a high-pitched rapper's laugh.

Travis sighed. "So what will they do now?"

"Dey best show us de money, or de Ghost has lost he patience. When that happens, heads roll and they don't know where it's coming from. Pull up about a hundred yards that way." He pointed to an area that seemed mostly stubble of some forgotten crop and sagebrush.

Travis slowed but the surface area seemed flat enough. He stopped and Elsie got out of the car with an attache case and walked away.

When he was a small silhouette on the skyline, he waved, did a crazy little dance, saluted. Travis heard the plane before he saw it, coming in low, a fairly new single engine Beechcraft A-36 appeared, skirting a butte and landed, bouncing minimally on the field. It wheeled in a show of dust and tumbleweeds, stopped, rocking a bit. After Elsie had entered, it took off again. Drug plane, Travis thought. For the money they were spending, it should have been a black Apache with cannon all over it.

с⁄эс⁄э

Travis got out of the car, stretched, opened the passenger side door. "You drive, all right?"

Emilie moved over behind the wheel. "Where to, boss?"

"Back to Vegas. That laptop is something that can't stay there."

"The hotel?"

"That's where they'd least expect to see us. It's in the safe at the front desk. It'll be a quick in and out, guaranteed."

She bumped the Dodge up onto the road and accelerated toward Highway 93 and Las Vegas, checking the rearview mirror.

с⁄эс⁄э

They stopped for a Coke and gas in South Las Vegas, and he bought a cheap pair of sunglasses from a rack to help take the edge off his headache.

"I figured out who you look like," she said. "A bigger Chris Isaak."

"Who's that?"

"A studly dude, singer. You've got a cuter broken nose, though. Anyway, how's the money being transferred?"

“Jeez, that almost gave me whiplash. Totally different subjects.”

“Yeah, yeah. Is it still coming in Krugerrands? Do we have to go back to those awful bomb sites?”

“Elsie said they were using PayPal. It was his idea. Should’ve gone that route in the first place.”

“PayPal?” She laughed. “I buy leggings online with PayPal.”

“Prepare to buy more.”

“But, Travis, twenty million? How can they do that?”

“With a smile. And a percentage. There is no dirty money at PayPal. Not after two-point-nine percent. They deposit the rest in a numbered offshore account and we don’t have to worry about laundering or counterfeit or anything. It’s all perfectly legal with no trail. Ghost takes care of that. The feds will never see a thing. We’re just like Fannie Mae.”

“Three percent of twenty mil, sixteen after Ghost gets their four, is four hundred and eighty thousand dollars! And the three hundred we owe Ghost. That only leaves fifteen million two hundred thousand.”

“Yeah. Just enough to pay off your student loan and get us some lunch money, right?” *So now she’s a math whiz. She sure toted that up fast.*

“Did I put ‘only’ in front of fifteen million dollars? I am Miss Piggy. But really none of it’s mine, anyway.”

He put his hand on her knee. “You’re an equal partner, partner.”

✾✾

“Pay the fucks,” Binaggio said.

“It’s what I’ve been trying to do, Tony. We could’ve gotten out at five million. Then ten. Now, it’s—”

“I know, I know. Sue me.”

"Easy to say since it's spook money. They are not happy, Tony bo-boni, as it comes right out of their war chest, so to speak."

"They never done anything right since fucking Watergate."

"You think that went right, do you?"

"You know what I mean."

"Luckily, they don't much care about JFK and the rest anymore. They're too busy puppeteering in Pakistan and points east. And fucking it up royally. I'll get the materials to them after the deal is done."

"What if the fucks renege?"

"I should think they've learned their lesson by now." Rafferty looked at Binaggio as at a slow child.

"No, the fucks! The blackmailers!"

"They won't. But, say they did, then the spooks unleash Homeland Security and the drones come in. The people we're dealing with are henceforth "terrorists" and hell follows after."

"Whyn't they do that in the first place?"

"You never really understood the fine points, Tony. You don't cut weeds with a chainsaw."

"Huh?"

"Well. *You* do. But you shouldn't."

❧❧❧

Travis and Emilie stopped at a Goodwill outlet where Travis found a worn Cardinals baseball cap and a large gray sweatshirt. That and the sunglasses should get him in and out of the hotel.

She sat outside with the motor running while he retrieved his laptop from the front desk and paid the bill for another week. He strolled out through the crowded lobby, the laptop in a paper bag.

"Anything in that room you can't live without?" he asked as they drove away.

"I'll miss that fantastic dress you bought me in New Orleans. Anything else is replaceable."

"We can go back," he said. "What's the worst that can happen?"

Her answer was to floor it.

"And another thing. Getting arrested would be bad, too," he said.

She slowed down.

എന്ന

Back in Henderson, they pulled up in the lot of a large drugstore to buy shampoo, a hairdryer, and her creams and makeup equipment. She had quit traveling light. He just needed some Tylenol. As she shopped in her tight jeans and snap pearl buttoned shirt, he had a flashback to the French Quarter drugstore where he'd first seen her. So much had happened in the short time since.

Another man paused, turned to watch her, and Travis froze for an instant, relaxed when he had a clear interpretation of what the other man was up to. The man, younger than he, in jeans and a T-shirt, had to pull his attention back to what he'd been doing, just as had Travis on that first day.

A small girl pulled at the man's back pocket, said "Dad" in about three syllables.

The man's face reddened slightly as he took her hand and turned.

"I'm tellin'," she said.

"Nothin' to tell, you little shit bird," he said.

But he smiled, and so did Travis.

CHAPTER 26

Breeze pulled up at Arnaud's in his lowered black truck with blacked out windows. Ignoring the dogs, he got out and pulled the large PVC tube from the back of the extended cab.

Cobb met him halfway to the house. "Anybody follow you?" he asked.

"Well good to see you too, you old fart."

"Oh, yeah. Breeze, you sight for sore eyes, I have missed you so dang much, they ast me what's wrong. 'Cobb, are you cryin'? Nah, I just miss that golden hair boy that Breeze, that Michel, I just can't—"

"Okay, okay," Breeze said. "No, nobody followed me." He put the big tube into Cobb's waiting arms.

"Did you look inside?" Cobb said.

"You said not to."

"So, did you?"

"How about gettin' me a beer. Long damn drive."

❦

Travis awoke before first light. He struggled out of a bad dream where his mother twirled in the cottonwood swing in her print dress, the sky darkening, and molten lava flowed behind her. Flocks of something chittering and squawking streaked by. His mother was Emilie, laughing, hoarsely yelling "Veve! Vulva!" The tire spun faster, and the tree was uprooted.

He was relieved that it was a dream, but when he felt for Emilie, she was gone. He heard her voice, or snatches of it from the bathroom.

"It's not right," he thought he heard her say.

He pulled the small pistol from beneath his pillow and shouted to her, "Are you all right?"

The door opened and she stood in the light in shorts and a T-shirt, a puzzled look on her face. "What's wrong?" she said.

"Who were you talking to?"

"No one," she said. "What's wrong?"

"Bad dream," he said. "I was sure you were talking—"

She held her empty hands out, as if to grasp the situation, or maybe show she had no cellphone. "You were still dreaming, Travis. I couldn't sleep. I didn't want to wake you." She took his hand, led him back to bed, but he couldn't sleep.

The dream kept him from feeling like doing anything else. They dressed early, and he told her where they were going next over breakfast at a little place called The Spot near the tack store.

She went outside while he paid the bill. He thumbed a toothpick out of the roller device next to the cash register, left a tip on the table from his change. She was in the car when he approached.

ᘒᘒᘒ

Travis pulled over in Cal-Nev-Ari. While Googling for something else, he'd read that the town of 350 was owned by a Nancy Kidwell and for sale: fifteen million.

"But, Travis, if we bought it, there wouldn't be anything left. How would we make a living?"

"That crop duster comes with it." He pointed to a faded yellow navy biplane, sway-backed under a makeshift canopy. "And I could maybe get her down to fourteen million. that way we'd be millionaires and we'd own the town too. You could do a little crop dusting to help with the utilities."

Emilie grinned her old mischievous grin. "What are we doing here?"

"Making a call." He started the car and pulled into a dirt lot next to an abandoned fireworks stand, where ragged flags fluttered and snapped. A payphone stood in the lot with a three-sided Plexiglas wind protector and possibly the only whole 1965 Nevada phone book left in the world.

"Reno calling for Mr. Rafferty, please."

"Reno! As I live and breathe—"

"Guess where I'm calling from, Jerry."

"Couldn't begin to."

"I'm calling from an eight-by-eight concrete bomb shelter they're using as a holding cell—oh, wait, no those guys are dead. I must be somewhere else."

"I can't begin to express my apologies about that, Reno, I just—"

"Jerry. Listen up. Take a look at the bottom of your pool. There's a large PVC container in the mid-to-deep end. It's not a bomb, so I would really suggest not getting any disposal guys to check it out. The contents are explosive, however. And copies of all of it are web ready. Will always be. Anything happens to me, my pals, etcetera, it'll go around the world in a heartbeat. And people, you included, will suffer badly. That's it. Got to run, Jerry. Key word, PayPal. Other key word, promptly." He hung up over Rafferty's protest.

He turned to Emilie. "They'll pay now, or suffer the consequences. They know that and they'll pay. So we've won. Now, we drive. Nevada is back that way. Arizona is about five miles that way. And California is five miles that way."

"Hence the name Cal-Nev-Ari," she said.

"Hence," he said. "I'll drive."

He opened the door for her. As he walked around the front of the car, he was only a little startled to hear the ignition. Then she backed up in a cloud of sand and grit, headed out toward bare desert, the passenger door slamming shut. He shaded his eyes, watching. She drove about two hundred yards out into the flat desert, stopped, and got out.

Again, he heard the Beech before he saw it. He was surprised, totally, yet not at all. He exhaled deeply. He'd met Em, The Ghost, Elsie all the same day. Had he put that together in some part of his brainpan?

She waved, but he couldn't see her expression, only a silhouette. The plane sat, its prop stirring up dust. He remembered Elsie's dance before taking off and he emulated it. She hadn't gotten in yet. Knowing her as well, and as little, as he did, he felt she would laugh. Or cry. Or both. She stood still a moment then entered the plane.

Then the plane was gone.

EPILOGUE

A vee of geese flew overhead. Travis could hear them, see them, through the thinning tree cover over the Marais Des Cygne. Fall coming on. He lay back in the gently rocking johnboat with his hands laced behind his head. "I'll live," he said to Cobb.

"Well, we sort of saw it coming. She was just too young, Travis. Flighty."

"Nothing flighty about her. She's young all right, but smart as hell."

"If it's any consolation, I don't want any money, anyway. Don't need it."

"It's no consolation. And she sent a hundred thousand by PayPal to get me and Ross started."

"Had a soft spot for you," Cobb said. "Right about *there*." He poked Travis with the butt of his fishing pole in the crotch, causing Travis to rock the boat perilously.

"Hell, I knew better in some corner of my mind, Cobb. It was a pipedream. But not the money. That was real."

"Her and Elsie and the Ghost. No shit. They had our number from the start."

"Yeah," Travis said, a little sadly. His phone sounded its siren whoop. He pulled it from his jeans pocket, pushed a key.

"Hey, Ross. How's the legal shit going?"

"Hardly hear you. But we're almost set up in Dallas. New Orleans was a cakewalk. You must have high-up friends there. How about Kansas City?"

"Done. I rented a small office there. Nice, though, for appearance sake. It's in Westport, second story over a bar."

"I got good news and bad news, which you want first?" said Ross.

"Bad. I'm a lot more used to that."

"Emilie is tight with Elsie."

"I figured," Travis said.

"The good news is, they're brother and sister."

"That's good news, I guess. For the next guy."

"Okay. Other news. Yvonne's my interim secretary. She's got a recording contract. And The Effigy is our new office in New Orleans. Someone got us a deal."

പ്രലന

"What are you going to call the outfit?" Cobb reeled in his empty line, smoothly recast the spinner over a spot where some branches poked up from the water.

"Meachem & Holt Security."

Cobb reeled his line in once more, attached the hook to an eye, tightened it. "You'll have to go back to work."

They tied up at the dock. The dogs were sitting around in a small circle, barking and muttering.

"Go see what the hell is with them. I'll get these fish," Cobb said.

Travis walked up to the house and the cluster of hounds. They parted and he saw what had gotten their attention. A small dog, a smaller version of themselves, tied by a piece of baling twine to the front stoop post. It was Oswald.

The note on his collar said, *This is good juju* (a small drawing of Emilie's veve) *for you and all the boys at coon holler or wherever the eff this is. His name is Oswald,* not *Jack. I got the dress back. You are a good ladies' buyer (smile) and a wonderful ladies' man. I dig the shit outa you, always will. XXOO times a million. Speaking of which, check your PayPal acct. It's way bigger than it was. Elsie says "word." Ghost says "You're Reno's boy," and I say "'til we meet again." (heart). Em.*

The End

About the Author

Guinotte Wise has been a creative director in advertising most of his working life. In his youth he put forth effort as a bull rider, ironworker, laborer, funeral home pickup person, bartender, truck driver, postal worker, ice house worker, and paving field engineer. A staid museum director called him raffish, which he enthusiastically embraced—the observation, not the director. Of course, he took up writing fiction.

Wise welds and writes on a farm in Resume Speed, KS. He welded a collection of short stories, *Night Train, Cold Beer*, that won money, publication, but not much acclaim in 2013 (Pecan Grove Press, available on Amazon). His novel *Ruined Days*, and a short story collection, *Resume Speed*, are under contract to Black Opal Books. His work has been allowed into numerous literary reviews and anthologies, including *Atticus, Thrice Fiction*, and *The MacGuffin*. Some of his work may be seen at http://www.wisesculpture.com and http://www.facebook.com/RenoPeteStCyr.

His wife has an honest job in the city and drives 100 miles a day to keep it.